Books by Alisa Allan

WINDS OF CHANGE - ISBN: 0-9761480-0-5
Cruise to Bermuda with a young woman who is forced to choose. Rekindle a past?... Or set it free?

AFTER MIDNIGHT – ISBN: 0-9761480-1-3
Cruise to the Mexican Riviera and the Canada/New England coast with two strangers who marry and clash in a blaze of differences.

THE BEST MAN - ISBN: 0-9761480-2-1
Cruise to Hawaiian Island paradise with a woman caught up in a tailspin of revenge after a failed wedding attempt, and finds herself in the middle of a bond that could not be broken.

BEYOND THE HORIZON - ISBN: 0-9761480-3-X
Cruise to the Caribbean with three friends who are taken away by balmy tropical breezes and become vulnerable to its magic, then discover a web of lies and deceit underneath its beauty.

ONE LAST TIME - ISBN: 0-9761480-4-8
Cruise to the Caribbean with a single mother and her son as they set off on a journey of adventure. Immersed in exotic ambiance, a woman lets go of a battle that threatens to drown her, but must eventually return and face it, and she must risk all she found to face it alone.

ANGEL MIST - ISBN: 0-9761480-5-6
Cruise to Alaska as a young woman discovers a calm to the haunts of her past, but she finds she would truly have to go home again before she could find real peace.

Visit us:
www.BonVoyageBooks.com
www.TravelTimePress.com
www.AlisaAllan.com

ONE LAST TIME

Alisa Allan

Bon Voyage Books
An Imprint of Travel Time Press

Bon Voyage Books
An Imprint of Travel Time Press

One Last Time
Copyright © 2005 Alisa Allan, All Rights Reserved

ISBN: 0-9761480-4-8

The reproduction or utilization of this work is strictly prohibited. This includes not only photocopying and recording but by any electronic, mechanical, storage and retrieval system or any other means hereafter invented, in whole or in part without the written permission of our editorial office.

This is a work of fiction. Any names, characters, places or incidents are products of the author's imagination or are used in a fictitious manner. Anyone bearing the same name or names is not to be construed as real. Any resemblance is entirely coincidental.

Visit us
www.BonVoyageBooks.com
www.TravelTimePress.com
www.AlisaAllan.com

Publisher SAN# 2 5 6 – 5 7 9 X

Dedication:

To all those fighting battles that must be overcome…
may you find your way and find the true peace,
that comes from within your heart.

CHAPTER ONE

The waiting room wasn't crowded, only three other people filled the chairs as Alana and Todd stepped inside familiar surroundings, too familiar, Alana thought as she took a seat. Todd immediately went towards a little red haired girl who sat on the floor reading a book and he plopped down directly in front of her.

"You sick? Cancer? Is your mom sick? I've never seen you here before, this your first time?"

Alana cringed at his words, Todd was always so blunt and forthright, and he always let his questions out in one long stream and didn't even think about them. He spoke with no qualms or hesitations and it sometimes took people back, took people off guard, as it did now. The little girl looked up at him but didn't say a word and Alana glanced over to her mother who was watching closely from a few feet away.

She smiled but the other woman's expression was distant and cautious. She knew her kind. One who believed it wasn't supposed to be talked about, if you didn't talk about it, it didn't exist, she'd run into them from time to time.

She was the same way before the cancer, the same as this woman who wanted it to go away. Funny, she couldn't remember clearly at that stage of the game, the beginning. Then again, this had consumed them so much, it was all she knew or could remember knowing, Alana supposed it was the shock that made the beginning hazy. Their life 'before cancer' seemed a blank to her now. She looked back to Todd who talked as if the little girl would answer, her ignoring him didn't dissuade him in the least.

"Dr. Lee is cool, you'll like him. He was a friend of my grandfather, my grandfather used to be a doctor here but, well, he died and..."

"Tiffany," The mother spoke and rose from her seat to approach them. "Why don't we go get a soda out of that machine we saw, we still have a few more minutes to wait."

Yeah, Alana thought to herself, just don't say the word and it won't exist. Don't say death, don't say cancer, don't say anything, she'd tried that too but it didn't work. It was going to be there regardless, and as much as you tried to ignore it, in the dark of night when you were alone, it was always there. Alana watched as they left the room and Todd went up to the nurse's desk.

"Hey, Ms. Nancy, you want to play tic tac toe?"

Before they began to proceed into the game, Alana was summoned for the appointment.

"Alana? Dr. Lee wants to see you now." With one hand Anne held the door open for her and with the other held the always-present clipboard.

"Todd, are you coming?" She asked her son who was in deep conversation now. It was another of his many qualities she loved about him, everyone was his friend. She thought she knew her son inside and out, but after the cancer discovery, she found herself more keenly aware of everything about him. Discovered things about him she might not have otherwise now that her senses were much more acute and attentive to everything around her. There was nothing she didn't know.

"You go ahead mom, I'll wait here."

Alana sighed, sometimes wondered if it was a little denial that crept into his demeanor because he seemed so indifferent at times in hearing what the doctor had to say. She looked up to Nancy who sat behind the counter smiling with the knowledge of what would be asked of her.

"Don't worry, Alana, he'll be fine, he knows I'm the meanest one here."

With a warning look passed silently to Todd, she followed Anne down the hall with reserved confidence.

"Todd's buttering up the nurse's, I think he plans on being a partner here one day, follow in his grandfathers footsteps."

Alana could only pray she'd see his future. "So being a doctor will skip a generation, I didn't have the backbone for this. I knew I couldn't do it."

"That always surprised me that you didn't. You were your father's constant companion, I would have thought medicine was the direction you would have taken, you were around it enough."

"Cancer meant death to me and I didn't want to be surrounded by it everyday. Funny how life works," Alana smiled sadly. "Now here I am with a constant struggle every morning when I wake up and try to find the courage for this fight day in and day out."

"Your father's with you I know, get some extra courage from him, he had quite a bit." Anne knew him well, had worked alongside him as a nurse for thirty years.

Alana didn't say anything. She wanted to feel him with her throughout all this, searched for signs he was beside her, but she felt so alone. As if the universe continued to turn, yet she stood in the middle by herself and never moved. He was in heaven with her mother, not that he wanted to die, but she believed he was content now to be with her.

"I try to find him, Anne, but I guess if he's sent any signs I missed them. I've been a little busy."

"You have his courage. You may not know it, but you do. He was so proud of you, Alana, whether you were a doctor or not."

"Not much to be proud of. I became pregnant and had a baby on my own, a single mother who works as a school secretary. Is that as typical and bland in truth as it sounds in my mind?"

"You were the twinkle in your father's eye no matter what you did. You could have ended up a sidewalk sweeper and he would have bragged you were the best in town. I can hear him now, 'Hey, Anne, did you see the sidewalk on East Street? Looks great, doesn't it? That's Alana's territory'."

Alana smiled with a slow realization, it was the first time in the many years she'd known Anne a revelation dawned on her. Her voice was hesitant. "You loved him, didn't you?"

"Who didn't?" She said it with a light air, not taking the question seriously.

"No, I mean you were in love with him." Alana stopped and faced her. "Why didn't anything ever become of you two? Did he ever know?"

The nurse now looked embarrassed, but spoke the truth. "He probably had his ideas, but there was only room for one in his life, and that was you. You were the only one he ever made room for."

She watched as Anne went back to her duties with a shy smile. How sad it had never developed. She felt his love for her long gone mother was so great, he never would have opened his eyes had he lived or not, and it was a shame, Anne would have loved him well. She missed him so much, especially now. His sudden heart attack and passing seemed to have put her life in a downhill spiral mode she had absolutely no control over. Since his death she had not seen one single ray of sunshine, not the faintest form of any rainbow beneath a cloud of darkness, and there was nothing that would give her indication it would turn around anytime soon.

Dr. Lee rose and gave her a kiss on the cheek instead of a strained nod or handshake had he been a stranger. They were friends, even like family to one another. Spent so many days, nights and tears together that formality of a handshake or a casual nod was not the greeting they shared.

"I would say you look great, but I'd be lying," he looked at her with deep concern, he could always see underneath the veneer.

"It's nice to know my insurance money is being put to good use, I'll have to call and let them know they're paying you to insult me." Alana paused, very rarely asked about other patients but she wanted to know about the little red haired girl. "The little girl in the waiting room, she going to be okay?"

"She will be." He answered without detail, but she didn't need the rest, it was enough. "I took you first because her appointment is going to be a little longer, yours is a pep talk, reinforcement."

Dr. Lee took her hands in his and she wanted to cry, she always wanted to cry with him. He was the only one she was comfortable enough with to break down. He understood everything, every emotion, every tear, every difficult step in this nightmarish process. And she had cried with him, never in front of Todd, not once had she broke down, but Dr. Lee knew that underneath the skin that covered her body, there was no hard steel.

"You know I don't make promises, but you have to believe it's going to be okay, Alana. Believing it takes care of quite a bit of the battle. You have to have more of an attitude like Todd."

"Denial? I don't have time for denial."

He smiled, almost laughed. "Not denial. Todd's a straight shooter, he knows exactly what's going on and has faith and hope buried deep, it isn't denial."

"It's so hard to carry that all the time, there's always the doubt of 'what if' that creeps in and takes over sometimes." She didn't bother to sit down, knew it would be a short meeting and was comforted by his old worn hands. "I try to be strong but Todd's strong enough for the both of us, I don't know where he gets it."

If her father were alive she would be having this conversation with him. He would comfort her, push her through this, but she was glad to have his friend, Dr. Lee. Even though she always had a hard time getting past the notion he was second best compared to her dad, but those thoughts were unfounded, she was only begin biased as a daughter would.

They'd been medical school colleagues, then partners, but more important they'd been friends. There was no better person for God to have sent her in this time of need, if indeed He had. That was something else she struggled with all the time. If He were with her, why was He putting her through all this?

They looked quickly at the x-rays he'd previously seen and explained over the phone, but she needed to see it for herself.

"The other preliminary tests came back and it appears we have all the cancer but I told you that's what I expected."

Alana sighed. He told her every step of the way how things were going to go, or how he thought it was going to proceed, but it was still good to see for herself and hear the words again to be sure. Even before she spoke she knew the answer to her question but had to be assured step by step.

"And now?"

"Now we wait."

"That's always the hardest part," she groaned.

"We wait, then more tests and see if it truly is gone or if it appears again."

"And if it appears again?" There were the tears, right there in her eyes and she couldn't stop them this time. In this long painful journey she knew this had been the last step. After this, it was either life or death, they both knew it. All the choices one had throughout life, but in the end it all boiled down to two things, there were no choices or options.

"I'm not going to answer that question right now, I'll answer it when it's appropriate."

"I wish my father were here." She couldn't stop the words from coming and her tears she'd tried to hold back broke through, desperate in her loneliness, even though Dr. Lee offered everything he could.

"And he would say the same thing." Dr. Lee laughed as if it were the reason she wanted him to be there, so he could disagree and give her something different, then he took her in his arms for comfort. "You know he wouldn't say any different than I just told you. Besides, he is with you, Alana, you have to know that."

He left me, left me alone and was now where he wanted to be, with her mother. She wanted to say the words out loud, but didn't. "You would think he'd have some pull up there in heaven and I wouldn't be going through this."

"You're strong, Todd's strong, if it weren't you two going through this it would be someone else that is maybe a weaker person and couldn't handle it. God only gives us what we can handle."

Alana chuckled with sarcasm. "Well He sure thinks I'm a lot stronger than I am. First my father, now this, I don't know what I did, but I royally pissed Him off."

"You should get away for awhile. This hit so soon after your fathers death, you didn't have a chance to heal from that before you were thrown into this. Maybe some time away is what you need now."

"Get away? With all this going on?"

"Nothings going to happen while you're gone, there's nothing we can do now. No chemo, no radiation, nothing but time on your hands. It's been a tough struggle, Alana. You and Todd somewhere warm and sunny seems much more bearable while you're waiting then just sitting around that tiny apartment of yours watching a clock tick. Doesn't it?" Dr. Lee gripped her arms playfully as if he could physically force her to go. "I'm making it an order, a doctor's prescription."

"I don't know. Todd has school and…"

"And he'll have school and you'll have work when you come back. It won't leave while you're gone."

She knew he was probably right and in that instant it crossed her mind it might be her last opportunity to get away with Todd. The thought kept running through her mind and she couldn't stop it. Everything they did could be for the last time, but wouldn't she be able to relax more after this was all behind them? Then again, it may never be all behind them. Maybe later would be too late.

"As a matter of fact, two weeks would be even better. If you don't want to make arrangements, I will and send you tickets," he threatened, and would do just that if he had to.

"I don't know when I'd be able to get away though, I have..."

"You have time right now, Alana, that's all you have. Time you may not have later." He certainly didn't want to make her feel any worse than she did, but sometimes she needed a push. "Alana, after all we've been through this past year we both know school and work are trivial matters, unimportant in the realm of life."

"As soon as I get back can I get answers then?"

"Just let me know where you'll be before you go." Dr. Lee ignored her question and gave her what he hoped was a secure hug of confidence. As confident as he was, he was a doctor and he was realistic, it could possibly be the last opportunity for the two of them to spend quality time together as the odds of the particular cancer they dealt with, were against them.

"Well? Just what I said, huh? Wait and see... wait and see... I heard him last time when he said it, I don't know why you had to hear it again mom." Todd reached over and patted her leg as they drove back to the school after their appointment. "I'm just teasing you, I don't blame you. It's just the way you deal with it. Some people have to deal with it in their own way."

"How old are you again?" She laughed. "You've developed way beyond your years."

"I'll be a teenager soon. You won't be able to hold me back then."

"I can't hold you back now." She laughed at his playful threat. "How about a birthday surprise?"

Todd's eyes lit up like Christmas. "What is it?"

"We'll go somewhere special and celebrate your birthday in style."

"Where? Where are we going?"

"I'll keep it a surprise as to exactly where, but you want to see the world, don't you?" Alana would only give him that little hint. "Well my little man, its fine time we set out to see the world. There's a lot of it out there to cover so we better get started."

Alana scoured travel sections, surfed the Internet, and called every travel agency that offered something interesting. She picked up every brochure she could, and finally decided that a cruise was the best way to begin their world tour. It enabled them to see so much more than just going to one place for a week or two. With the possibility that their time may be limited, she wanted to get in as much as she could.

Other than the summer camps or beach vacations, they'd never ventured out for much more. It was always 'Oh, one of these days'. Well, that 'one day' had to be now, it had come and she would plan their dream vacation, a chance for both of them to leave cold Chicago behind. Hospitals, doctors, treatments, all of it would go away, at least for a little while.

It was set and arrangements were made. She booked two weeks on a cruise ship that offered alternating itineraries so they could get in even more. She also decided to plan a little mini pre-vacation, a few nights in San Juan, Puerto Rico, only a short flight from Miami, and then a few days after the cruise in Miami. They would see more in fourteen days time than they'd seen their entire life.

****

"Look at all this stuff. You are aware that the airline will only allow you to check two bags each, aren't you?" Jenna walked around and looked at all the things spread out in Alana's small living room.

"I'm trying to tell Todd that."

"This is excruciating." Jenna picked up Todd's snorkel gear. "You two will have so much fun and it's killing me I can't go."

"I didn't tell you to use all your vacation up the first two weeks of the year."

"And it was totally wasted. Two weeks with the guy I thought I'd spend the rest of my life with. How was I to know he had issues? Something wrong with a person who has to clean out the bathroom sink with bleach every time he washes his hands, always made me wonder what the hell was on his hands."

"Then it wasn't totally wasted. If you hadn't had the two weeks, you might have ended up with him and in the middle of a divorce by now."

"I would have had a clean house," Jenna looked around. "I don't see your snorkel gear."

"Yeah right," Alana said sarcastically.

"You're at least taking a bathing suit, aren't you? You look great in a bathing suit, even if it never gets wet."

"I'm not that bad. I'll get in the water, shallow water." Alana had been cleaning out her purse and looked up now to see Jenna pick up the photograph on top the television, the picture of Alana with both her parents.

"I don't know how you can at all."

"It was a long time ago, Jenna." Alana's voice revealed a slight tinge of the pain that was still there, it was obvious it hadn't gone away.

"Something like that never leaves a person." She placed the frame back in its place and turned with worry, she worried about her often.

"We haven't had much of a chance to sit down and talk lately. You mentioned a little while ago that you felt like you were drowning all over again. Do you still feel that way?"

"Everyday," Alana answered honestly, and as much as she loved her dearest friend, she was still alone in a pain she fought hard not to show.

Jenna couldn't stay long, had to go out of town on business and her flight left that evening. Todd had gone with his best friend Tommy's family out to dinner and although they'd invited her along, she'd declined, wanted to finish last minute packing.

Tommy's parents treated Todd like another son, and they'd all become such good friends. She was often grateful for quiet moments every so often when they cared for him so well at times, but that evening felt she should have gone to dinner. After Jenna left, the apartment seemed enormously quiet.

Alana picked up the picture Jenna held in her hands earlier and three happy faces stared back at her. How were they to know at the time, what life had in store for them? There was never a moment she'd felt alone when they were on this earth. She loved her son like nothing else she'd ever known, but as mature as he was, Todd could only understand so much at such a tender young age. Even after her mother's death she hadn't felt deserted as she did now. Her father always went out of his way to make sure she was happy and loved, such a devoted father till the end, but her question always returned, so where was he now?

He'd left her and was where he wanted to be, with her mother. The tinge of guilt hit her, the guilt that it could have been different, maybe it should have been different and Alana wondered as she often did, if her father had wished that were the case. All the years her parents had to suffer apart because of death, now each where they wanted to be, where their hearts were, with each other. And she was alone.

CHAPTER TWO

"This is so cool, Mom, my first plane ride and now I know where we're going." Todd settled back in his seat after he buckled his seatbelt and tightened it. "San Juan has forts, real forts with canons and stuff, we learned about it in history class last year. And all the pirate tales we learned about too. Tommy and I were in the class play about Christopher Columbus, remember? And we played pirates, it's going to be great, Mom, this is the best birthday."

Alana smiled that he didn't know the full details of their vacation, she'd told him nothing, he'd seen it displayed as their destination when they arrived at their boarding gate. But she didn't say a word about what else was planned and let him think it was the only place they were going. She smiled just thinking about the look on his face when she took him to the ship in a few days but kept the secret to herself as the plane lifted off from the cold tarmac of Chicago and headed towards warm Caribbean islands.

Late winter was the perfect time to leave. The bustle of the holiday season over and done as the city turned from a Christmas wonderland to a dull metropolis as a cloud of winter covered it. It hadn't bothered Alana, it was a holiday she'd been glad to put behind them, there was only so much cheer to be created in a hospital room and as for the cloud of winter, why shouldn't everyone in Chicago feel the way she felt all the time?

As excited as he was about San Juan, the flight alone would have been enough and if Alana thought he would be a little afraid she didn't know why she worried. Her fears subsided as Todd's face never peeled away from the window. He watched as the plane took off and the ground seemed to expand and stretch. Roads and buildings faded smaller and smaller.

"Look Mom, there's the city. I think I see our building," he pointed down below. "Look how small everything looks now."

Even as they rose higher, when all there was to see were the tops of white puffy clouds, his face never left the view, now a view of only clouds and nothing else. It looked like you could easily bounce from one to the other on what appeared to be huge soft cotton mountains, and Todd looked across the immense space, saw nothing but pure white haze. Sometimes a small translucent spot in the denseness gave a view to what was below.

"You're awfully quiet now, you okay?" She wondered if the altitude had hit him.

Todd was quiet and his eyes never left the window and it was a few moments before he answered. "I guess this is what it looks like when you're looking down from heaven."

His soft words came out of nowhere and sent a chill through her. Barely audible, she wondered if he meant to speak out loud.

When they reached San Juan he was disappointed when the flight was over, but thrilled at receiving a set of plastic wings from the Captain, and thrilled at the adventure that lay ahead in the new city. Todd wanted to explore a fort before they even checked into the hotel but Alana won the argument and they ventured by taxi to the hotel on Brumbaugh Street. There were incredible views of San Juan Bay, and it was right in Old Town so they could easily explore on their own.

Pastel homes and stores lined cobblestone streets, carriage riders pulled by horses, and they felt instantly welcome in San Juan, Puerto Rico with its old world charm that captivated them both. Reminded them how far away from Chicago they were. Alana hadn't realized they needed to get away so badly, but as she viewed the city, and Todd's face, realized how free it would make them both feel. The first time in a long time they could take such pleasure.

"We're going to the fort, right Mom?" Was the first thing Todd said when they hit the street after checking into their room.

"Of course, but we're going to compromise and walk to the fort so we can see other things along the way."

Armed with a walking map they began a stroll through history as they started towards the 19th-century paseo. Paseo de la Princesa was where long ago Spanish nobility strolled and enjoyed the balmy Caribbean air that breezed in from the sea. Alana too breathed deep the air, could feel every strained nerve in her body begin to release stress with each refreshing breath.

They continued on to a building that for centuries was one of the most feared prisons in the Caribbean. Todd made up stories about the long gone pirates it once imprisoned. Then a walk along the seaside promenade revealed the city walls that once were able to withstand any stronghold placed on it. Again Todd could imagine in his vivid mind the battles that took place and the pirate ships that attacked from the sea.

Everywhere Alana looked she saw beauty and was drawn into the history. Next was the Plazuela de la Rogativa, also known as the Plaza of the Procession, where a statue marked its center. It depicted a time in 1797. It was spring and a fleet of British ships led by Sir Ralph Ambercrombie sailed into San Juan Bay with the intent of launching an assault and take control of the colony.

When they didn't succeed they tried to block the city from the water in hopes of starving the residents into surrender. Soldiers were stationed in the inland towns and they didn't see help arriving anytime soon, so the governor ordered a divine plea. A religious procession ensued and all the women of the town formed an assemblage and used torches, ringing bells, and the like as the ladies walked. From their viewpoint in the sea, the ruckus and the moving lights indicated to the British that reinforcements had arrived and their plan foiled. They quickly sailed off.

"Ha!" Todd laughed loudly. "Yellow belly's scared off by a bunch of women!"

Todd's excitement soared when he saw El Morro. Castillo de San Felipe del Morro. Its fortress walls part of a network of defenses that made San Juan La Ciudad Murada, The Walled City.

"Look, look how big it is. This is too coooool."

Every nook and cranny of the fortress had to be explored, and there were many both inside and out. From the outside you could view the Bacardi rum distillery and leprosy island. Again, Todd's imagination ran rampant with the stories he could imagine taking place so long ago.

A cemetery bordered one side and Alana explained that Puerto Ricans used to take their dead out to sea when they passed but the tide would return them to the shore. So they buried them where they were found. There were many cemeteries by the sea in Puerto Rico.

"How about we take a cab back, I think you've had enough for one day."

The disappointment on his face was immediate. "But there's still so much to see, we've only walked this much and there isn't that much more." Todd pointed to the map and traced with his finger the rest of the way they were supposed to go. Then his face changed to loving consideration for her. "Unless you're tired, Mom."

"I'm just fine, but..."

"If you need rest..."

Alana saw the look of pleading and couldn't deny him. "I can keep up if you can. We'll finish the walk, but we're taking a break for lunch then head back to the hotel. It will be an early night for you, young man."

They stopped several more places then unexpectedly came upon La Capilla de Cristo. A very small old stone building with the Alter dedicated to the Christ of Miracles and both of them fell silent. It served as a reminder of their own battle they fought, one they tried to leave behind in Chicago but couldn't escape all together.

A reminder of the miracle they searched for in their souls, but their prayers hidden to secrecy in their minds, neither one spoke. It wasn't as if they never talked about it, the cancer was all they'd talked about for so long. What more was there to be said?

"Didn't you say you were hungry, Mom?" Todd was the first to break the silence.

"Yeah, and we're out of water."

They ordered sandwiches from a small deli store and took them back to a bench on Plaza de Armas to eat. It wasn't as crowded as Alana would have thought for such a beautiful day. A few people that passed she guessed were locals that tended to business, others tourists like them on a journey of discovery.

"Hey, mom, maybe you could find a husband here, right here in this square."

Alana almost choked on her sandwich. "I don't want a husband, and why do you think I can find one here anyway?"

He held the map and read the information pointed out about the Plaza they were in. "It says that in the old day's families with unmarried daughters used to parade around the square in the hopes of catching the eye of available men. I bet it would work for unmarried mothers too."

Alana had to laugh. "I don't want a husband and if I did, I certainly wouldn't want to 'parade' myself around a square for one."

"You ought to have a husband," he sighed and spoke in his most serious tone.

"You're the only man I need in my life."

"But you've never had one, I think..."

"Stop thinking, Todd, we're on vacation, we aren't supposed to think."

Alana didn't know why he kept bringing up the subject, but he'd mentioned it at least a dozen times in the last few months. She couldn't date if she wanted to, certainly couldn't think about a husband with all she had going on.

"Hey look, can I go play ball with them?" He pointed over to a few kids kicking around a soccer ball and was on his feet already walking away before she answered.

"Stay within eye shot."

Alana stretched out her legs and enjoyed the sunshine, had she been able to stretch out completely she probably would have fallen asleep. Now that she'd eaten and sat down for probably the first time that day, other than while on the plane, she realized how exhausted she was and would have gotten up right then to leave but Todd looked to be enjoying himself so much, she didn't have the heart. Where did he get the energy? It amazed her.

"Excuse me, is anyone sitting here?" The man indicated the seat beside her and Alana instinctively pulled Todd's lunch trash aside.

"No, you're welcome to it."

The two sat in silence for several minutes and she'd almost forgotten anyone else was there until he spoke.

"I'm surprised the square isn't more crowded. I would have thought this sunshine would have brought them out in droves."

"Isn't it normally sunny?" She asked.

"Just had two days of rain."

"Oh, I must have picked the right day to come then, just got in this morning." Alana smiled quickly at him but her attention turned back to Todd in the distance.

"Perfect timing. Will you be here long?"

"A few days."

"My name's Matt by the way."

Matt reached out to shake her hand and when she squarely faced him it was the first time she had a chance to notice how handsome he was. Dressed casually, she didn't know he'd just come from playing golf, but she would have guessed had anyone asked. Dark hair and dark eyes but it was the bright smile that caught her. A bright smile that sent a feeling through her, one she hadn't felt in so long it scared her and she almost physically recoiled.

It was a simple feeling of attraction. Shake his hand Alana, she told herself. So he was handsome with a nice smile and you noticed, shake his hand. After a brief hesitation she hoped he didn't notice, the hand obeyed the mind and she reached out and shook his hand with what she hoped didn't look like a contorted smile.

"Nice to meet you."

It was a short, simple statement and she offered nothing more in the way of friendly conversation, nothing more of anything as she turned her attention elsewhere again.

"So you just got in this morning, where are you from?"

Okay, shaking his hand was one thing, now he wanted to share personal information. Why couldn't she sit here and have a decent conversation with a nice man? What could it hurt? Had it been that long that she didn't even know how to converse anymore? So what? So he was handsome and you were instantly attracted to a man who sat on a bench next to you who probably waited for his wife.

He was just being pleasant, she argued in her head. He didn't want to date you, wasn't going to ask you out. It had been way too long since she'd been in a normal society of normal people and not doctors and nurses and hospital staff. Now she couldn't even behave like a normal person.

She basically ignored his question and rose to leave without a backward glance. "I've got to run."

Then she ran off like a frightened child who'd been offered candy from a stranger. No pleasantries of farewell, not even a 'have a nice day', Alana was gone. Todd was quite a distance away and when she turned around halfway to him, the man was still there. Now in conversation with an older woman who sat in the spot she'd been. He was probably discussing the strange tourist he'd just met with a stranger who was graciously friendly, as opposed to her.

All he'd wanted was simple chitchat, he was being sociable, but her instant attraction to him caused panic as if he'd have wanted more. It had become an automatic defense to put a wall up between her and the opposite sex, a defense that had been fine tuned. Now she felt foolish she couldn't even handle an innocent exchange of words from a friendly man who simply wanted to engage in conversation to pass a few minutes of time.

"Hey, Mom, it worked!"

"What worked?" She didn't know what he referred to.

"You caught his eye. Just like in the old days, remember? The story about this square? You caught his eye." From the distance he was, Todd couldn't see the face clearly, but he knew it had been a man sitting next to her.

"Todd Gibbs you have one wild imagination. He was a stranger who sat down and shared a moment of conversation," Well, she thought, not shared. It was more one sided but he did sit down, that part she didn't lie about. "If I caught anything, I probably caught something from that dirty bench. Now come on, it's time we showered, changed and rested. It's been a long day."

CHAPTER THREE

They ended up walking around the hotel a bit as Todd made friends, so open and friendly and he always had to talk to everyone. Later, a shower was enough to invigorate them to enjoy a nice dinner in the restaurant downstairs, but after they returned to the room, exhaustion caught up to them once more and they fell asleep by nine thirty.

When Alana opened her eyes, she expected to see early dawn. Instead, the bedside clock told her it was only eleven thirty, of the same evening. She'd been so tired she would have thought it was morning but it was dark and she'd only dozed off for two hours.

Now wide awake, she attributed it to the extra strong coffee after dinner that had a delayed reaction in her system. She looked over to the other bed and could see clearly because of the moonlight that streamed into the room, saw Todd huddled comfortably under the covers with the slow even inhale and exhale of slumber. She smiled in the dark. He'd had such a wonderful day, couldn't stop talking about it when Dr. Lee called to check up on them.

"It was the coolest, Dr. Lee. Forts and pirate stories, and I played soccer too."

"And your mother? Did she play soccer?"

Todd laughed, "No, she was picking up men in the Plaza. I thought we'd find her a husband."

"A husband? I'm sure she wants a few souvenirs, but I'm not sure that's the kind she's looking for."

Todd explained the Plaza as he'd explained their entire day in detail. Then talked to his wife Mona and promised to send lot's of postcards.

"What is this about you picking up husbands?" Mona asked when he'd handed Alana the phone.

"Todd wanted to 'parade' me around San Juan. Guess he thinks I'm desperate."

"Todd may be on to something. Your father wanted you to have a husband, but I'm not sure he would have approved of those kinds of tactics in a strange city," Mona laughed at the thought.

"Maybe Todd is taking up where daddy left off. He was always trying to pawn me off on someone."

"Pawn you off? He carefully viewed potential prospects."

"I think he hired half the doctors he did because they were single."

"He worried so about you being alone," Mona said.

The words struck her. If he worried so, then where was he? She kept asking the question over and over, it kept sticking in her brain, but Alana didn't voice her feelings. "I used to think he wanted to go back to fixed marriages so he could marry me off to someone of his choosing."

"You know, he didn't get so bad until about six months before his death. Maybe he had a premonition, wanted to make sure you'd have someone before he left."

"Now I probably never will, and I'm just fine with that." She looked over to Todd, there were more important things on her mind and he was all she needed.

"I remember him telling me once, whoever it was that was meant for you it had to be someone special."

Alana smiled inwardly at a memory that came to her mind. "He said it had to happen in a special way for me to take notice. He always wanted for me what he and mom had. I'm not sure anything like that would ever exist between two other people. And I…"

"What?" Mona questioned when she stopped talking.

"Nothing, just some childhood haunts and guilt's."

"You were six years old, Alana, you couldn't have done anything."

Mona misread her guilt and Alana hadn't explained. She now lay in the dark and thought of the conversation as she tried to get back to sleep but it was a fruitless venture, sleep wouldn't come. For fear of waking Todd, she couldn't turn the television on, or the light to read by, so she dressed quietly in the bathroom and went downstairs to the lobby. Alana decided a late glass of wine would maybe counteract the earlier caffeine.

The casino was full of both happy and unhappy people. She looked in briefly but it didn't draw her in as it would others who sought promises of quick riches. The past year proved luck was one thing that was not in her favor. Games of chance took their toll on others as Alana opted for a table in a quiet corner in the bar and ordered a glass of Chardonnay.

"If you're going to have a few glasses, I always like to suggest our half carafe, it contains about two and half to three glasses," The waitress suggested.

"I'm hoping the one glass may do to put me back to sleep, but thanks anyway."

"Sleep? It's a lovely night, early yet, maybe you should be out doing the Salsa somewhere." The waitress smiled at her but saw it was the last thing on her mind. "Well, if you change your mind about the carafe at least, just let me know."

Alana opened her book and just briefly, it crossed her mind how pathetic she looked to others. Sitting alone in a hotel bar, novel in hand and wine for one. San Juan was exciting, the noise alone sent adrenaline through one's system as bells and whistles could be heard from the casino, shouts of cheer on occasion, people laughing, and music from somewhere in the distance.

For the first time in a long time she felt a little restless as she remembered how normal life could be. The book wasn't going to be enough to pacify her solitary boredom, or help put her to sleep, so she ordered the half carafe of wine. What the hey, she thought, she was on vacation, wasn't she? And when was the last time she enjoyed a nice leisurely glass of wine, even if she did have to drink it by herself.

"So, you just got in this morning, where are you from?"

Alana's head shot up from the book she hardly concentrated on and saw the man from the square, she'd forgotten his name, but his smile was still as gorgeous as it was that afternoon. Instinctively, as if mechanically operated by a little button somewhere in her brain, an invisible wall came up to shut him out. If he hadn't started rambling on and sat down, she would have made a quick excuse and left.

"That was the question I asked when you ran off this afternoon so I figured I'd just start from there. Of course it could be my downfall, maybe that's why you ran off because you didn't want to tell me." Matt sat down opposite her without waiting to be asked. "If that's the case I can ask another question, or I don't have to ask any questions. You don't have to tell me, just a nice polite question that's thrown out there simply for communication purposes. Actually let me guess..."

He continued on without stopping for a single second. "Minnesota? No, you'd have some sort of Minnesotian accent. Is that a word? Minnesotian? If it seems like I'm talking nonsense, I am. The way I look at it is you really are a polite person and you're not going to run off while I'm talking. So I'll just keep saying things, anything. And you probably won't get up and walk away from me until I stop. But you can join in anytime, just throw something out there, it's really easy. Anything? Something?"

He paused only slightly before he continued. "So maybe you're from California? No, you'd probably be wearing in-line skates or something. Okay, so you don't want to tell me. I said that was fine and it is, so we'll talk about something else. Rather I'll talk about something else, you seem to be a good listener. I just finished a book today. Probably the most boring book I've ever read and I've read quite a few books. It started out with this man who traveled the Grand Canyon by foot and every square inch of that huge, dusty canyon was covered in this book. Started out at this one dusty rock, big boulder that kind of looked like a large arrow or something, then when he went around the bend there was another one, this one shaped like..."

He rambled on for awhile explaining every square inch, shape of rocks, colors of the dirt and menial, boring details to his fictitious tale.

"Okay, okay, I give. Uncle. Stop." A slow smile appeared on her face while he talked on and on, now she smiled full in resignation.

He had worn a few of her reserves down, at least managed to make her feel like she didn't have to run out of the room screaming. Made her feel she could possibly still be normal after all. Besides, if she hadn't given in, somehow she knew he would have covered every rock in the Grand Canyon even though he made up the story. And he was right that if he hadn't of blabbed on about it, she would have left.

"Now we're getting somewhere. I don't want to appear forward but I'm assuming you're here alone? There isn't going to be a husband walking around the corner any minute is there? Some big guy with a black belt in karate?"

Alana took note he hadn't mentioned seeing her with Todd that afternoon, so he didn't know she was there with a son. As handsome as he was, it didn't erase the fact that he was a complete stranger. She didn't want him to think she was totally alone in an unfamiliar city so her answer sounded a plausible tale.

"No, no husband will come walking around the corner, I'm here with a small group, some nursing associates for a few conference meetings." It was a lie but she knew quite a bit about the medical field now, with what they'd gone through. Could probably answer any question he could throw at her.

"I find you again, you have a voice, and no husband. My nights looking better compared to the disaster in the casino," he said.

There it was again, that smile that did something to her. Made her feel like a sixteen-year-old girl who passed by the cute boy in the school hallway. What was it about that smile? It made her feel comfortable as they chatted easily for a while, and Alana was surprised that after her initial lie of who she traveled with, the rest of the lies came easy.

She told him her name was Jenna and she was from a small town in Virginia. Let her be someone else, just for this one night in time, she didn't want to be her. She didn't want to be Alana Gibbs whose life had been consumed by cancer over the past long months. Was it so wrong for her to want to enjoy one evening without thinking about that life? Pretend she had another?

"Jenna," he stated simply.

They talked well into the early morning. The wonderful day in San Juan relaxed her and made her more open to possibilities than she would have imagined she could be. Of course she attributed some of her flirty giddiness to the wine that kept flowing and Matt was enough to make the most celibate nun take a second glance.

His dark eyes warm and kind, they pulled her in as if by some inexplicable mystical power. And his smile, the easy way he smiled at her made her feel like one of his old friends he'd known for years. It was what she needed, an old friend to take her away, even if just for a little while.

She wasn't a nun, but she'd certainly been celibate for quite a long time. Outside the air was balmy, the sea calm and soothing as the water lapped along the rocks. As they walked along the promenade in front of the hotel, Matt pulled her close to him but it was Alana who leaned in and pressed her lips to his. Alana who decided her years of celibacy would come to an end.

It was almost four in the morning when she rolled and encountered another body. She'd fallen asleep for only a short time and now her mind was groggy, couldn't immediately comprehend where she was, then smiled in remembrance of Matt and what they shared. It was a quick moment of emotional exposure she allowed herself, and then it was replaced by panic.

What had she done? It hadn't been a dream, it was real and she was in Matt's bed, a stranger. And she'd lied to him, about her name, about where she was from, what she was doing there, lied to him about everything. Anything he'd asked about had been a lie. And she was naked in his bed. Made love to him with a passion so strong it terrified her, and he didn't even know her name. Quietly, but as quickly as she could, she dressed and left the room.

****

"Hey, Mom, this is awesome. There's so much stuff down there." Todd took his snorkel mask off and dropped it on the sand beside her.

"Did you use up another camera?" She smiled, squinted her eyes to the sun. He'd used up one underwater camera already and she was glad she'd purchased several.

"Almost, you ought to see it, there's all kinds of fish. I think I saw an octopus too and I got a picture. I'm going to walk a little further down and snorkel there, okay?"

"Sure, honey."

Sunshine and relaxation they'd sought, so they packed a day bag with swimming and snorkel equipment, water, and all the necessities for an entire day at the beach. A taxi ride to the little fishing village of Las Croabas, near Fajardo, and Todd made the decision for a sailboat over to a small sandy key. They could have taken a motorboat, but he wanted to do it like the pirates did.

"Mom, we're in Puerto Rico, we have to do as the Puerto Ricans do and I know back in the old days they didn't use a motorboat."

They sailed a small wooden sailboat across and Alana had to admit the hour-long voyage was much more relaxing in the sailboat than it would have been by motorboat. It was midweek and not as crowded as it was on the weekends so when they arrived there were only ten people or so scattered about. It felt like their private beach for the day.

Alana could only try to escape thoughts of Matt but her mind wouldn't let her. On the sail over she closed her eyes to take a short nap in the sun while Todd helped their Captain. An older gentleman who fully appreciated the child's outgoing attitude about life.

Matt was there when her eyes were closed or open and she couldn't make him leave. Maybe it was because she hadn't been with a man for over three years, not so intimately anyway, and she remembered well the touch of his masculine hands. The softness of his lips, the way he held her so close after they'd made love and she felt so protected in his arms. As if he made all her troubles disappear just by being next to her. And he had, hadn't he?

For a few brief hours she had no troubles. She was Jenna from Virginia, a nurse in San Juan with a few associates for some lectures, conferences and such. Alana found herself making up lie after lie when she had to, or if it wasn't a lie, she exaggerated the truth a bit and tried to avoid direct questions all together. Changed the subject or skirted the issue in avoidance, but sometimes he'd pressed for an answer and she made one up.

She'd never done anything like that before and wanted to escape the memory now, mentally pounded herself for hours and tried to figure out what possessed her. How could she have done such a thing? Never once in her thirty-five years had she'd been so impulsive with a quick rash decision to sleep with a stranger. Alana didn't date, never dated, yet there she was wrapped in the arms of a man she knew nothing about. And she found it beyond odd, but she didn't regret her decision, even though she was glad she wouldn't have to see him again. To avoid him, she purposefully planned the day away from Old Town to lessen her chances of running into him somewhere.

He was doubtless trying to do his best to avoid her also. Matt was alone in a beautiful city and in all probability only wanted a one-night-stand anyway and lucked out when he met her. She was only more than willing to forgo a long-term relationship in lieu of a few hours of lust. He'd hit the jackpot with a woman named Jenna. She would be the locker room talk next week, maybe after tennis, or a round of golf, or after a workout at the fitness gym. She didn't know and didn't care. Hell, she knew nothing about him. Alana wanted to literally slap herself upside the head, but in the next moment she'd suppress the smile as she thought of him.

She didn't see him the next night, but thought about him still. He didn't stay in the same hotel but she gave it a thought that if she went down to the casino she'd probably find him there. It was how he'd come to be there the evening before, he'd been gambling and just happened to wander into the bar for a drink.

Why couldn't she stop thinking about him? Had she been that sexual deprived? It hadn't been something she thought about anymore, too many other things occupied her thoughts and her mind, but she certainly didn't think one night of passion would have created this constant desire. Maybe it was the vacation. She'd relaxed just enough to let those long forgotten feelings in. Only problem was now, she couldn't get rid of them.

When morning came, Alana woke to the sun that poked through the window and could tell from the light it had only just begun its rise. As she glanced over to Todd's bed she launched herself up when she saw it was empty. Glanced over the small room quickly with one scan of her eyes and he was nowhere, hadn't fallen out of bed, wasn't in the bathroom. Where could he have gone? How long had he been gone? He didn't get up this early, very seldom did he rise before he needed to, and she wasn't going insane, Todd wasn't there.

Alana rushed downstairs and searched the restaurant, lobby, pool, any area she could. Then in her panic, practically accosted the first bellhop she saw.

"Have you seen my son? A little boy about this tall, blond hair, probably has on a baseball cap, a blue one."

"I jus come on duty, ask Rodriguiz if he still here."

"Do you know where he would be?" She looked around the lobby area one more time but still no sign of Todd.

"Oh, he walking out," he pointed towards the door where a man exited and Alana ran to stop him.

"Excuse me, have you seen a little boy about..."

"Todd? I see Todd."

He smiled and Alana felt only a little relief. He may have seen him, but until she did, only then would she feel better.

"Where is he? Where did he go?"

"It was before sun, he said he was going to church."

"Church?"

Alana ran through Old Town as if she had meant to jog that morning. A regular morning routine like others she passed, only they weren't frantic, and when she rounded the corner and saw him her sigh could have woken up all of Puerto Rico. He was on his knees and his hand held the bars that protected the Alter dedicated to the Christ of Miracles. Her fast run came to a halt and she walked slowly towards her silent praying son. Relief spread over her like rain.

She gasped for air, had never run so fast in her life and it took her several minutes for her legs to stop shaking and her stomach to settle from its queasiness. Alana stood for a long time without saying a word and Todd finally looked up with large eyes and offered his excuse for scaring her nearly to death.

"I'm sorry, Mom. I figured if I prayed early, I could get mine in before God got so busy."

She sat beside him on the ground, leaned her back against the bars and closed her eyes. She wanted to cry, the tears were there just under the surface, but she didn't. Daddy, I need you now, please, Alana pleaded in her mind. Help me, I'll never ask anything of you again, you can rest in peace with mom, just help me get through the rest of this.

****

A rental car that day gave them the opportunity to explore the rest of San Juan at their comfortable leisure. They started with a forty five minute drive along the north coast to the east central part of Puerto Rico. Past the little village of Palmer they proceeded on to the tropical wonder of the 28,000-acre rain forest of El Yungue, the only tropical rain forest in the U.S. National Forest system. Beautiful cascades and waterfalls greeted them and instead of stopping to climb the observation tower they enjoyed the picturesque view from stops along the roadside.

El Yungue had over 100 billion gallons of rain each year, which was bestowed on them part way through. And Todd didn't have to listen hard or look very long to find the coqui, a small tree frog that proliferated in abundance in the habitat, and they serenaded them with their chorus of song.

Map in hand, Todd navigated their way to Luquillo Beach where they stayed for a few hours along the sun washed shore, then stopped to get dinner on the way back to Old Town where they returned the rental car. It was then she noticed her son was awfully quiet as they walked along the sea wall promenade towards the hotel.

Alana put her arm around him and pulled him close. "You okay?"

"Yeah, I guess."

With typical mother instinct, she automatically felt his head for fever and found none. "Feeling all right?"

"This is our last day, Mom, our days in San Juan are over and I'm just a little sad about leaving, that's all." Alana smiled and he saw her. "Well gosh, mom, you don't have to look so happy about it. Didn't you like San Juan?" He seemed offended she found it humorous.

"I liked San Juan, but I'd like to see other places also. I never said we were going home after this."

"We're not?" His usual jovial cheer began to return. "Where are we going?"

"Hmmmmm..." She teased as if she wouldn't tell him.

"You can't do that, come on, mom, tell me. Please?"

"Let's see, we're going back to Miami, then on to the Cayman Islands, Roatan, then off to Barbados, Grenada, St. Lucia, Antigua and Tortola."

Todd looked a little worried, it all sounded great but it concerned him a little. "Are we never going back to Chicago?"

"Of course," Alana didn't want to think about Chicago and what awaited them when they returned. As much as she would have liked to run away and never go back and face it, she assured Todd it wasn't in her plans. "You know the cruise ship you saw this morning? It wasn't the one we'll be on, but tomorrow we'll be going to Miami and boarding our own, we're going on a cruise after we leave here."

"We're really going to go on one? Just like that huge one? And go to all those places?" It was more than he ever could have hoped for.

"Really."

"This is the best day of my life, Mom." Todd ran ahead a few feet and jumped and turned at the same time.

"You said that yesterday, and the day before. And you know what? You'll say it again tomorrow."

****

When Todd fell asleep that evening, Alana quietly sat on the edge of his bed and stared at him, hoped that every day of their lives could be like this, every day the best and the next even better. All she had right now to hold onto was the next two wonderful weeks ahead. It was all she could focus on, all she saw in front of her and forced to the back of her mind were thoughts on what lay beyond the two weeks of freedom. It tried to nag at her, but she forced herself to try and let it go for just a little while.

She had no problem doing that two nights ago wrapped in false comfort of a strangers arms. Stop yourself Alana, he was probably gone, even if he weren't he wasn't pining away for you. Probably hadn't given you another thought. But what if he were still here? Why couldn't she go to him? After tonight she would be off for fourteen days to sail the Caribbean and he would be off to his part of the world. In weeks to come the entire affair would fade from memory, so what could one more night hurt?

She couldn't find a logical answer to her question, so Alana stood on the outside of his hotel room. The entire walk over she placed herself into the person she was two nights previous. Jenna, single, carefree Jenna in San Juan to meet with a few nursing associates. Alana hesitated, but Jenna had the courage to knock on the door.

He could have checked out yesterday for all she knew. If not, what if someone else were in the room? Maybe he was married, his wife in town now, and she would answer the door. Maybe another girl he'd picked up, a girlfriend. What was she doing? She had no business being there, had no business to be greedy, should just take the memory of the one night they'd shared and be happy with that. She was about to turn away when the door swung open suddenly and he stood in front of her.

"Oh my God you scared me," Alana held her hand to her mouth as if to hold her lurching heart inside. "I was about to leave, I didn't think you were in." She felt foolish, like he'd caught her spying or something.

"I didn't expect you, but I'm glad you're here. I was headed out for a drink, care to join me?" Matt's smile was welcoming, glad to see her.

Alana felt so much more assured when he smiled at her. That smile she hadn't been able to get out of her mind and in one instant she was full of the boldness she needed to remain there.

"Do we have to go out for it?" Her coy flirting wasn't something she did on a normal basis, wasn't something she'd ever done at all, but she wasn't herself. She was someone else now, and after tomorrow she would never see him again, what did she care.

"Or in, in is good," he held the door wide and she stepped inside.

It was a nice room now that she could notice it. Alana hadn't seen much of it the other night, when they got there they didn't turn the lights on before they ripped off each others clothes and stumbled in the dark to the bed. But the lights were on now and she hadn't had anything to drink, not one glass of wine to loosen her nerves a little. He spoke as if he'd read her mind.

"Wine?"

"What are you having?"

"Scotch."

"The same for me."

She didn't turn around to face him, instead she walked over to the window and looked at a glorious view of lights as he poured them a drink from a wet bar. Alana heard the clanking of the ice and it was so quiet she heard the pouring of liquid, and then if possible, she heard every fiber of carpet crunch beneath his feet as he walked towards her. What was she doing here? Just leave Alana, leave, she tried to talk herself out of it but it didn't work. He had taken her away the other night and she wanted to go again, wanted to be someone else, in someone else's life for a little while longer.

"Thank you," she said and took the glass offered.

"How did your meetings go?"

"Fine," Alana didn't hesitate with her lie.

They were silent, but it wasn't an uncomfortable silence. There was a sexual tension in the air and each of them knew why she was there, no need for small talk to get in the way. Alana felt bold but not so bold as to make the first move, not without a drink to give her false courage, but she found she wouldn't have to make the first move. Matt walked slowly over to her, removed her drink and set it down then pulled her into his arms and kissed her hard. Forget the drink.

They made love with the same fiery passion as before, even more so if that was possible. Their skin melted together as if fused and bonded as one and Alana knew that if she'd ever made love like this before, she wouldn't have remained celibate for so long. He filled her senses completely with every touch, every caress. She felt like she couldn't get enough of him, couldn't get close enough even though they were naked skin to naked skin.

Afterwards, Matt ordered room service and they lounged on the bed with little sandwiches and fruit, talked with a comfortable ease.

"Are you going to sneak out on me again?" Matt referred to their first night together.

"I didn't sneak out, you were asleep and I didn't want to wake you."

"I felt so cheap and used," he teased and she laughed.

"Okay, so I won't sneak this time. Just don't fall asleep."

"Oh, believe me, I won't," he turned her palm over and kissed the tender spot inside with just the slightest touch of his lips.

They made love again and she fell sound asleep. It had only been two hours sleep, but it was the soundest sleep she could remember having since she didn't know when. Before the cancer, everything was before the cancer. Curled in the comfort of his arms against warm skin of the man responsible for making her feel so alive, she couldn't help but think, if only her life were different.

But it wasn't. And as she looked at the glowing bedside clock, she knew she had to leave, moved to get up but felt his arms tighten around her.

"Don't go," Matt said when he felt her stir.

"I have to."

"I won't ever see you again."

"I know," Alana whispered in the dark.

CHAPTER FOUR

When the plane took off, Alana watched San Juan fade into the distance, bid a silent farewell to a man who'd never know her name. The flight to Miami was smooth and trouble free, and unlike the flight to San Juan when Todd wanted to fly longer, he couldn't wait to land this time knowing a cruise ship awaited them.

"Mom look, that's our ship, you picked the best one, it's the best one here." Todd had to hold himself back from running through the port.

The ship glowed in the afternoon sun, beckoned them aboard to share a wonderful adventure and it was impressive in its size and grandeur. Todd was in wonder and awe of everything from the moment they stepped aboard. He talked to everyone throughout the process of embarkation and there wasn't a person that saw him that didn't know how excited he was.

They checked out their cabin first, and with everything else, Todd thought it was the 'coolest'. The décor was bright, decorated with blue and yellow and featured a balcony to watch the sea float by, a small vanity area and plenty of storage for their things when their bags were delivered and unpacked. As lovely as it was, Todd's favorite thing seemed to be the toilet. When you flushed, it made a huge suction sound.

"Man, I'd hate to be sitting on that thing," he said.

They began their tour in the atrium that soared high above and from there around every corner and down every passageway was a new surprise.

"Mom, it's like a whole city on one ship. We don't have this much stuff near our apartment. And we can just walk out our door, and it's all right here."

When they got to the buffet restaurant they were serving lunch and Todd piled his tray high but ate every morsel. Alana was glad to see his hearty appetite.

"We can eat like this everyday?"

"You can. I don't think my waistline would hold as much in a week as you just ate in one sitting."

Around every bend there were new places to explore. Restaurants, lounges, a library, game room, nooks and crannies one could hide away discreetly and watch the sea roll by. Or places to mingle and meet new friends. Entertainment venues abounded and Todd already looked over their daily newsletter to plan their activities.

"This is like a 24 hour summer camp." He'd already highlighted several things he wanted to do.

She looked over his shoulder. "You have a few things that overlap, better look at the times more closely."

"It's a good thing we have two weeks."

"We might need even more."

Later that afternoon they called for the mandatory muster drill and Todd took his duty as a passenger very seriously. He donned his lifejacket, waited for the signal that blared through the hallway and the speaker of the room, and knew exactly where to go because he'd studied the map on the back of the door.

Alana loved the fact they didn't have to go far for anything, didn't have to drive through a strange city to search for a nice restaurant, or a library, or a place to enjoy a good cup of coffee. All one had to do was walk down the hall, maybe go up or down a few decks, it was all so easy.

The biggest worry they had that evening was the question of where to eat. As they dined they felt like two special important people, every whim would try to be accommodated. The service was friendly and impeccable, their waiter shared a little of his country freely with them, encouraged highly by Todd's curiosity.

"Maybe I'll work on a cruise ship when I grow up, look at all these people here. Week after week the passengers change, it must be the coolest job."

"The coolest," she teased.

"Too bad Jenna couldn't come, she would have loved this."

"We'll just have to do it again when she can come, won't we?"

Todd laughed. "We haven't even been through one night of this cruise yet, and I can hardly wait for the next."

Alana promised herself at that moment in time, that if things worked out they'd go on a cruise every year, maybe even two, or three. Again she made a silent plea to her father, to pass on a good word to God.

Afterwards, Alana went off to enjoy a show and Todd went off to explore more, and each held a small two-way radio just in case they needed to contact one another. Todd found himself on the basketball court on the quiet top deck with a basketball but no one else interested in a game. Excitement on the ship was found elsewhere by other passengers. Few wanted to brave the risky sky as scattered showers threatened the night and he was about to leave when he saw a lone man walk by.

"Hey mister, wanna play?"

The man stopped and looked to the young boy after he'd realized it was him he spoke to. Basketball was not something he'd thought of as entertainment for the evening on a cruise ship, it hadn't been on his agenda, but at that moment, he couldn't think of anything better to do.

"It's starting to rain harder, we might get rained out."

"Just water. You chicken?" Todd challenged in his easy friendly way and the man laughed.

"Should I be? How good are you?"

"First time I've ever played."

Todd pretended a boyish innocent smile and the man burst into laughter then, found the young boys easy and pleasant way a breath of fresh air compared to a few he'd met that day. His grandmother had met a group of people and Matt concluded all of them escapee's from an old folks home, certainly they couldn't have left on their own.

His conversation with one elderly woman centered on the combination of what happened to her when she had both prune juice and bran cereal for breakfast. Then she'd added coffee to the mix. It was more than he cared to know.

He looked at the hopeful kid and thought a friendly game of basketball would serve well to take his mind off things he didn't want to think about. Specifically a stranger with silky dark brown hair and bright blue eyes he'd left somewhere in San Juan. Physically he left her there, mentally she followed him everywhere.

"Okay, you're on kid." Matt took off his jacket and rolled up his sleeves.

It rained on and off but never hard enough to stop them from playing. So wrapped up in the game, Todd didn't realize what time it was until he heard his mother on the two way radio she'd given him to keep in touch.

"Todd?"

"Oh, hang on," he snatched the radio quickly from his pants. "Yeah mom?"

"Where are you? You're late." Her voice scratched through the small speaker he held in his hand.

"I'm sorry, I'm coming now," he turned his attention back to the man with an apologetic smile. "Sorry, I gotta go. But thanks for playing, nice to meet you sir." Todd extended his hand as his grandfather had taught him, just as a gentleman would.

"Could we dispense with the sir? The name's Matt. Matt McCray." Matt shook his hand and the boy's firm grip didn't go unnoticed, he'd been taught well.

"Nice to meet you, Matt. You don't play so bad, play again sometime? Tomorrow night?"

"I'll keep an eye out for you."

"See ya." Then he ran off but stopped and turned around. "If you're going to stay out here, you might want to practice that long shot, needs a little work."

Matt laughed. He hadn't missed a single one and the boy was only being facetious. How old was that kid again? Had he asked? He dribbled the ball around by himself as the rain came a little harder with every moment that passed but it went unnoticed. His mind was elsewhere, he couldn't stop thinking that the crackled voice on the radio sounded familiar, it sounded like her.

Every laugh in the distance sounded like her. A woman in the distance looked like her. He'd stepped into an elevator that day and the entire space smelled like her. Now five words filled with static, barely audible, a scratchy sound through a small two way radio, and he thought it was her. He was getting desperate.

****

Their first full day on the ship was a sea day. It was easier for them both to do things together and then go off on their own at times. Todd to the arcade, Alana to the art auction, or taking advantage of any other activity offered. They'd meet up at specific times, or call on the radio if they needed and it was when they met in the cabin that evening to get ready for dinner that Todd informed her he'd made dinner plans for them, wanted to dine with a friend and his family.

"I told him we'd meet him at seven."

Alana shook her head and laughed. "Todd Gibbs is there anyone on this ship you don't know yet?"

"There's so many nice people mom, and they're from all over the place too. The guy that comes in and takes care of our room is from the Philippines, and the lady that gave me ice cream today is from Bulgaria. Bulgaria mom!"

Alana dressed in a brightly colored dress and looked forward to the meeting of Todd's friends. Jonathan was a year younger than Todd, and his parents, Amy and Robb, were pleasant company as they enjoyed dinner. They were from Miami and had an older son in college, Jonathan had come as a surprise, but a pleasant one and they decided to keep him, Robb teased.

"Figured it was easier than going through the trouble of sending him back," he looked to his son and winked.

"I told you to have another." Jonathan countered. "If you had, I wouldn't have been in your hair all the time, I would have had someone to play with all the time, like Todd."

Todd laughed. "I told my mom the same but she got me a hamster instead."

"Something that could be contained," Alana smiled.

"Can we be excused now please?" Jonathan looked hopeful and Todd chimed in also.

"We were going to go to the kid's center for awhile, then play basketball."

"Do you have your radio, Todd? I don't want you late again." Alana looked to his pocket and noticed it there. "Make sure it's on."

"If you ladies don't mind, I'd like to be excused myself?" Robb looked hopeful now and Amy sighed.

"I'm surprised you lasted this long. Go on to the casino, I'm staying for coffee and dessert if Alana won't leave me too."

"I'm not going anywhere, I ate too much and can't stand up anyway."

She and Amy enjoyed the extended time alone to chat over coffee and the dessert she didn't think she could eat, but she finished the chocolate concoction easily. Todd had a knack for meeting people, and he had a knack for meeting the right people it seemed. That's why it was easy for her to agree to meet up with them and spend some time the next day.

"What are your plans for tomorrow? Want to join us on an island tour in the morning? I thought we'd see the island then head to the beach for the afternoon." Amy sipped the espresso she'd ordered. "Oh please do, Robb is a bear on the beach, can't stand it."

"I'm sure we can work something out." Alana saw the next day forming nicely, company for Todd and company for her. "I did have plans for the afternoon though, maybe you could come with us? But I'd have to call in the morning and see if there's space. I'm surprising Todd and taking him to swim with the stingrays."

It was decided they would see if there were room on the excursion, and they would all spend the day together. Afterwards, they went to the casino, and Robb was happy to hear he wouldn't have to do the beach. If Alana's excursion didn't have room, he would find something else to do for the afternoon, but the beach wasn't his priority.

"I was going to go get Jonathan now, it's about time he got ready for bed."

"I'll go find him, I'm ready to call it an evening anyway." Robb spoke up as he played his last hand of poker. "I've donated enough for one night. I've got to pace myself for losses throughout the week."

"I hope it wasn't me that ruined your hand." Alana looked the culprit. "My luck isn't the best, but I didn't think it would rub off so easy."

"I have my own bad luck I carry around," he laughed. "Do you want me to send Todd in?"

Alana looked at her watch. "He still has a little bit of time left, I gave him a late curfew."

While Robb went in search of his son, the ladies walked around the shops then settled port side, found a nice spot at a café in the atrium area. Sounds of the fountain behind them soothed their tired bodies and music filtered throughout, it was the perfect spot to help them wind down after a long day.

"There you are." Robb's search for Jonathan found him playing basketball.

"Hey, dad." His son didn't look at him as he took another shot but missed and continued to play with Todd.

Matt left the game to introduce himself. He wiped his hands on a small towel that hung out of his pocket and the two men shook hands.

"I'm Matt McCray. Care to join us? I need some help, these boys are tearing me up."

"Robb Myers. Sorry to say, I wouldn't be any help. Not a basketball man, golf's my game."

"I don't usually make it a point for basketball, but Todd makes it hard to refuse his challenges. And don't let their size fool you, these boys have been giving me a workout. Way I look at it, it lessons my gym trips in the morning." Matt laughed and wiped his forehead with the towel. "I play a little golf myself, always look forward to a few rounds in the Caribbean, maybe we can get together if you're interested."

"Always interested. The wife does the beach and I try to run the other way. I wasn't planning on tomorrow, but if you want to get together I might be able to work something out."

"We could head over to Britannia."

"This is my first cruise, I'll be in your hands." Robb beamed, excited to have so quickly found someone to take him away from wherever his wife would drag him to. Knew she'd be more than pleased to not have him grumbling beside her. "We're taking an island tour in the morning though, would the afternoon work?"

"My plans exactly. My grandmother is with me, she likes to see the island then come back to the ship. Afternoon couldn't be better."

"Since we're all doing the same thing, why don't you join us? Someone mentioned they have vans or large open air trucks, we can all pile in together."

"Why not?" They'd planned on just getting a cab, and he knew his grandmother always enjoyed the company of others. "Bring your clubs and we can just be dropped off at the course and get a cab back on our own."

"Great. Eight o'clock? Meet outside on the dock somewhere?"

Jonathan heard the last of the conversation. "Where are we going tomorrow dad? Can Todd come too?"

"His mother has already made plans to do just that, they'll be coming with us also."

"Awesome!" The two boys clapped a high five together.

When they left, Matt and Todd continued for a few more minutes of basketball.

"It's cool that you and Mrs. McCray are coming with us." Todd met his grandmother that day when he saw them eating lunch by the pool and stopped to talk for a while. He liked her, thought she was funny.

"Does your dad play golf? Maybe he wants to join Robb and me in the afternoon."

"He's not with us."

Todd didn't elaborate on his statement and Matt assumed that his father simply hadn't joined them on the trip, maybe he couldn't get away from work.

"I'd better go before mom has to call me again." Todd passed him the ball and grabbed his water bottle.

"You didn't get in trouble last night because you were late, did you?"

"Nah, she never really gets mad at me. She's a pretty cool mom." Todd smiled as a thought dawned on him. "Hey, I almost forgot already, you'll meet her tomorrow."

When Todd left, Matt put his shirt on and leisurely walked along the upper deck then stopped to lean over the banister that looked down onto the pool area and the hot tubs. Other cruises found him in similar places late at night. It surprised him now that his evening entertainment on this cruise was looking forward to a basketball game with a kid.

Matt never thought about children, not really anyone else's or having any of his own. Married for ten years and never once had he wanted them, didn't even think he liked them. He didn't think they were a bad thing, all his friends who had families he rarely saw, so he wasn't around kids often. It was just that he hadn't thought he wanted any in his life.

But Matt now had to confess, he enjoyed Todd's company. The boy's gregarious personality and his adult manners reminded Matt of a young gentleman instead of a child. He'd spent a good hour with them that afternoon and even his grandmother commented on how good-natured he was. They laughed as Todd told them of their last vacation which his mother let him plan and they'd gone camping.

They discovered along the way his mother was not the outdoor rustic type and didn't do well with cooking over fires, or having to use a bathroom similar to an old time outhouse, a basic hole in the ground with a bench over it. Or an outside shower that left most of you exposed to the elements. When she tried once to use a makeshift bathroom in the woods he constructed with a tarp, she mistook a rabbit hidden underneath a bush for a snake or some other sort of wild animal and it sent her running and screaming for cover.

Previous cruises and vacations, his once a year jaunts with his grandmother, had Matt busy with other activities. Sometimes he took his chances at gambling in the casino or met a few male passengers and hung out for a beer or two. Before he was married and after his divorce two years previous, he would sometimes take pleasure in the company of a pretty single woman. But even though he could, this time he paid no attention to the beautiful women he passed, he didn't give them a second glance and found the most satisfaction from an evening basketball game with an outgoing small person.

Matt wasn't interested in the least in a woman's attention, the only woman that occupied his mind was basically a stranger he knew little about. Only what little she shared with him, which was minimal. A nurse from Virginia named Jenna that he would never see again.

CHAPTER FIVE

As opposed to long ago, the Cayman Islands today boasted tourism and the international financial industry as the basis of its strong economy and prosperity. At one time, with limited natural resources, the Caymanians turned the sea into prosperity. Outstanding sailors and turtle fisherman, many became some of the finest ship's captains and seamen in the world.

Located in the western Caribbean, three Islands comprise the Cayman Islands, the largest being Grand Cayman, separated by a channel about seven miles wide from its two sister Islands of Cayman Brac and Little Cayman. A British Crown Colony located 480 miles south of Miami, Grand Cayman was 22 miles long and 8 miles at its widest point.

Limestone outcroppings, the islands were porous and lacked rivers or streams. Because of that it gave the Caribbean Sea that surrounded it excellent visibility most times, sometimes well over 120 feet. This made for one of the most famous dive places water enthusiast flocked to. Recognized as the 'birthplace' of the sport of recreational scuba diving, it offered healthy coral reefs and drop offs to explore.

A hot cup of coffee in her hand, Alana had been on deck before sunrise and watched as they sailed through turquoise and azure water. It was everything she'd hoped and just standing there alone, taking in the beauty, made her spirits soar and now she was even more excited about the day of exploration ahead. If Grand Cayman couldn't help her get rid of her ridiculous thoughts and visions of a man she'd never see again, she didn't know what would.

Once she called and found out space was available on the afternoon excursion, Amy decided her and Jonathan would join her, and Robb was only too happy to be let off the hook to enjoy an afternoon of golf. Robb secured a vehicle for their small group, and the two women were the last to appear. As Robb and another man busied themselves loading their golf bags, Todd introduced them to Mrs. McCray, he'd told her that morning about another friend who was coming along with his grandmother. Todd had been sure Alana would really like her, said she was 'old but funny' was how he put it.

Alana smiled, "Mrs. McCray, so nice to finally meet you. You're the grandmother of Todd's friend?"

"I am, but please call me Diana," she smiled and looked to Todd. "Your son is quite the young man, I've become smitten with him."

She laughed and looked at him proudly. "Quite the charmer he is."

"And this is her grandson mom, this is Matt." Todd pulled her by the hand towards the back of the truck and finished his introductions. "Matt, this is my mom, Alana."

When Matt turned around, she almost outwardly gasped in shock. Breathe Alana, breathe, was all she could say to herself. He stood directly in front of her again, the man she couldn't stop thinking about, the man who invaded her thoughts whenever she allowed the memory in. He stood before her now and she couldn't breathe. This was Todd's friend? The one Alana assumed was Todd's age?

Her son hadn't mentioned his name, why hadn't she asked? Hadn't mentioned his age, why hadn't she asked? She assumed it was another young boy like Jonathan, why had she assumed anything? Say something, Alana, say something, anything. Then you can tell everyone how sick you feel and can't go, maybe fall to the concrete and bust your head open. Or better yet, you could throw yourself over the dock.

They were all ludicrous notions of course, but if she thought they'd work, she probably would have tried. She felt blindsided and foolish, instantly guilty of all the lies she'd concocted, lies about her name, her life, everything. She hid the sting of shame well, the smile she walked up to the truck with remained frozen on her face, she was so intent on not letting any emotion show through, it was an automatic smile so plastered she wondered if it would ever come off. The shock forced it to remain, probably forever.

"Alana," he stated her name with an even tone and then simply nodded his head in acknowledgement.

Robb saved them both when he announced at that moment they were all set to go and everyone made their way into the truck and seated. Alana found herself next to Mrs. McCray towards the back, and when she could breathe again, stop her heart and stomach from lurching, she found she could actually talk. Even carry on some kind of conversation, or participate anyway. Alana wasn't quite sure how she did it, but just kept moving her lips and hoped she didn't blubber like the embarrassed idiot she felt like.

The women's conversation centered on the ports they were to visit. Mrs. McCray had been to several of them and Alana appreciated the information and tips she gave. Matt basically ignored her, no words, no looks, she was invisible.

"Hey mom you didn't say, is Jonathan going with us this afternoon?"

"Yes, I called and they have space."

"And where are we going again?" He asked it innocently as if he could trick her into saying.

"I told you, it's a surprise."

"Ah... surprises, aren't they great?" Matt's words didn't really mean anything to anyone else except her. Weren't directed to anyone but her and no one noticed the sarcasm, but her, and the tinge of anger.

Her saving grace, other then when he sat in front, was the driver animatedly talked proudly about his island and no one had to engage in conversation. He pointed out things along the way and everyone else in the truck probably absorbed it all. But she had a problem comprehending anything. He pointed to something on the right and Alana looked left, something on the left and Alana looked right. She hoped no one else noticed her brain wasn't up to full function again just yet, more than likely wouldn't be until she was out of this truck and somewhere else, anywhere else, and she didn't care where.

The driver didn't seem to be the safest choice as he passed cars haphazardly and once went up on the curb but Todd and Jonathan loved it, Amy shrieked at times and others seemed indifferent. It was nothing compared to what Alana had just been through and still endured. She barely noticed anything, not even the large bus that almost scraped against them as the two vehicles tried to share the small road.

Their first stop was the Cayman Turtle Farm in West Bay, the only one of its kind in the world that housed thousands of sea turtles from six ounces to six hundred pounds. When Christopher Columbus first discovered the islands, he named them 'Las Tortugas', meaning The Turtles. It was said there were so many turtles that the islands looked like they were covered with rocks.

Todd was excited to hold one, held him out far away but smiled as he did. He was also fascinated by the large lizards on display.

"Look, Mom, it looks like a dragon. Did you get a picture?"

She took the picture, plenty of pictures as she clicked away at everything he wanted, but one she didn't need was when their driver insisted they all get together for a group shot.

The driver took her camera out of her hands before she could stop him. "Everyone over there and I will take picture."

"Oh, no thank you..." Alana began to object but Todd intervened quickly.

"Come on guys, this is great."

Todd and the others began to gather but they were alone in their enthusiasm.

"Beautiful picture it will be." The driver kept insisting and Todd kept encouraging.

"The camera is a little tricky, you may not be able to..." Alana tried to discourage him somehow but even saw how foolish it was to do so herself, it was a throw away instamatic, how complicated could it be.

"You push here, right?"

"Right," she sighed and joined them when Todd called again.

How had she gotten here? Alana questioned. Dear God, this situation was uncontrollable and there didn't seem to be a thing she could do about it. She thought she smiled when the camera clicked the nice looking group with paradise behind them. Rather, Alana thought, the illusion of paradise behind them. It may look like it, but it sure didn't feel like it.

"What do you think about Mrs. McCray? She's just like I told you, isn't she." Todd made it a statement instead of a question, sure of his words.

"Yes, Todd, she's very nice. I like her."

"And Matt's cool too, isn't he? I tease him, but he is a pretty good basketball player."

"You could have told me he wasn't your age, I was expecting…" She stopped herself. Todd hadn't done anything on purpose and he hadn't a clue the turmoil she'd been thrown into. "I was expecting a little boy and his grandmother."

He laughed, had just realized he hadn't explained. "Oh, yeah, I guess so. But he is cool, isn't he?"

"Cool," she answered quickly, and then grateful for the interruption of Amy.

Their next stop was appropriate. Hell. A little town one could send a postcard from, a gift shop with trinkets, and a small area that had steaming rocks. And of course the tourist picture could be taken behind a piece of painted plywood you could put your face into and become the devil.

Surely God would take notice one day that he'd passed right over her when he waved the luck wand around. How much worse could her life get? It was bad enough, now, how appropriate, she was actually in Hell. Had her life become some sort of joke for the amusement of angels? Maybe it was penance. She thought about the guilt of her life then, the thoughts that had lingered over the years, maybe it was her that was supposed to die not her mother, and this was the price she paid.

It had been an excruciating morning. On the way back, Alana didn't look at much the driver pointed out, her gaze concentrated on the road ahead. He said they were headed to drop off Matt and Robb at the golf course, and then back to the ship. Just drive, don't talk and point, and don't slow down, just drive. Alana remained silent but screamed the words in her head.

Mrs. McCray went back to the ship to rest even though Alana invited her along with them. Figured there would probably be room on the boat for her to observe, but she said she'd rather eat lunch and rest that afternoon and maybe they could get together later. Alana asked so as not to be rude, and as much as she really liked the woman, she hoped she didn't seek her out later.

As she suspected, swimming with the stingrays was a wonderful surprise for Todd, and the activity provided great relief from the morning's anxiety for Alana. They boarded a boat at the dock that took them out to a site where they snorkeled first. Alana watched from the boat as Todd, Jonathan and Amy took to the water. She didn't mind too much being in the water as long as her head remained above, so she declined the snorkeling of course.

Todd was ecstatic when he returned. "We saw tons of fish. Yellow, blue and I saw a really big orange one with white stripes. All kinds of colors and a turtle, a huge sea turtle swam right by me."

Todd and Jonathan took off towards the front of the boat for the trip to stingray alley and Amy sat next to her.

"It really was beautiful down there."

"I'll see all of Todd's underwater pictures." The thought of being underwater was enough to almost make her panic.

"You don't go in at all?"

"A little, I wade in shallow water. I can't swim." She used it as excuse but Amy continued.

"They have a snorkel vest, it's easy to float."

"No, I'm content in shallow water."

Amy didn't question her again as she looked towards the island where a dark spot of clouds hovered. "Uh oh, looks like storm clouds over there. Wonder if they're overtop the golf course? Poor Robb, he's in his glory playing golf, I hope he's not rained out."

Alana didn't say anything and Amy continued in the direction she hadn't wanted the conversation to go. All she could do was hope she sounded normal.

"That Matt's a darling, isn't he? Jonathan mentioned the name, but I thought he was a kid until Robb told me he'd met him last night. Surprise, huh? Or did Todd tell you he was older."

"Todd told me nothing. Like you, I expected a kid."

"Far from that."

Amy looked to Alana but couldn't read anything into her smile. She knew Alana was single, and Matt was single, and she thought maybe there would be an attraction of some sort, but Alana remained bland, only shrugged her shoulders when she commented.

"Seems to be nice."

Amy nudged her playfully. "Oh come on, he's gorgeous."

She decided it was a fact she couldn't play off, it was the truth after all. "He is, but I'm not interested Amy. I know what you're getting at, but I'm not interested."

Alana hoped her voice was enough to put an end to anything further. Hoped their new friendship wouldn't be over so soon by Amy trying to push it, or trying to slyly get the two of them together somehow. Well meaning people had a way of thinking they were doing something good. By him being there, her week would already be filled with uncomfortable moments and she didn't need Amy to make it worse.

"It was a thought." She smiled and that was the end of the subject.

They reached their next destination of stingray alley. A sandbar where other boats gathered and the Captain assured her she didn't have to put her face in the water to see them. Instructions were given to walk with very flat feet across the sand, and when you fed them, to keep your thumb inside your fingers. They weren't dangerous, and wouldn't bite, but would perhaps mistake your thumb sticking out for food.

"Mom, look at that big one. He's coming right for you."

Todd pointed behind her and she didn't want to turn around so she just closed her eyes but felt him brush past her leg. She didn't want to be around all the creatures swimming by her, she was only doing this for Todd. They weren't shy by any means, came close enough to touch you, and after a short time she retreated back to the boat.

"That wasn't so bad, was it?" Todd asked when he joined her only when he had to, when it was time to go.

"I can say I did it. Let's put it that way." She pulled the towel around him tighter. "I think you need more sun block. Dry off good and we'll put more on."

"That was fun though, wasn't it?" Todd worried a little she'd forced herself on his account, knew how afraid she could be of the water sometimes.

"It actually wasn't so bad."

"You having a good time, Mom? Feeling okay? You were a little quiet this morning."

They spent so much time together, there wasn't a thing they didn't notice about the other, they were literally an extension of their own flesh and blood.

"I'm fine," she wiped his wet hair from his forehead. "And I'm having the best time. You?"

His broad grin was all she needed in answer.

When they returned to the ship, Alana sent Todd in to take a shower and promised Amy they'd catch up later for dinner. Then she used the payphone with her pre-purchased phone card to call her best friend.

"Alana, I didn't expect to hear from you, everything's okay isn't it?" Her first words were concern.

"Health wise, everything is fine."

She sighed with relief. "So how is it? Are you having the time of your life? I'm so jealous, work today was horrible and all I could do was think about you two basking away in the sunshine, in someplace beautiful."

"It is beautiful."

"Okay, don't lie to me, Alana, you never have and don't now. What's the matter?"

Alana sighed into the phone. "You'll love this. I met a guy in San Juan and had two glorious nights of wonderful sex." She could hear the audible gasp from the other end of the very long distance line. "Yes, believe it or not I broke my celibacy with a stranger in Puerto Rico. How outrageous is that?"

"He must have been unbelievable. I've been trying to talk you into a date for years and you'd have no parts of it, now a stranger?"

"A few glasses of wine, a warm night and a gorgeous man. Who knew it would be my downfall?"

"But you said it was wonderful, what's the matter?"

"Fantastic. Unbelievable. Here's the kicker. Ends up, he's on the same cruise, here on the ship, here in the Cayman's, as a matter of fact, believe it or not, Todd was the one who met him innocently. He's been friends with him since the first night on the ship."

"I can believe that, Todd meets everyone. He's going to make a great president one day. I think he's already running for office now."

"How could I be so unlucky?"

"What's so unlucky? He's on the same ship. You said it was great, so you have more sex. Where's the problem with this? Is he married or something?"

"No, but forget the more sex. I shouldn't have done it the first night but then I really shouldn't have gone back for more. But I did, and I did it as someone else."

"You're confusing me now. What are you talking about?"

Alana sighed deeply, "I lied to him. Told him my name was Jenna and I was alone in San Juan with some nursing associates." Alana paused when she heard her laugh but once she started again she rambled on. "Yes, I used your name, I knew you would love that but it was the quickest one I could think of, and I know enough about the medical field that I could skirt any of those questions if they came up. A few glasses of wine, a walk along the sea with the moon and stars and I was taken over the edge into some sort of fantasy world. Threw all caution to the wind. So he's here now and I lied, about everything."

"So what? Something like that isn't the end of the world if you're attracted to each other. He probably lied too."

"He didn't talk, didn't even look at me all day and I can't blame him. The grandmother was rather nice though. But Matt, I think he would have slit my throat like a pirate if he'd gotten me alone anywhere, and I can't blame him. Todd just thinks it's the greatest thing to make friends and..."

"Wait, wait, wait. I think you lost me at the grandmother. First the image of beautiful Puerto Rico, you and a gorgeous man and it all sounds so romantic. Then the hot sex. And all of a sudden a grandmother pops in out of nowhere and totally destroyed my dream bubble. How did somebody's grandmother get into this story?" Jenna was trying to make sense of it all.

"That's who he's with. I'm used to emotional chaos in my life so it shouldn't be too bad for the next week as long as I can avoid him," Alana looked around as if she'd see him somewhere and she certainly didn't want to.

"All I've ever asked is that you go on one date. How many times did I want to set you up and you told me it was too much trouble. You should have let me handle that end of your life, I would have done a fine job. This serves as proof that left on your own you're a disaster!"

Alana laughed. "I knew I could count on you for encouraging words."

"I still say have the great sex for a week."

"I knew you'd say that too. Besides the fact that he hates me, Jenna, I think I've already caused enough trouble for myself."

****

They met for dinner again and Alana almost backed out, worried Matt would join them, but he wasn't there and relief spread over her. She hadn't seen him since that afternoon when they dropped the two off at the golf course but she couldn't stop Robb from bringing him up a few times in conversation about his golf game. Every time he said the name it sent some sort of small electrical jolt through her body.

After dinner the boys took off to the arcade and although Amy and Robb tried to talk her into the show, Alana decided an early night with her book was what she needed. The day had worn on her and she was exhausted in more ways than one. She suffered both a physical and mental exhaustion and she wanted to retire to solitary comfort.

She stopped by the buffet area first to get a cup of coffee to take to her room. Alana had agreed to let Todd stay out till midnight and would need the coffee for extra energy to keep her awake till then.

"You're the best mom, love you." He'd said, and kissed her before he ran off.

It was his vacation and there had been so much to deal with, and there would be so much to deal with when they got home, and they only had now. No one promised them tomorrow and as much as she tried to leave the cancer behind, leave it in Chicago when she left and not think about it, she knew it only waited for their return. It wasn't going away just yet.

Alana took her coffee to a quiet spot on the deck and leaned against the banister to watch the passing wake below. The gorgeous moonlight cut a path across the immense ocean and a calm breeze caressed her face. She had to admit it was a little easier to relax in the Caribbean surroundings, so much so that she'd gotten herself into trouble and as if he'd read her mind and knew she was thinking about him, she heard his voice from behind her.

"Well, if it isn't Jenna from Virginia. Oh, excuse me, Alana from Chicago. By the way, how many lives do you have?" Matt's voice emitted a loathing mockery.

Alana didn't turn around but remained where she was. Her eyes never wavered from the light path of the moon, but she physically sensed it when he leaned on the banister next to her. So close, yet not touching her at all and she could almost feel the heat of his anger.

"If a one night stand was all you wanted, I can deal with that. What I can't deal with is lies. I don't know why, but for some reason I thought you were different than other women. A moment of stupidity on my part, guess I just have a knack for picking the lying cheats."

"I don't expect you to understand," she said.

Alana could hear the obvious hostility in his voice and couldn't blame him if he hated her. Didn't know what he meant by her being a cheat but she wasn't going to ask. The lying part she'd take blame for, but she wasn't going to question the rest, she would let him have his say and get it over with as quickly as possible. Here it was. The shame and guilt of what she'd done broke through the subsurface and was blasted in her face.

"Couldn't you have just told me the truth? Let me decide whether I wanted to sleep with a married woman?" Then Matt laughed but it was a mocking sound as he laughed more at himself than anything. "I can't believe it, I probably would have slept with you anyway."

He'd lived with a cheat for ten years, and even when he knew his wife was cheating, he didn't pursue or have any interest in another woman until they were separated. Matt knew how it felt to be betrayed and the same feeling went through him when he saw Alana's face. Not only was her husband betrayed, even though he didn't know it, but Matt had been betrayed too. And he felt it.

Alana spoke quietly, there was nothing to do but tell him the truth now, at least the basis for what she'd done. She wouldn't explain the why.

"I wanted to be someone else. For one night, only for a little while, I didn't want to be Alana from Chicago. I wanted someone else's life, not mine. I'm sorry, and I don't expect you to understand."

"You know what irritates me the most about this whole stupid thing? It would have been better to have just lived with the memory of a beautiful woman named Jenna that I met in San Juan and shared a few unforgettable nights with. It would have been better to not know the truth, because I liked her. That wonderful memory is destroyed now, because I discover she doesn't even exist."

Matt walked away and left her alone with her regret and embarrassment. She didn't know why he thought she was married, nor did she care, she wouldn't bother to tell him the truth, let him think of her what he would. It wasn't as if he could ever be in her life anyway.

Had she used him? Yes, but it was mutual, neither one looked for anything more than what they had. He fulfilled a need that burned deep, the need for comfort, for someone to look at her the way he did without pity and without sadness, without thinking of the cancer that consumed their lives, as others she knew did. To just look at her, want her, and take her to fiery heights as two carefree adults who simply wanted to share a few special moments. Even if it was in a magical make believe world.

Alana felt that was the only way. Maybe she'd been selfish in her quest but neither of them asked nor wanted for any more. She never meant to hurt him, never dreamed he'd discover what a fraud she was, but for two beautiful nights in San Juan she was somewhere else, far from the pain of her world. She experienced total escape wrapped in a pretend life that wasn't hers as she became someone else who could fully enjoy a moment's passion that had eluded her for many years. Was that so wrong?

CHAPTER SIX

The largest of the Bay Islands, eight of them collectively known as Las Islas de la Bahia, Roatan is approximately 34 miles long and 4 miles wide. Gentle, lush hills and clear turquoise water offered visitors a taste of its simplicity 30 miles off the coast of the Republic of Honduras.

The result of an enormous crack along the ocean floor, which lava from the earth's mantle welled up through, this crack formed the Caribbean plate. It buckled and formed the Bonacco Ridge which the Bay Islands rested upon. Now it was occupied by friendly, hospitable people, and offered brilliant blue waters and palm fringed white sand beaches, an exotic tropical feel of unspoiled beauty.

"It's beautiful, yes?" The cab driver questioned as he drove them to yet another secret destination Alana hadn't told Todd about.

"Magnificent. There isn't a care in the world out here is there?" Alana took it all in, didn't think about the cancer, the hospitals, the question of life or death. None of those thoughts had a place here in such beauty.

"We sure don't have places like this at home." Even Todd appreciated the brilliance of the new place they were ensconced in for the day.

Alana was grateful Jonathan, Amy and Robb had previous plans. Afraid another accidental meeting of Matt would have occurred had she planned anything with them, so she and Todd had taken off on their own.

The surprise she planned was a canopy tour. Hiding in the jungle were platforms and you were attached to a body harness then to a zip cord hanging above the trees. In mid air you floated from platform to platform until you reached the bottom.

Alana's heart filled at the sound of pure joy in Todd's laughter as he flew through the air. On one leg of the journey he turned upside down with delight, Alana opted not to, not as daring or brave, but she still enjoyed it tremendously. When they reached the bottom he wanted to go again and she couldn't deny him. There wasn't much she denied him.

When they were through, as they walked on a path through the woods, Alana kept a keen eye for the lizards and other land crabs. Small creatures that scared the wits out of her with their unexpected appearance and she shrieked a couple of times when she saw something. A fact both Todd and their driver who escorted them found amusing.

"My mom doesn't do woods well," Todd explained.

"There is much to see here but you are in no danger," The driver told her, tried to reassure her but his words didn't make her feel better.

She crept along with her eyes peeled to any moving thing, sped up to catch Todd and the driver whenever they got any distance ahead of her. Out of the corner of her eye she saw something on the pathway and the movements made her instinctively think it was one of the small lizards, or another innocent crab trying to quickly get out of her way, but when she actually looked, it wasn't either. Instead, a huge, long, slithering snake came out from the underbrush and quickly crossed her path. She screamed that time and it wasn't a small shriek as the one's she'd done previous, this was more a scream that sent birds flying and other animals running as noises emitted from the deep woods.

Both Todd and the driver turned in time to see the snake dodge for cover and Alana turned around the other way to get away from it. In doing so she twisted her ankle but didn't care, kept going a few feet before she stopped and no longer saw it.

"That was so cool, did you see that? It was huge!" Todd was thrilled then looked to his mother to see the stark fear on her face. "You okay, Mom?"

"Oh, I come second after the cool snake, now you ask if I'm okay." She laughed and teased him as he now stood beside her along with the driver. "I'm fine. Is my hair completely gray now? It feels like it should be. Have we had enough of playing Indians for the morning? Is there a beach somewhere?"

Alana started to walk then remembered she'd twisted her ankle because she felt the pain.

"You are hurt?" The driver took her elbow to support her.

"Scared as hell and I guess I twisted my ankle but I'll be okay, the walk will work out any kinks. Too bad it won't help with the nightmares I'll be having."

"Must have been ten feet long, what kind of snake was it?" Todd was still excited over seeing it.

"Hard to say, but we have no poisonous snakes on the island."

"I think it was a Boa Constrictor." Todd exclaimed, the only snake he knew the name of.

"Great, a wonderful story to tell, I was almost attacked by a Boa Constrictor." The thought of it still frightened her, even though she knew it was an exaggeration.

"He was so cool mom, did you see him? I mean, I know you saw part of him, did you see all of him?"

"See him?" She laughed. "If I hadn't of jumped out of the way he'd have run me over!"

When Alana put more pressure on her foot, she could feel more pain but she walked ahead and tried not to flinch. She still wanted some beach time, figured she wouldn't have to move once she placed herself in the sand so the driver took them to a lovely beach where they stayed for two hours then headed back to the ship.

By the time the driver got them back to port, Alana's ankle was twice its size and with the help of Todd she hobbled along the dock at a slow pace. She put her arm around his shoulder and the slight brace of him helped her a little, but he was so small she didn't want to put all her weight on him.

"It isn't broken or anything, is it?" Todd was concerned but she reassured him she was fine and he believed her, had no reason not to as she put on a brave face and tried desperately not to lean on him too much.

"Just twisted I think. I'm fine, other then the nightmares I'm going to have from seeing that monster, he was the size of a Buick."

"I can't wait to tell Tommy. Hey, I'll send a postcard from the ship, I'll tell him in the postcard."

Todd referred to his best friend back home and Alana was sarcastically glad she was able to provide a story for him.

"Great."

Matt watched the two from a distance, could see that Alana tried as best she could not to put much pressure on Todd, used him only for slight support and it was obvious she needed someone stronger to lean on and someone taller. Leave them alone, Matt told himself. They're fine. It would take her awhile but she'll get there just like everyone else, just slower.

He continued to observe them from his distant position until she almost tripped and when he saw her face twist and contort in pain, it made him wince himself. When they stopped for her to rest a moment he knew he couldn't just stand there, it wasn't in his nature to ignore it.

"I can't just stand by and watch this. I don't know what your mother did, Todd, but do you mind if I give a hand?"

"Hey, Matt, sure," he was only too glad to have the help, felt as if he wasn't doing much to assist her.

"I know this might be a little unconventional, but short of a wheel chair I think it's the only way we're going to get back to the ship before it sails." Matt easily put his arm around her back then the other behind her knees and effortlessly swooped her up into his arms as she let out a squeal.

"I don't think I need all this, I'm fine, really." Her voice tried to be pleasant as Todd stood by, she wished he weren't there at that moment so she could let Matt have it.

"What happened anyway?" Matt ignored her and directed his question to Todd.

"You should have seen it, the snake was at least ten feet long, huge. And it came out of the bushes, right after mom. Well, it just wanted to cross the path but she was right there. She jumped back and he ran away when she screamed. Should have heard her, the birds started squawking and you could hear little crabs and lizards running off everywhere."

Matt couldn't help but laugh. "Must have been a sight."

"Todd, isn't that Jonathan up there? I'll be okay, why don't you go ahead and ask him if they want to meet us for dinner tonight? Go on ahead and walk with him and I'll meet you in the room. Start your shower when you get there."

"You sure, Mom?"

"Go, hurry before you lose sight of him," she strongly encouraged. When he did she fumed at Matt. "Put me down right now."

"For you to walk on your own? Yeah, you looked like you were doing a really good job of that."

"I'll crawl if I have to, put me down," she squirmed a little but he only gripped her tighter.

"Believe me, I'd like nothing more than to put you down but at the rate you were going, you'd miss the ship. As much as I'd love to leave you here, I couldn't do that to your son. He's a good kid, I can't blame him because his mother has 'Sybil' issues and doesn't know who she is. I'm not doing this for you."

"It never crossed my mind," she huffed.

He was still so angry, and Alana was angry because he was angry with her, if that made sense. She was hurt that he didn't understand and yet she knew he didn't know the full truth of why she lied. Still, she let him get to her.

His arms held her tight, her body pressed close to his and Alana's arm wrapped around his back to his shoulder because she couldn't just let it dangle. She knew what his skin felt like underneath his shirt, remembered the way his breath felt on her face, his smell so close to her wafted through her mind and recalled clearly nights she struggled to forget. Stupid, stupid snake. As scared as she was of it then, had she known something like this would happen she'd have stepped on its head.

"We're almost there and I can walk the rest of the way. I don't think my husband would appreciate me being carried by another man." It was all Alana could think of to make him put her down. He thought she was married so why not try to use it to her advantage. But her plan backfired when he laughed and she felt even more foolish at being caught in another lie.

"Sorry, that lie won't work. Your name and single motherhood came up in a conversation with Robb somehow. My mistake, I'd assumed you were married from a comment Todd made, that I mistook to mean his father just wasn't on this vacation. So it means you're not a cheat, but doesn't change the fact that you played me."

Matt refused to put her down when they got on the ship and carried her directly to the ships doctor who confirmed that it wasn't broken. The heat and having to walk so much just after it happened was probably the cause of the majority of the swelling. Immediate ice and rest would work to reduce it.

"I told you I was fine," she huffed with a childish 'I told you so' attitude.

"Like I'd believe you, the truth doesn't seem to come naturally for you. Where's your cabin?"

"You don't have to carry me to my cabin."

"I'm not, I'm going to drop you off at the nearest elevator."

****

With her foot elevated on pillows Todd propped up for her, they dined in the room from a tray he'd fixed from the buffet. With one of the crew's grateful help he bought her a sampling of everything and included a plate with several desserts to choose from. They shared and each had a taste of it all.

"I'm sorry this ruined our plans to have dinner with Jonathan tonight," Alana said.

"Its okay Mom, this is cool, eating dinner in bed. Like a picnic."

And it was. They had a great time as they chatted about their day and continued to laugh at the huge snake that now had grown to at least twenty feet in length, and every time he told the story, it grew more.

"I guess the sand on the beach is the best place for you," he commented.

"What do you mean?"

"You don't want to go in the water, or the woods. The sand is what's in between."

She laughed. "I guess you have a point."

"Why are you so afraid of the water, Mom?" He'd never asked the question before and it surprised her he asked out of the blue now.

Alana looked at him and pondered his question, debated telling him the truth or play if off. She decided the latter. "I guess because I can't swim."

"Granddaddy could swim, how come you never could? How come he never taught you?"

"I didn't want to learn, never interested."

"I miss him too." Todd picked at a piece of coconut cake and looked directly at her with a knowing look on his face when he could see his comment caught her off guard. "I see you sometimes and I think I know when you're thinking about him."

"You know quite a few things, don't you?"

"I know he's probably here on this trip. He's with us."

She was glad he'd felt him. "That's what people keep telling me."

"You don't think so?"

"I don't know. I want him to be."

"I think you've just been so wrapped up in everything, you haven't opened your eyes to anything else."

"Is that what you think?" She looked at her son with such love. "I think he might be right inside of you, you're acting more his age than your own."

"He's going to make everything okay, Mom, I know he will, he loves us." Todd was through with the cake and took her hand in his. "Open your eyes mom and see, he'll make everything okay."

Alana didn't say anything, couldn't say anything for fear of the tears that threatened. There was so much she wanted to believe, everything he'd said, but she'd never been able to find a reason to.

Todd made sure she was extra comfortable before she made him leave and go have fun so he was off again to explore. Mrs. McCray liked to sit in the central atrium with a cup of hot tea and listen to a piano player and it was where Todd headed later that evening when he looked all over the ship but couldn't find Jonathan.

"Evening, Mrs. McCray."

"Evening, Todd." She smiled at him, he was such a little gentleman and she enjoyed his company, especially since Matt didn't seem to be his jovial self these days.

"Did you have a nice dinner?"

"It was lovely, you?"

"Ours was great. We had a picnic on the bed in the cabin so mom could rest her ankle."

"Oh? What's wrong with her ankle?"

"A snake scared her in the woods today and she twisted it. The biggest snake I've ever seen and I saw one in the zoo one time, but this one was even bigger. It was huge. Matt saw us trying to get back to the ship and mom's ankle was making her real slow, so he carried her back. He didn't tell you?"

"I guess he forgot to mention it. It isn't going to ruin the rest of her cruise, is it?" She asked the question with sincere concern.

"No, the swelling's better already but we just want to be on the safe side and rest it as much as possible tonight. By tomorrow I think it'll be okay. Hey, my birthday is next week, we'll be in St. Vincent. Isn't that the coolest thing?" He grinned widely at his announcement.

"Are you taking the cruise after this one?"

"Yeah, great, isn't it?" The young man beamed as he spoke.

Diana smiled, "How wonderful, so are we. Matt and I will be on this ship again too."

His face lit up in surprise. "Wow. That'll be fun, lets do some stuff together. Maybe you and Matt can celebrate my birthday with me?"

"I'd be honored. At your young age, you've got much to celebrate. At my age, I go to sleep every night and wonder if I'm going to wake up in the morning."

Todd became silent for a moment as he watched the activity around him. When he spoke again, this time his voice was not so lively, the sparkle in his eyes just slightly clouded.

"Yeah, sometimes I do to. Go to sleep at night and wonder if I'm going to wake up in the morning. Are you afraid to die?"

"Why would you possibly worry about such things?"

"I have cancer. I get really, really, sick sometimes during the treatments and stuff, and sometimes I'd be afraid to go to sleep, I didn't want to close my eyes."

Mrs. McCray was stunned into silence at his confession. The young boy had just poured his little heart and soul into her lap and she didn't know what to do with it, didn't know how to react to the revelation.

"I... I didn't know."

"I'm okay with it. I don't think I'm afraid to die, but sometimes there's a doubt. I guess that's normal, huh?"

"I imagine." Diana still had a hard time finding her voice.

"Like when I first saw this ship. I was so excited but I've never been on a boat like this and there was that uncertainty, you know, a little nervous. I wondered what it was really going to be like, and I had my doubts. Kind of the same way I feel about dying."

She was amazed he could put it into such simple perspective. He'd obviously had time to deal with it, he was so easy and casual as he spoke and she suspected it wasn't something he'd discovered just yesterday but something he'd been dealing with for quite some time.

Todd continued in his easy manner. "If I knew when to expect it, I'd probably not worry about it, like if the doctors gave me a date at least I'd know. I don't worry about it so much anymore, it could still happen anytime I guess, but like I said, I used to worry about it more when I was really, really sick. Like during treatment and stuff and in and out of the hospital. I'd be afraid to go to sleep because I didn't know if I would die by morning."

"Yeah," she said softly, still didn't know quite what to say. It wasn't a conversation she would ever have considered with such a young man. So boldly honest, forthright and unabashed in his confession and she offered the same. Diana spoke the truth, said what came to her mind. "Same here, if I knew which night I'd die, I'd probably wear my best pajamas."

Todd's spontaneous laughter rang out loudly and made her giggle too. And when he continued, her heart poured out to him as he described the past year he'd lived. But what came through to her the most, was that his main concern was the pain he knew his mother endured, she always looked strong but he knew she suffered so deep at the thought of him dying. And his worry over her was evident.

"We lost granddaddy not long ago, and I never knew my grandma, or my dad. There'll be no one left for her, not family anyway."

He told Mrs. McCray of some of the long rough times in the hospital. Once, Alana decorated his room by actually recreating his bedroom at home, complete with his video games and fish tank. How she'd shaved her own head when the chemo and radiation treatments caused him to lose all of his hair.

"We laughed so hard one of my IV's popped right out. Should have seen her, she was bald and on back of her head she had someone paint a face so when she turned her back it looked like you were still talking to someone. So then I just laughed harder and another IV popped out."

Todd laughed easily at the recollection. It had been a bad place, a bad time, but a good memory he relived with pride and love. His mother hadn't been one to pull him along with false hope, she'd taken his hand and they'd walked through it side by side every painful step of the way.

Mrs. McCray listened intently. The little boy was so knowledgeable about an illness that would possibly kill him. All the medical jargon he spoke should have been reserved for someone much older than his young years.

Todd spoke very matter-of-factly, it was obvious he'd come to terms with what could possibly be his fate. Diana wondered why God would keep her there for so long and threaten to take such an incredible spirited soul as Todd's instead. It didn't seem fair.

She now understood the look of sadness or possibly fear, she wasn't certain, that she'd seen in his mother's eyes a few times when Alana looked at Todd. Diana had caught a quick glimpse of something and didn't understand at the time, couldn't begin to imagine the pain that burned deep inside this young mother's heart now that Diana knew what jeopardized their lives.

Diana liked to travel, liked to meet different people wherever she went and would often, as people do, guess about the lives of others. A nice young family she imagined to be on the biggest vacation of their lives, others she would guess well traveled, or the young newlyweds or older couple celebrating an anniversary or special occasion. When she'd first met Todd and Alana she took a guess at what their lives were like, and imagined a recently divorced mother who simply wanted to get away with her son.

Young women, and older for that matter, were always attracted to Matt and she hadn't seen that in Alana. So she attributed it to possibly a nasty split with an ex husband and she wasn't interested in any sort of relationship. Diana's guess to what their lives were like hadn't come close to the truth Todd explained to her now.

"Hey, where's Matt tonight?" Todd asked the question in his normal jovial spirit as if he hadn't just talked of his possible death. His straightforward conversation on his illness was over and he effortlessly moved on.

"I haven't seen him since dinner, if I were to guess, he may be standing over a blackjack table."

"I have a little more time and I thought maybe some basketball..."

"Well," Matt had come from around a corner and unexpectedly seen them. "My two favorite people."

"We were just talking about you." Diana smiled as he kissed her cheek. "Have you cleared your pockets already?"

"Blackjack was not kind this evening."

"I doubt playing basketball with Todd will be kind either. Every time I've seen you play he seems to get the better of you," Diana smiled with weariness and Matt noticed immediately.

"You okay?"

"Past my bedtime, so I'm off and you two go play."

"I'll be easy on ya tonight, you know, you being a little older and all." Todd grinned and threw out the challenge in his playful way.

"Ouch, that one hurt," Matt playfully winced. "I can't think of anything better. The casino has enough of my money for the moment."

Matt wasn't sure the time spent with Todd was a good thing. It was already an uncomfortable situation with his mother and the best thing would be to remain indifferent to this young boy. But it was hard to do with someone with a personality such as Todd's. When Todd ran across him, he would always stop and talk, join him for a quick moment and the same with his grandmother as well.

That morning Alana was with him and though she smiled respectfully and said hello to his grandmother, she didn't stop. Said she was in dire need of coffee so couldn't stay, the invisible tension understandable only between the two of them and no one else suspected the pointed, uninterested remoteness.

Matt found it difficult not to enjoy Todd's company. He didn't seek him out on purpose, quite the opposite, and he couldn't avoid him and wasn't going to risk hurting his feelings by ignoring him. So they went off together to the basketball court.

"Where's Jonathan tonight?"

"I think he's chasing after a girl."

Matt laughed. "Ah, puppy love. Is she cute?"

"I guess," Todd shrugged his shoulders.
"What about you? I've seen you talking to a few."
"Nah, I don't have time for girls."
"I hate to tell you this, but one of these days you will. Unfortunately, it will be all you'll be able to think about. Just giving you a warning now." Matt tossed him the ball.
Todd looked at him curiously. "Is that what you do? You have someone special you think about all the time?"
"Nah, it's kind of like a cold, it will hit you, but you'll get over it." He lied.
They played for an hour until Alana found them.
"Todd, you're late, and I couldn't get you on the radio."
"Hey Mom, what are you doing up? How's your ankle?"
"I'm up because I had to get out of the room for awhile so I figured I'd come look for you. Where's your radio?"
"I forgot it, I'm sorry." He ran over to her with concern and apology she had to look for him. "Does your ankle still hurt?"
"It's fine. It's late and you've had a big day, time for you to get to bed." Her voice revealed she wasn't happy with him. She hadn't expected him to be with Matt and when she saw him she almost turned around and left.
"I'm out Matt. I'll be right back mom." Todd threw the ball onto the court, ran to get his water bottle and before she could stop him ran off down the stairs for a refill of water and left her alone with Matt.
His strong bare-chested upper body seemed to shout out at her as it gleamed with sweat, and muscled strong arms she remembered could be so gentle, tender and kind at one time. Stop thinking Alana, stop remembering, stop thinking, and stop looking at him. It was fairly dark where she stood so she hoped he didn't notice the gaze of her eyes.
Matt didn't say a word as he walked over to retrieve his shirt thrown over a deck chair. He would ignore her, it was probably for the best neither of them said another word to each other for the rest of the week. And he would have ignored her but Alana felt she had to say something. Even though her voice had an edge to it when she spoke, it was the truth. She was appreciative that he saw no need to take any anger he felt towards her, out on Todd.
"Thank you for being so kind to my son."
"He's a good kid," Was all he said.
Todd rushed past her, ran over to Matt and gave him a high five. "Want to do something tomorrow?" Then Todd looked to his mother with a smile as if he'd just had a brilliant idea. "Hey, how about breakfast? Want to have breakfast together?"
"I…" Matt was thinking of an excuse until Alana spoke.

"Todd, I don't think we need to make breakfast plans. It's a day to sleep late and you'll probably be in bed until lunch."

"Then we can plan on lunch together," he looked to each other and wouldn't give up until he had a definite answer.

"Let's just wait and see what comes. I'm sure you'll see Matt tomorrow, this ship is only so big." She said it with a slight edge and Matt picked up that it wasn't big enough for her.

"Okay," he sighed. "Thanks for the game, Matt. Next time I might have to let you win just so you'll keep playing with me."

Matt smiled. The same smile that once drew her in close now pushed her away, for it was gone when he glanced back at her before they left.

CHAPTER SEVEN

Their last day for that week's short cruise was a sea day, and Alana was grateful she could let her foot rest and not have to traipse around an island. She and Todd had eaten breakfast in the dining room with Jonathon and his family, and then the two boys had run off. Alana found him much later.

"There you are," she tipped her son's hat down onto his face and smiled at Diana. "Hello, Mrs. McCray." Alana liked Diana, under different circumstances, like Todd, would have enjoyed her company.

"Mom, Mrs. McCray has a bird, the kind that talks. It says 'Good morning', and some words she won't tell me."

"Then I guess we'll have to leave that to our imaginations, won't we?" She laughed as she put her arm around Todd. "I thought you were going to see the movie with Jonathan?"

Todd hadn't realized he was late and he quickly said goodbye with a quick kiss for her and after he left, Alana took the opportunity to talk to Diana as she'd wanted to do, but hadn't the chance.

"I really hope he hasn't bothered you. I see him with you quite a bit and if you want to come up with some sort of sign for me to intrude and find something else for him to do, I'd be happy to. You most likely just don't want to be rude."

"Oh dear child," she sighed and smiled. "He has been the highlight of my trip."

"He can be quite a handful, but yes, he's quite a highlight too."

"You're a lucky woman to have been so blessed." Diana looked her directly in the eyes with compassion, a silent conveyance for a mother's pain without saying the words.

"Yes, I am."

The quiet communication didn't go unnoticed to Alana. Whatever happened, she had to appreciate the fact that she had been blessed with Todd, even if it would come to only a short while, it was a blessing to have had him in her life.

Alana was sure she hadn't misread her meaning. It surprised her Todd would have said anything, he hardly ever spoke about it to others outside of ill patients and a few very close friends. And with other patients he talked about it as if it were his job, something he was chosen to do as he used his buoyant charm to uplift those not even close in degree to his grave critical condition.

Even though Mrs. McCray was a pleasant woman, they'd only just met and that's what bewildered Alana the most. She hadn't known him to talk about it with strangers but neither said anything else on the subject.

"How is your ankle healing, dear? You look like you still have a limp, does it bother you much?"

"Not so much." Alana leaned down to show her the swelling was only slight now. "I think by the end of today it should be back to normal. I don't plan on doing anything but lying around in the sunshine."

"No place better I can think of to heal yourself. And I should think a few frozen drinks could take away any leftover pain quicker."

Alana laughed, but she was becoming too comfortable there and didn't want to stay for fear of running into Matt. It disappointed her when she felt she should go.

"I think I'll take your advice and indulge myself today. Its better advice than any doctor would have given, and sounds much more fun. Have a good day, Mrs. McCray."

"You too, dear."

Neither one saw the other as Alana left the table and a few moments later Matt joined his grandmother.

"You just missed Alana. Todd's mother?"

Of course his grandmother didn't know that he didn't have to be reminded who Alana was and he almost laughed but didn't, Matt gave no response to her statement but wished he could have thought of something before she spoke again.

"Such a nice young lady, I'm surprised you haven't taken a liking to her."

"Don't do that grandmother, I'm not interested. She isn't my type anyway."

"She's beautiful, just your type."

"Katherine was beautiful also, that didn't mean a thing."

"I told you before you married that snake ex-wife you were making a mistake. She was a reptile in someone else's beautiful human skin."

Matt had to laugh at her accurate description, he could now with the pain of divorce over, but he still carried the pain of her betrayal. He didn't think he did until Alana reminded him with her own lies of deceit.

"Alana had the proper upbringing you can tell. Very pleasant woman and..."

Matt now stopped her mid sentence. "Yes, she's very nice. But Grandmother, quit trying to pair me with every woman under the age of fifty. If I ever find someone I want to settle down with again, you'll be the first to know. And I expect you to dance at my next wedding if there will ever be such a thing. Until then, let me be." Then his voice softened when he realized it came out so strong. "Please?"

"You have time. We're going to be together again for another week after this."

"What are you talking about?"

"Todd told me they're booked on next weeks cruise also. Lovely, isn't it?"

Matt almost openly cringed but quickly stopped himself from any obvious display of irritation. "No, we're not going to be together. You and I will be together. Alana and Todd will be together. We are two separate entities. Two completely different families who just happen to be on the same cruise, we didn't come together."

Matt knew it sometimes felt as if they had and couldn't for the life of him figure out how their lives had become so entwined. Virtual strangers a week ago, then lovers, now family members interacted together as the lovers, rather ex-lovers, tried to ignore each other and stay out of each other's way. How crazy was that? A golden case for Sigmund Freud, or better still Jerry Springer, except nobody was sleeping with anybody, as was often the dilemma on the Jerry Springer show. Yeah, he had to remind himself of that, didn't he? And he'd have a whole other week to not sleep with anybody.

The sea day passed quickly, Alana rested in the sun and took Diana's advice as she and Amy enjoyed a few frozen cocktails by the pool as their sons enjoyed the day together and Robb and Matt occupied themselves elsewhere. Todd had already told her that Jonathan and his family would be on the next cruise, but she learned from Amy that Matt and Diana would be there also.

"I talked to Mrs. McCray last night, they're going to be on the cruise next week also. Isn't that great?"

Alana almost moaned out loud and what came out was automatic. "Wonderful."

"Robb's excited to get in more golf with Matt but I told him not to hope for much. I had many plans."

Alana's face was to the sun, she kept her eyes closed and revealed nothing, but inside her mind reeled at the news. She'd been looking forward to getting back to Miami and starting a new cruise for much longer without the worry of Matt. Now she would be faced with him again.

That evening Todd made plans for their dinner and he included every one of their new friends, including Diana and Matt, and it was comfortable and lively as everyone talked to everyone. Except Alana and Matt who never talked directly to one another. The boys wanted to be excused immediately after dinner, and Mrs. McCray insisted Matt stay when she too decided it was her bedtime.

The four were left like a nice cozy little group to enjoy coffee and dessert. Only Alana and Matt's insides churned.

"I think it's great we'll all be together again next week. What are the odds of that?" Amy beamed.

Odds had never been in her favor, is what Alana wanted to reply, but of course didn't. "It's wonderful for Todd. He enjoys my company, but I can only do so much. He and Jonathan get along so well."

"It's the perfect ship for children with so many things to do, they can't get enough. And of course they'll have Matt to play basketball with them."

Alana wanted to leave, but when they finished, Amy insisted they go to one of the dance clubs to continue their evening. It was large and crowded with floor to ceiling glass that surrounded three sides, dark woods, glass-topped tables and deep cushioned chairs with brocade upholstery that were comfortable and inviting.

Neither she nor Matt wanted to appear suspicious in refusing so quickly so each went along casually. She would have had a good time had she not had to face Matt, especially alone when Amy and Robb danced. They couldn't understand why Matt and Alana didn't take the same opportunity but each refused when it was suggested.

Matt had been patient but could take no more so he took the opportunity to leave when they were alone. "Tell them I went to the casino, a blackjack table calling my name."

"I'll tell them you're just a rude person who actually hates them. Maybe that would stop them from trying to push us together."

"If only it would," he sneered.

She hadn't looked at him when he spoke, now watched his back as he exited. Maybe she could cancel the next week, it crossed her mind but she couldn't, she wasn't going to let him ruin the time with her son.

When the ship docked in Miami, Alana and Todd, and Amy and her family all piled into a van and went to Bayside Marketplace. It offered shops, a band, restaurants and various activities to enjoy. They took a boat ride to Star Island and Todd was fascinated. It was an enjoyable day and Alana was glad Diana and Matt couldn't join them when Amy asked.

But it was only temporary, she was faced with them again when they re-boarded the ship for the second half of their journey but Alana had set in her mind to enjoy it. She got through the meals Todd planned with them for the next few days at sea and kept an angry distance when their paths crossed. When their first island stop of Barbados came, Alana was only too glad to be able to leave the ship and get away from Matt.

****

One of the few coral-capped islands in the region, Barbados rested in tranquil beauty just east of the Caribbean island chain where unspoiled charm awaited travelers. And Bajans welcomed visitors 'home' with open arms. Although common to nearby islands, volcanic peaks would not be found, it was relatively flat compared to island neighbors who shared turquoise sea, but none less magnificent.

A bustling cosmopolitan area could be found in Bridgetown while the countryside offered rolling hills, quiet roads and scenic beaches to while away the time. It was another beautiful clear day in paradise when the ship pulled into port.

Alana couldn't have been more anxious to get off to start her day. She gathered her bag together and met Todd on the top deck where he enjoyed his morning with Mrs. McCray. After a quick chat, she made their excuses and wished Diana a pleasant day. Just in time to miss Matt who joined his grandmother.

"I've got to go, I'm meeting Jack in just a few minutes. Do you want to walk down with me?" Matt asked.

"No, I'm waiting for Ellen, that woman you met last night? She's going to the Botanic Gardens too but we don't have to meet the rest of the group for another thirty minutes or so. You go on, don't let this old lady keep you."

Matt reached down and gave her a tender loving kiss on the cheek. "You will never be an old lady."

"You have a good day at golf, I hope it improves your mood."

"What do you mean?" He was confused as to why she thought his mood needed improving.

"Your disposition is always so upbeat on our vacations, but you've been so quiet this time, I don't want you not to enjoy yourself."

"I am enjoying myself as always grandmother. Just taking me a little longer this time to get the work stress out of my system and relax. We're starting a new project and I hope they're getting along without me." It wasn't all a lie. As part of a commercial development group he worried about every new project. "The Royal Westmoreland awaits, I'm meeting Jack and a few others from the ship and this will be the day all my stress is relieved. I'll be a new man the next time you see me."

Matt could only wish the golf would do it, probably would work wonders if he didn't have to come back to the ship and inevitably run into Alana again. But he would make it a point to improve his attitude for his grandmother, it was ridiculous for him to let a strange woman have this sort of effect, and Matt knew he had to shake this mood one way or another, had to shake thoughts of her one way or another. If not he would be completely insane before the week was over.

The course was touted as one of the finest in the Caribbean situated in 500 acres of the most breathtaking scenery in the West Indies. Just thinking about it improved his mood. That is, until he saw Alana and Todd on his way out. It made him wonder where they were going and what they were doing. Then he stopped himself, wasn't his business, why did he even wonder?

Couldn't he just take the anger inside and transfer it to his eyesight? Every time he saw her his pulses soared. He was a man with desires, had felt her skin, kissed the tenderness of her lips and enjoyed the pleasure like never before. His anger at her betrayal boiled, but his masculine senses lost all control.

Todd stopped and shouted across the short distance, Alana simply walked on. "Hey, Matt, we're going to swim with the turtles, wanna go with us?"

"Golfing today, buddy, but you have a good time." Matt waved and thought to add something for Alana's benefit. "Hey, Todd, watch your mother, don't let her trip over herself again."

To anyone within earshot it would have seemed as if it were friendly joking. Alana knew otherwise.

Matt tried to figure out what was going on inside his mind and couldn't. He'd had his share of relationships, both before his wife and after his wife, and although one-night-stands as a single man were few, they were consensual. Neither wanted anything from the other but sex and it worked well.

Wasn't that the case here? It's all either of them had wanted in San Juan. So she lied, initially, it's what angered him the most because his wife had lied to him for years and he felt a betrayal, but what incensed him more was the memory Alana stole from him. This perfect stranger came into his life so unexpectedly and gave to him so tenderly, so passionately. When he saw her and realized it wasn't real, all a game she played, that's what infuriated him more than anything.

As the days passed, Matt secretly watched her interaction with Todd, the way she playfully tousled his head or pushed his hat down over his eyes. When she protectively put her arm around him as if she would save him from any harm or when she looked at him, he saw such pure love it was hard for him to believe she was the deceitful fraud he'd labeled her in the beginning.

He found himself wanting to know this woman. There was so much more behind the soft innocent smile, something about her he wanted to be close to. Then he'd come to realize there was also something about her he wanted to run from, so he held onto his anger because he knew she had the power and ability to break his heart for the first time in his life.

His ex-wife hurt him, but by the time the divorce came he hadn't loved her, if he'd ever truly loved her at all. So she hadn't broken his heart, she was incapable of that and it was still intact. But with Alana, he knew it would be different. There was already a crack.

****

They took a cab to Royal Pavilion Beach where they met the tour provider who would carry them, along with six other passengers off the west coast of the island on a boat to snorkel, swim and feed the Hawksbill sea turtles that gathered for food.

"Mom, every day we're doing what I want to do. You don't snorkel, barely get in the water, isn't there something else you want to do?"

"Nothing, just to be with you makes it a wonderful day."

"I'm serious. Isn't there something special you want to do?"

"I'm doing it, spending time with you. I may not want to get my face in the water but you know I enjoy the sun, so I sun, you snorkel. Works great."

"You're getting so tan I hardly saw you in the dark last night when you came out to get me from the basketball court," Todd laughed.

"Speaking of basketball, I know sometimes Jonathan can't play with you, but maybe you shouldn't bother Mr. McCray so much."

"He likes to play mom, I don't bug him about it or anything, he just likes to play. He's kinda good for being old. Well, not that he's that old, but you know what I mean."

"Yeah, I know what you mean."

"He's cool, isn't he?" He asked with an innocent look.

"Everything to you is cool."

"But I mean, he's really nice, and fun too. Maybe we could do some things on the islands this week." Todd would have planned it all if he could. Get Matt and his mother together as often as possible, but he hadn't been able to.

"Maybe," she shrugged it off as best she could.

When Todd went into the water, Alana leaned over the side of the boat and watched the sea turtles. There must have been a hundred of them everywhere and he kept pulling his head out of the water to shout at her.

"Mom, did you see him? He was right next to me!"

She didn't have to be in the water to experience it with him, felt just as delighted as if she were right next to him, felt his joy all the way to the inner core of her heart. "There's more coming, Todd," she pointed behind him.

It seemed like he was in the water for hours and when he finally came out she wrapped a towel around him, pulled him close and rubbed his back. If he was getting too old for her motherly affection, he never protested. "There were hundreds of them, I saw them all around you."

"I saw a gigantic one. Swam right next to me for a long time and he was almost big as I was."

"I think he was." A man said when he came out of the water behind Todd.

"Did you see him too?" Todd's eyes were big.

"Biggest one I've ever seen here."

The man talked about his past trips to Barbados and Todd was fascinated in all he told him about the undersea world. He told him what to look for and what to stay away from, and explained different kinds of fish and coral as the boat carried them to another snorkel site over a shipwreck.

Todd found it the funniest thing that the five-striped Sergeant Majors allowed tiny yellow wrasse to cleanse parasites from their teeth. However, if the larger fish hurt the wrasse, the wrasse would spray a chemical over the Sergeant Major and other wrasse would no longer clean that fish. It would eventually die from parasites.

They snorkeled together and Alana could see Richard and Todd come up several times as Richard continued to explain things. Perhaps the fish they'd seen or how to clear his snorkel properly and Alana watched and smiled from her always comfortable seat on the boat.

Since her father passed away, she felt Todd craved male attention at times. He missed his grandfather who had been such a major influence in his life and although he didn't seek a substitute, he didn't have trouble connecting with people to fill a tiny piece of the void, even if it were temporary travelers. Alana was just glad that at least this time his new friend would not be a threat. She would guess correctly that his traveling companion was of the same sex as he.

Along with a male traveling companion who wasn't there that day, Richard also traveled with his sister and her husband who had waited on the shore of the beach while he went out to snorkel. His companion, Kevin, suffered from seasickness the night before and stayed on the ship for the day.

After they enjoyed a little time on shore, and lively conversation, Alana felt comfortable in accepting their offer of an island tour with them in the open air car they'd rented. Since they expected Kevin to join them they'd rented two cars so there was plenty of room with Alana and Todd in Richard's car.

Having been there several times before, Richard made an educated tour guide. They headed north on Spring Garden Hwy to Speightstown and turned east on Hwy 1E. The Wildlife Reserve was perfectly timed as the monkeys were ready for feeding and across the road they visited St. Nicholas Abby.

They drove up Cherry Tree Hill that was lined with mahogany trees and it was a magnificent spot with an excellent view of the Scotland District that covered the hilly parish of St. Andrew. Richard told them it was one of the most beautiful views on the island. Not only did it overlook the rugged Scotland District, also the mighty Atlantic Ocean and Cattlewash Beach, the longest beach in Barbados. Back in the jeep and past Lakes Beach where the road turned South East, they drove along the coast and continued down.

"Most people don't visit the East side of the island but it has the most beautiful views." Richard explained and Alana had to agree with him.

They reached a crossroads and Richard asked Todd to pick one.

"Straight, left or right?"

"Huh?"

"You decide where we're going, either way is great."

"Right?" Todd said it as a question, without much conviction, and they laughed.

A right dropped them down into Bathsheba. A favored resort for Bajans that few tourists frequented and Alana thought it a shame, it was picturesque in its beauty.

Small homes and the odd rum shops here and there lined the roadside that ran along the sea. Rugged in its terrain the dramatic coastline offered wide open beaches and striking rock formations. The bay was one of the most painted landscapes in Barbados, also known as the soup bowl because of the crashing breakers that was standard most times of the year. It was a popular surf area and they were pleased a few chose to brave the waves that day as they got a quick show.

"Oh wow, did you see him?"

"They have many local and international surfing championships here. As you can see, quite rough for swimmers and you certainly can't snorkel, that's why most tourists don't see it. They go to the calmer beaches instead. Obviously this side is more for its beauty."

"They don't know what they're missing. It's breathtaking." Alana marveled at the paradise surroundings. Wondered what it would be like to live with this kind of scenery through your window every day.

They drove on towards Sam Lord's Castle located in the parish of St. Philip. A beautiful Georgian mansion built in 1820 by notorious buccaneer Samuel Hall Lord who acquired his wealth by plundering ships, lured them onto reefs off the coast by hanging lanterns in coconut trees. By doing so, it fooled the Captains of ships into thinking the lights were for their destination of Bridgetown and they would wreck on the reefs and be looted.

"You have now been around the entire island." Richard pulled into a gravel parking area off the main highway. "Now it's time for lunch, a cutter sandwich?"

"I'm starving," Todd exclaimed as he jumped out of the car. "What's a cutter sandwich?"

"A staple here in Barbados, a flying fish sandwich."

"Oh wow. Cool!"

Alana had to laugh, everything was always 'cool'. She gave Todd money and he went to purchase their sandwiches with Richard and Eric while Alana and Rita, Richard's sister, waited on a nearby bench.

"So, are you in love with Barbados?" Rita asked.

"Beautiful doesn't even begin a worthy description."

"One of our favorites. We come here on cruises but we've also come and stayed on land also. That's why Richard knows so much about it and he loves to drive it every time we come and is in his glory with you and Todd. He loves to show it off as if he were a local."

"I feel like I've had my own personal private tour guide."

At first Alana had her reservations, she really didn't know these people at all after only an hour on the beach with them, and she wondered why a situation such as this made her feel more comfortable than she would with someone she'd met on the streets of Chicago at home. But sometimes you could trust your gut and she was glad she had. Alana would have been one of the other tourists who'd missed the East side of the island and it'd been the highlight of her cruise so far. They also would have missed a day with wonderful people.

After cutter sandwiches they headed back to the ship where Todd was to meet up with Jonathan and his father for some wave runner fun and Robb promised to get the boys back onto the ship before it sailed. Rita's husband decided to call it a day, but Richard invited all the ladies to join him for a couple drinks before they had to be back on the ship.

Had Alana known what that innocent little offer would lead up to that evening, she may have backed out, but the day had been so fun and she went along without any hesitation.

CHAPTER EIGHT

He took them to a lively place that boomed with steel band Caribbean music and most of the patrons were locals with few ship passengers sprinkling the barstools. The place was crowded and boisterous, and Alana found her uncertainties lessen with each beat of rhythm as people yelled out to greet them as if they were old friends.

"Ahhh, welcome home beautiful lady," The bartender smiled warmly at her, made her feel she'd actually been there before and had come home.

Drinks flowed from the bar where two people danced atop it and more on the floor outside of the bar area. It had been such a wonderful day and after a few drinks she could feel herself relax even more. Richard was so open and gregarious, they all joked and laughed together, and Amy too liked Rita and Richard just as much.

With feeling so comfortable, the effects of a soothing day and the drinks added, Alana had no qualms when Richard asked her to dance to an upbeat steel drum island song. It was when he insisted they dance on the bar she became slightly hesitant, but the small group of friends encouraged her on.

"Come on, you'll never see these people again." Richard took her hand and tugged her along.

A cheer went up from the crowd as they clambered on top the bar and after only a few seconds of discomfort, she forced her inhibitions back to the recesses of her mind and let the calypso music and the drinks full of rum flow through her blood.

It surprised her when she began to move easily to the beat with confidence, encouraged by Richard as she moved along with him, reserves tossed aside out the open window. She was so into dancing and laughing that Alana hadn't noticed when Matt walked into the bar.

After they dropped off his clubs at the ship, and the other two men who'd gone with them, they had a little more time to catch up and Jack took him to a local bar he frequented mostly on the weekends. But they found it just as lively on that weekday when they stepped through the door.

"Don't even think the next time you come to Barbados we won't have a rematch. I don't know what was in you today but you keep that swing up and you'll give the pros a run for it. Wouldn't be a bad life, ever think about that? You could move here with me, we could relive some of our wilder college days. Spend the days on the course." The golf game had not gone in Jack's favor and he ribbed Matt as they walked towards the bar.

"I'd starve, go insane or both. A good day maybe, of course it's always a good day when I can blow you away on the golf course, but if I had to make a living at it, hell no." Matt shook his head to give emphasis to his words. "And I wouldn't want to go back to our college days, we were broke then remember? Had to make up signs, 'Will work for beer'."

When they walked inside Jack whistled low. "Man oh man. Yeah, let's leave the college days behind, for a split second I'd forgotten how the girls matured into women. Would you look at her? Forget the golf, why weren't we here all day?"

Matt glanced up and saw Alana gyrating to the beat of the music with a tan blond man who'd taken off his shirt and swung it in the air as the crowd cheered. He then pulled it around the back of Alana's neck and pulled her closer to him and they swayed together as if one.

She was dressed in a simple black top that bared smooth shoulders and a black and orange colored flowered sarong around her waist. The opening on the side revealed dark sensuous leg only a glimpse at a time and her silky hair fell loose. Their movements seemed perfectly timed as if choreographed and he wondered if like her dance partner, her clothes would fly off any minute.

His expression never changed and Jack looked at him and saw no reaction. "No comment? Have you gone blind? That divorce really did something to you, Matt, normally you'd be all over that."

"Can I get a Banks please?" Matt ordered his drink. "Make that two," then he turned to Jack again. "What do you want?"

Jack laughed with a knowing, "Ahhhh, I get it now. She's on your ship, isn't she? Looks like you might be a little late." He looked towards the duo again whose hands were interlocked above their heads as their bodies pulsed together side to side. "I can't believe you'd give that away."

"Not mine to give," he stated flatly.

Jack made up his own story as to the connection the two may share. "So I guess that's the problem? Just haven't gotten that far yet and wham... someone else moves in. I wouldn't have wasted any time with her, should have known there were going to be more behind you. Haven't I always told you to watch your back?"

"Yeah, and I didn't listen to you. You knew my ex-wife better than I did."

"I know her kind better than you. They're all the same, probably that one too," Jack nodded towards Alana. "But damn its fun till the bubble breaks."

"How do you know if they're all the same, you've never stuck with one long enough to find out?"

"I probably would have settled down if I didn't have that shit hole of a marriage of yours for inspiration. It ruined me for life." Jack knew he wouldn't take offense to his comment.

"Yeah, Katherine managed to ruin quite a few people."

"You're not still gun shy, are you? Is that why you haven't moved in on her?" They looked as Alana was now laughing and being helped down from the bar as Richard picked her up by the waist and set her on the floor with effortless ease.

Matt tried to skirt around the issue of Alana. "Gun shy? No, Katherine didn't ruin me, I only referred to the other broken marriages she caused along the way. She didn't keep her affairs to single men and after the divorce stories filtered in. All of a sudden everyone had a comment or knew of an incident with her, they didn't have the guts to tell me while I was married to her, but felt after the divorce they thought I wanted to know it all."

"Present company excluded. I tried to tell you."

"You were the only one." Matt had known for a long time before his divorce that his marriage was over. The only way she hurt him was the betrayal he'd felt because he'd spent so many years in the charade, all the while being faithful.

"Think you'll ever get married again? Do the whole two and half kids and white picket fence thing?"

Matt took a drink of his beer and for some reason automatically, completely unconsciously, looked at Alana. If he did, why did he think of her? Because there was something there, and it was intense, powerful, and completely insane at the same time.

The first night they shared was sex, pure and simple. But the second time, when she came to his room, she'd left a little bit of herself behind and he held onto that now, couldn't let it go even in his anger. Talk of Katherine reminded him of how stupid he could be. Was he being completely blind and reading more into something than he should? Being taken in his one sided obsession with a woman who laughed and danced in the arms of another man?

What Alana was doing to him was no fault of her own. She avoided him, didn't speak to him, or even acknowledge him in any way. It wasn't as if she led him to believe there was something between them, it was only what he felt inside. Was Jack right and they were all the same? Matt had no answers to anything, his confused state of mind nothing but a jumble of nonsense that bordered madness and he couldn't help but think of how simple his life was just a short week ago.

"Right now I'm certainly not thinking about marriage, it isn't something I'm actively looking for by any means. I guess I'd need a serious relationship to test commitment waters again, and my last one that could be considered half way serious only lasted five months."

"I've thought about it a couple of times."

Jack's statement surprised him and Matt laughed. "You? The one who designed an escape ladder on his balcony to make it easier for a woman to leave and not get caught by a girlfriend if she showed up at the front door?"

"I'm not that bad anymore. Well..." He paused before he went on. "Should I say I'm smarter than I used to be, I've learned never to give a house key to a girlfriend. It saves me from untimely visits now. If I even think about giving a key, that's kind of my own sign to tell me that maybe I'm serious about someone, maybe I'm ready to be faithful, kind of like a sacred symbol of undying love if there is such a thing. Some people give rings, I'll give my key, but I don't know when, I haven't given a key to anyone since college."

"I don't suspect you ever will. Who knows, maybe you'll surprise me one day. Guess we won't know till it hits us." Matt took a long drink of his beer.

"I wonder how we'll know? Neither of us knows anything about it, what something real feels like."

Matt laughed a little. "My guess would be a sledgehammer."

He tried to ignore the fact that Alana was in the same vicinity, on the same island, in the same world. Amy stopped and said hello, even chatted for a moment, but Alana did the same as he was doing, barely noticed he was in the room, or rather, like him, she just pretended not to notice.

He and Jack joked and talked. They finished catching up on everything they hadn't while they played golf that day and he avoided her entirely until she walked by him towards the back of the bar.

"Looks like your foot is better."

"Much," Was Alana's short response as she walked on without looking at him.

Jack shook his head. "You've been out of the dating scene way too long if that's the best pick up line you have. Hell you might as well step out of line and let me in if that's the best you got."

Matt couldn't explain it to his old friend, couldn't explain it to himself. The longer he sat, the more agitated he became. He could hear her laughter from across the room and it didn't matter where she was, and as crowded as the bar was, you'd have thought the other noise would have drowned it out but it didn't.

He glanced up when she danced atop the bar again and watched when they all made a toast with rum shots. She was having fun, not a care in the world and it incensed him she had the ability to make him so miserable. What was she to him? Why was he feeling this way? He had no answers but knew he had to do something. Against his better judgment he rose from the bar to leave.

"Jack, it's been a pleasure to see you and thanks for the golf game but I'm going to have to cut out of here. I can't explain, but I'm going to take the little dance queen back to the ship."

Jack didn't have to ask who he referred to. He'd seen his eyes wander, seen a distant look as he was distracted elsewhere. They were old friends, if Matt ever wanted to explain it, he would. He smiled broadly and slapped Matt on the back as he gripped his hand.

"Now that's the way to get back in the race, just take control. Hey, you know I was only teasing before, sometimes they're not all the same."

"Getting soft in your old age?"

"Just holding out hope. Who knows? Let me know how it works out and I'll see you in a few months stateside when it gets warm. We'll replay that round of golf because you had an unfair advantage, I never would have played you had I known it was the aggravation of a woman behind your swing."

When he approached her, Alana stood somewhat off from the crowd, and with the music blaring they couldn't be heard by others.

"Come on, I'll take you back to the ship."

"That's okay, I have a ride." Alana turned away, irritated that he assumed she'd go anywhere with him. He'd been angry with her, fine, stay angry with her and let her be. It was easier that way.

"I really think it's time you got back," he gripped her by the elbow and she whirled her head around to face him again.

"Who are you to tell me it's time to do anything?"

"I'll take you back to the ship, I think we should talk."

"You've been making me miserable for days, and now you want to talk when I'm finally..."

"Finally showing your true self? At least you had the decency not to bring your son to watch your display. Where is he by the way? Do you know?"

Alana glared at him then turned to the small group of friends with a large smile as if it had been a pleasant encounter. "Hey guys, we were about to leave anyway so I'm going to catch a ride back with Matt."

"See you tonight? We'll meet at the bar on top at seven for drinks?" Richard asked.

"I'll be there."

She smiled and waved as they walked out the door and as soon as it shut she exploded.

"Who the hell do you think you are, how dare you...?"

Matt opened the taxi door and held it for her. She didn't say another word until they got out at the dock then she automatically took up where she left off.

"How dare you come in there and drag me away like a child. The only reason I came with you was because I didn't want to cause a scene. You hate me, fine, then why don't you just leave me alone, why couldn't you have just let me be? What business is it of yours if I choose to have a good time?"

This wasn't what he'd planned but should have expected it. He merely wanted to talk, maybe call a truce, and probably hadn't gone about it in the right way but the pent up sexual tension and jealousy got the better of him. The better of them both as they matched their anger step by step and it all flowed horribly and quickly out of control.

"What was your name tonight? Brenda? Tiffany?" He asked sarcastically.

"I hadn't decided yet, was thinking of something exotic, like Lolita. Does that suit me?"

"Perfectly. That was quite a show you put on in there. Where is your son while you've been practicing your new profession as 'Lolita the bar top dancer'?"

"It isn't any of your business."

"Maybe I'm a little worried about him while his mother is sitting around drinking all day. How do I know you haven't forgotten him on a beach somewhere?" Of course Matt didn't mean the words, none that he said, but he couldn't stop himself.

"I know where my son is, what the hell do you care? You're not his father, he isn't your responsibility, and I certainly don't have to answer to his whereabouts."

"A little careless, isn't it? In a foreign land, God knows what could happen to you at that bar and if you weren't thinking about your son in case something happened to you, I was. Somebody had to worry."

"Go away, Matt, leave me and my son alone. We don't need you." She shouted the words loudly, angry at the feeling that she did so more to convince herself of the words than him. Alana tried to walk faster, they were moving into dangerous emotional territory and she didn't want to be there.

"Quit trying to run away from me, you still have a limp and look ridiculous." Matt softened and spoke with more tenderness. "Do you want me to...?"

"To sweep me off my feet again? No thank you."

"Look, Alana," he grabbed her arm and stopped her in mid step, had to catch her when she almost fell. "I don't mean any of this. Truth is, I haven't been able to stop thinking about you since that first night we met and you've been driving me crazy. We're going to be together for another week, how about we call a truce and start over."

Alana looked directly into kind eyes that enticed her into a peaceful shelter. Eyes of an old comfortable friend who would help her carry the weight of her pain, help her stand strong when she wanted to fall. Someone to trust her worries to, if only for a little while.

Faces and bodies were dangerously close as she felt his breathe, less than an inch and their lips would touch. How she wished she'd met him a year ago before this all began, the cancer, the pain she endured every day now. She knew he would have been her rock of strength to hold her above waters that raged and threatened to drown her at every turn, but she hadn't met him a year ago, and he couldn't help her now.

They'd met in another life, one she'd invented that wasn't real, a pretend life she'd created, and they shared an intimacy she would forever cherish. But this time instead of stepping out of her life he wanted to come in, and there wasn't room for him here, it was full of other more important things.

How could she possibly invite him in now and have nothing to give but the immensity of her anguish over the cancer that could possibly kill her son? And she was an emotional wreck, how could she be close to him for the rest of the cruise and not have his memory drive her crazy afterwards? It was already driving her crazy now, and they'd only shared two nights together.

Alana stood motionless and pondered her fate, knew she had to turn her back on him now. The longer she waited, the worse it would become and right now, maybe not ever, she had no life to offer. She was not one to invest her feelings in someone on a whim. Her face remained hard and un-giving, the conviction in her voice real, but her heart a different story as she felt it crush beneath the weight.

"It was sex, Matt, unadulterated sex without emotion. It was sex with you in San Juan, it will be sex with someone else tonight and probably tomorrow night. I'm sorry if you read something different but it was nothing more than unattached sex. Maybe the next time you hook up with someone, you might want to keep your heart out of it because it has no place in the bedroom."

With the hate of her words, she knew she'd hit her mark when she saw the damage they'd done. Instantly wounded, his eyes clouded over with false belief and everything spiraled out of control as Alana pushed it all over the edge. She could envision it as a tangible thing in her mind as it crashed against imaginary rocks below.

"So that's who you are?" He said quietly when he realized he could still speak. "Well, if you aren't the prettiest piece of work I've ever seen. Beautiful little pretend mom, perfectly innocent sweet face you show your son and when he closes his eyes at night you're the lying whore about town. What kind of mother are you? You don't deserve to have a son like Todd."

"You fucking son of a bitch!" Alana's voice burst with fatal venom. The words he'd pierced her with shot through like fire and her hand reared back and smacked him hard across the face.

Caught up in her own deception, the instant she heard the words it validated all her fears. Maybe that was the reason she would lose Todd, maybe that was the reason God would take her son away from her, because she didn't deserve him. Later, she would understand why he'd said them but in that one instant she couldn't understand any of it.

****

Dressed in black khakis and a black silk shirt, Matt met his grandmother for a pre-dinner drink in the quiet atrium area that had become her favorite place. He ordered a straight scotch and sat down next to her.

"That's what I'd have ordered too after the bout you had in port today." Diana raised her eyes, she never heard a word but she'd seen them go at it.

"I hope I don't hurt your feelings grandmother but I don't want you to take this lightly. I don't want to talk about Alana, not now, not ever."

She looked into his hard eyes and almost listened to him but continued regardless. "I may be old but I remember things. You two were pretty heated, and people don't get angry like that with someone unless they feel something."

"She feels something for someone, but not for me." He had no trouble bringing up the recollection of her admission to a stream of lovers every night, wondered when he'd forget it. Jack had been right after all, they were all the same.

"It's you, or she wouldn't have smacked you silly." Diana laughed. "I haven't seen anything angrier than when I swatted a hornet's nest. All this time I thought you two barely knew each other, figured you definitely weren't interested. Now I see you actually made it a point to avoid each other."

"Obviously not enough, but I'm sure it won't be a problem from now on. I really don't want to talk about this."

Matt's voice was stern and again she debated whether to continue but felt she had to, something pushed her on. "If you're afraid of logistics if you fall for each other, you have offices in other places. I don't see why you couldn't have one in Chicago, it's a big city. Those little details can be worked out. She's a sweet girl, Matt."

Matt laughed, the cynical sound boomed to the other side of the open atrium. "Sweet little Alana, a woman even you couldn't see through. To put it into perspective for you grandmother, I probably would have stayed married to my ex-wife for ten more years if it meant I'd never have crossed her path. Truth is, I feel worse for Todd than I do for me, I'm just stupid, I did that to myself, but Todd has no choice. He's just an innocent boy with a mother who doesn't deserve him."

Diana's fear rose and her voice was a soft whisper, "You didn't tell her that, did you?"

"It's the truth. Did I deserve the slap across the face for it? No, but I'm not going to tell you the details and ruin your reputation for being able to 'read people like a book' as you always say. Just trust my judgment that she doesn't deserve him."

"Oh, Matt, you didn't," Diana sighed deeply, "That poor girl."

"Curse me, blame me, and think what you will but believe me the remark was warranted."

Diana knew her grandson. If he'd known, he'd never have said such a remark to a mother going through what she was, no matter what the circumstances. And he'd never have been so cruel and justify it, Matt wouldn't have let anger turn him heartless. At least by knowing he could set things right for himself.

"I thought maybe Todd told you."

"Told me what?" Matt questioned and motioned for another scotch.

"You'd better order two and make them doubles. If you thought you needed it before, you're really going to need it now."

CHAPTER NINE

Between St. Lucia and Grenada, one of the most mountainous of the small Antilles, was St. Vincent. 18 miles long and 11 miles wide with a rather quiet capital city of Kingstown, it lie in wait as the ship sailed towards its harbor. More village-like than a metropolis city, St. Vincent was in a natural state and one could see the Caribbean in untouched beauty. Black sand beaches, tropical valleys and deep forests were among some of its delights.

Alana had gotten coffee and Todd juice after she woke him up before dawn and now they stood in sunrise splendor as she sang soft and sweet. "Happy birthday to you, happy birthday to you, happy birthday dear Todd, happy birthday to you."

"Thanks, Mom. This is great, look how pretty everything is."

Although still groggy, he was excited to be up and see the dawn break on his birthday, it instantly made the day more special. Alana held him close to her, remembered every detail of his birth thirteen years ago. Every ounce of her love that poured into that moment had grown so much stronger over the years when she wouldn't have thought it possible. Her son, her love, her entire life, it was all here in her arms as the first shades of pink tinged a blue black sky. God had given her his birthday, both thirteen years ago and now, and for that she had to be grateful. Despite her efforts, a few silent tears escaped her eyes and rolled down her cheeks.

Under her dark glasses were swollen red eyes from her night of tears. She'd cried at the thought that maybe she didn't deserve her son as Matt had said, but her senses eventually took back control. She'd long ago argued with herself to find a reason God would take him away when there was none to be found. And she knew Matt's angry words were not aimed at her, but who she portrayed herself to be. He'd let the rage of her words in, and in defense, he too lashed out with cruel intent to inflict the same.

Then she cried at the emotional mess she'd made of her heart, wanted so badly to share it and yet there was no room, Todd was there and she filled every small space with him. She'd cried, as she did at the end of each day, at the question of whether it would be the last time they would see the wonder and beauty of such places they were seeing, just as she would cry at the end of the day in St. Vincent. Silently and alone she shed her tears without Todd ever knowing.

Would it be the last time for them to share a spectacular sunrise or sunset? The last time they would ever be able to walk along that beach, or feed the monkey's or walk through a rain forest and listen to the couqui's? People may only get to those places and do those things once in a lifetime and it was enough. It wasn't a question of whether they would ever go back again given the opportunity, rather the uncertainty of whether it would be possible at all.

Would Todd be there to share it with her again? Or one day able to join a few college buddies on a dive trip? Maybe bring a new bride for a honeymoon or take his future son's or daughter's to swim with the turtles? San Juan, Grand Cayman, Roatan, Barbados and all the other islands they would see. For years to come they would all be there with welcome paradise for the weary traveler. But would Todd?

Their agenda for the day was an excursion booked through the ship. One that would give them an island tour, a boat ride, and some beach time to enjoy. The sun glistened bright now that it had risen and it promised to be another fabulous day. When Todd left to go back to the cabin to shower and dress for the day, Alana remained with another cup of coffee when she heard Matt's voice from behind her.

"An apology doesn't seem adequate for the things I said last night, the things I said were beyond cruel but they didn't apply to you, not the real you."

Alana turned to see the regret in his eye and he continued before she could object.

"I know you're not that person, but things got way out of hand and saying I'm sorry doesn't seem to be enough but it's all I have right now. We're going to be on this ship for quite a while longer, I don't see any reason we can't at least be friends."

Matt's eyes were kind and warm, apologetic, but there was something else. There was a knowing there, she knew Mrs. McCray had told him. Alana didn't see pity, with his smile that felt like a warm embrace he offered her solace, support to share her torment if she chose, friendship, even if only for a little while.

"I'm sorry also, it wasn't like me to, well..." Alana stammered along, the scene was ugly and she still felt the sting on her hand. "I've never hit anyone before. I'm really sorry."

"Don't be sorry, I deserved it for what I said, but I honestly didn't mean it." Matt extended his hand for a handshake. "We're in the islands maybe we can do what the pirates did, a peace treaty or something. I can have papers drawn up if you want it official. I think they might have exchanged gold coins, maybe land or something. I could probably come up with a cow or two."

Alana couldn't help but laugh. She'd been so tired of this... thing between them. She couldn't find another name for it but she was so tired of feeling anxious, nervous, frustrated, and everything else when she saw him or was around him. His first friendly comment to her instantly released some anxiety.

"We're stuck with each other for a while, I don't see why we can't clear the air a little."

Then he joked, "I'm doing this for purely selfish reasons. If you're mad at me you might not let Todd come out and play basketball, and I don't find adults nearly half as amusing as your son."

"That's at least one thing we're in agreement with. I feel the same." She looked at his hand and still hesitated. "If I shake your hand, does that obligate me to take your cows? Would I be breaking some kind of pirate law if I refuse them?"

"I can probably talk them out of making you walk the plank but I can't promise I can keep them from making you row the ship."

Alana shook his hand and held on a few moments more than necessary, passed between them a silent gratitude for his gentle offering of compassion. "If that's the case, I'm not going to do it without you."

"I'll even take the nightshift for you." Matt held her soft hand in his. It was all she offered for now, if she wanted more from him he was there to give, if she didn't want anything, it would be her choice. "I have to tell you, when I couldn't find you last night Todd told me what your plans were and I got tickets for your excursion today because I wanted to be sure to see you this morning. Grandmother can go, but if it makes you uncomfortable I don't have to go." Matt was willing to walk on the eggshells that surrounded her.

"Don't be ridiculous. Todd would love for you to be around today, it's his birthday." She smiled at Matt with their silent truce between them.

"Then I'm glad I'll be able to share it with him."

Todd was excited to see them among the group when they all met on the dock, it made it a perfect day for him. They boarded the bus that took them through town and a guide explained about their fair island and along the way they stopped at a botanical garden which Diana thoroughly enjoyed, Todd even seemed to enjoy her knowledge of flowers and plants. When Matt and Todd went off somewhere, Mrs. McCray brought up something she wanted to talk about all morning.

"I hope you don't mind I told Matt about Todd's illness. It wasn't my place to tell anyone your business but when he told me what he'd said to you, I felt he had to set it right. He never would have said that to anyone had he known."

"I don't mind. I understand you did what you felt needed to be done, thank you. It was hard for me to think he'd go off and spend the rest of his life thinking I was a horrible person, but..." Her words trailed off unfinished.

"I don't understand things these days. Back in the old days we courted, got married, had our families, raised our children. Everything seemed easy and simple back then. Hell, these days us old women have to ask the man, and scream it too. Half of them deaf the other half can't remember they told you 'yes'."

Alana laughed at her tale but had to try and put something straight. She and Matt would not be 'courting' as she suspected. "Oh, I don't think Matt and I will be anything more than friends, it won't be any sort of dating relationship, Mrs. McCray."

"At my age, I take companionship where I can get it. We can all get by without a lot of things in this world, but companionship isn't one of them. Matt's a good man, Alana. I know your plate is full, and I may be his grandmother, but even I can see he'd make a tasty side dish."

Alana burst into laughter so loud at the analogy that people turned to stare. It took her several minutes to stop.

"What's so funny?" Matt asked as he and Todd looked confused when they walked up.

It only sent her into more laughter and she of course couldn't answer and it was Diana that spoke up. "We were laughing at that old bald man over there who keeps making eyes at me. As if," she said with the twist of a teenager.

The boat they boarded was a wooden replica of a large pirate ship and with the backdrop of the island, they set off to sea. At one point the ship stopped and invited any who wanted to swing from a rope tied to the mast over the blue waters and jump. Todd was a little leery until Matt went before him. He hung onto the rope, swung out and when he let go went soaring into the crystal clear water.

It gave Todd the confidence he needed and once he went he couldn't be stopped. Not only did he just swing into the water, he also became brave enough to let go and somersault to an appreciative cheering crowd too chicken to try it themselves.

Alana jumped with worry and could only clap with the others when his beaming face came up out of the water.

"Relax. You jumped so high I thought you were going overboard. Don't worry about him, he won't hurt himself." Matt had just come out of the water and sat down next to her while he rubbed his hair with a towel.

"I'm worried about your grandmother more, I think she wants to try it."

He looked over and laughed. Diana stood and clapped for Todd as if it counted for Olympic points. "I'm surprised she hasn't. Last year in Mexico I drove the Sea Doo and she was on a tube behind me, had a blast."

"You went with her last year also?"

"Every year since I was five. And only because she had to wait till I was fully functional, you know, walking, talking, and potty trained. Every year we go for at least a week somewhere, most times the

Caribbean. When I got older I thought she'd stop but she kept planning for our yearly event and I've kept coming with her."

"So I guess when you got married, your wife came along?" He'd told her one of their nights in San Juan he'd been married for ten years and divorced.

"She didn't include her. Would tell me where and when we were going and to be packed. Never mentioned one word about taking her along and when I mentioned it the first year I was married she said 'Hell no'. That was that," Matt laughed. "They didn't get along well."

"Todd's grandfather used to take him on their 'manly' outings, camping, fishing, the usual boy stuff. Some of the best days of his life, both of theirs actually. My father died a year and a half ago and as much as I wish he were here, I'm glad he didn't know about Todd. He was a doctor and I know if he wasn't able to help Todd, it would have killed him."

"Last couple of years certainly hasn't been kind to you." Matt paused. "I understand now, Alana. I understand why you wanted to be someone else when we first met. I can't say I know what you're going through because I don't, because I've never been faced with anything that could even compare. I can only imagine how hard it must be and it tears me up to think of what your life is like." Matt couldn't stop himself, he had to touch her and took her hand in his for just a moment. "I know why you lied. I know why you wanted to step out of your life. San Juan, the moon, the stars, the music and a willing victim, it was a perfect opportunity. I would have done the exact same."

"I'm glad you understand and don't hate me anymore."

"Angry yes, hated you never. You could have confided in me though."

"It's not something people want to be part of. Cancer is an ugly disease and people would much rather hear that your life is full of roses than sit and listen to dreadful tales of sickness. Like maybe if they don't talk about it, it doesn't exist."

"I'll listen anytime you want to talk."

Alana smiled gratefully but was quiet.

Mrs. McCray never attempted the swing even though Alana waited to protest if she had, and they almost had to pry Todd's hands off the swing rope when it was time for the boat to leave. Although he bought his snorkel gear he never used it and spent the entire hour there putting on a show for the others. Between him and Matt, each tried to outdo the other to the joy of their new fans onboard.

"Mom, this is the best day ever."

Todd plopped down next to her wet and dripping. Alana wrapped the towel around him and pulled him close for warmth as the sun moved directions and they were shaded. She glanced up at Matt who looked at them from across the boat and then she smiled and hugged him tighter.

"It is the best day, isn't it?" Everyday she had Todd for one more day was always the best day.

For the first time since the vacation started, Alana felt happily and completely relaxed. The company of Mrs. McCray had been more of a pleasure then she ever imagined and the situation with Matt was no longer filled with tension and unease in each other's presence.

They enjoyed some time on a beach and when they returned to port, before getting on the ship, Todd invited them for his birthday dinner. Matt looked to Alana before he felt he could answer and she reassured him.

"Of course it wouldn't be a proper birthday dinner without the two of you, please come," she said.

"We'd love to." Mrs. McCray answered.

They set up the meeting time and place and Alana told them she'd see them at dinner, she had to use the payphone before boarding. Todd didn't want to wait so walked ahead with Matt and Diana.

"Don't run off looking for Jonathan, start your shower immediately Todd and wait for me to get there before you leave the room. I'll only be a minute."

"Are you calling Jenna, Mom?"

Matt had to hold back his laughter, looked up smiling with question in his eyes and Alana stammered a little with explanation. "My... It's... a friend... Jenna is my best friend's name."

When Jenna picked up the phone on the third ring Alana sighed into it. "You're home, I thought your machine would pick up."

"My happy sailor, how's Todd?"

"I haven't seen him ever look better."

"I imagine him every day. I literally close my eyes and picture what he's seeing, what he's doing. Oh, Alana, I knew this would be wonderful for him." Then Jenna's voice changed to quick impatience. "So, the sexy Puerto Rican guy? Tell me, tell me."

"He isn't Puerto Rican, I just met him there."

"Whatever, he's a great lover, that part I remember. So catch me up, what's happened?"

"Oh Jenna, it was horrible."

She gasped on the other end of the phone line. "You had sex again and it was horrible?"

"No, we didn't have sex again."

"I get it, he couldn't make it happen and it was horrible. You can probably get some Viagra down there..."

"No, Jenna, it isn't that."

"You found out he was actually a horrible person."

Alana laughed, "If I can get a word in edgewise. You move way to fast for yourself, and me, just slow down."

Alana explained the previous evening which was the horrible part, then the day in the beautiful island of St. Vincent paradise.

"Yada yada yada, so you still haven't had sex again. Alana, you don't have time for all that bonding junk."

"Jenna!" Alana scolded but laughed.

"Well, I'm just trying to push you along, you don't have much more time, and them going on the cruise this week is fate. Destiny, the stars, the stars aligned with the moon, the moon behind the sun, whatever, its something there. And it means something."

"It's another week, Jenna, that's all it means, nothing else. Except for the frustration of having to watch him play basketball with his shirt off, I can deal with it."

"He loves Todd, like everyone does, and he liked him before he knew about him so it's not a pity thing. He likes Todd, Todd likes him, you like him, he likes you, is there something I'm not getting here? Where's grandma in all this, is there someone she doesn't like? Where's the problem?"

"She's wonderful, you'd love her."

"So everyone loves each other, include me in the group hug, but please explain to me why you're not in his bed again." Jenna sighed.

"I'll never see him again."

"So what? If you don't, you have a great memory of a wonderful two weeks in the Caribbean with a sexy hunk. How much more dreamy can you get."

"It isn't good for Todd."

"What isn't good? For Todd to see his mother have a relationship? It's what he's wanted for a long time, and if you don't want him to think anything's going on, which I know you don't, you're not going to flaunt a relationship in front of your son. I take it he has his own cabin, surely he's not sleeping with Grandma."

"He has his own cabin but..."

"So you go there for little midnight meetings. Yeah, you sneak around like teenagers but as far as Todd is concerned, you're friends."

"And afterwards we never see him again." It wasn't a thought she wanted to think about, but it was fact.

"That's the beauty of it. Okay, that's a little harsh, but so what, you never see him again. To Todd it was just a nice man he met and you spent time together."

"Leave it to you to make a sordid affair sound like the right thing to do."

"Then you're going to?" Jenna sounded elated.

"No, I don't know, I don't think so. Oh, Jenna, it would be so much easier if he'd just play basketball with his shirt on."

****

They enjoyed a boisterous dinner that evening for Todd's birthday. Along with Matt and Diana, of course there was Jonathan, Amy and Robb, then Richard, Kevin, Rita and Eric. They were all only too happy to join in the celebration.

The conversation flowed from one to the other. The wine flowed among the adults and Alana laughed when she overheard Richard and Diana having a playful debate on the topic of whether teens should color their hair purple or not. Richard argued it was a form of personal expression and Mrs. McCray countered with the fact that parents didn't want to spank their children anymore and gave them freedoms they weren't old enough for.

The waiters brought out a birthday cake and they all sang. When the adults enjoyed coffee, the young boys were antsy to play basketball and allowed to be excused. Mrs. McCray and Matt followed soon after, Mrs. McCray to her cabin, Matt to work off his dinner with the boys after he changed.

Alana felt a little guilty he'd left, had the feeling he enjoyed the others company but she thought he might have left because he didn't want her to feel uncomfortable. It felt like they were coupled together and maybe he thought she didn't want to feel that way. So the first part of their trip they would stay away from each other because of anger, the second because of passion. Go figure, she thought to herself.

And she didn't want to, but she immediately missed him when he was gone. My God, in one single day she'd gone from one extreme to the other. Last night she slapped him across the face, this evening she wanted to be close to him. It was all this paradise and crap that totally screwed with her mind.

After dinner the rest of them converged on the sports bar instead of a show. Out of earshot of others, Richard rambled on about Matt and it was like talking to a male version of Jenna and he made her laugh so hard tears rolled down her eyes and her sides ached. Alana didn't tell him details, didn't tell him the situation at all but Richard picked up on the attraction and made up his own story. Even down to what type of guy he would be in bed, and if she hadn't had him yet she had a treat coming.

When she looked at her watch she realized it was a little after midnight. "I've got to go," Alana announced. "My son is probably waiting up for me, worried. A little change of roles, isn't it? Maybe I should stay for one more so he'll see what it really feels like, a little payback."

"Please stay for one more," Rita pleaded. "If I have to listen to these two discuss what the best golf course is any longer I'll club one of them over the head. Tell Matt he started something that has to be finished, make him join us tomorrow sometime. Dinner? Drinks?"

They had coupled them, and it surprised her when she felt okay about it, even liked it. Then of course that fear in the back of her mind crept in just a tiny bit. Don't get too close Alana.

"And bring Mrs. McCray," Rita continued. "Because if I lose the nerve to club them, I know she'll do it for us."

Amy stood along with her. "I'd better go make sure Jonathan is in also, I'll walk with you Alana."

"Alana love," Richard pulled her down to whisper in her ear. "I want to hear all the details tomorrow."

Alana laughed and playfully swatted him when she left.

"What lovely people, I don't think I've laughed that much in weeks," Amy commented, "And your son we can all thank. He seems to be a miniature cruise director. The meet and greet welcome committee all rolled into one little person."

"He has a knack for people."

"No one in that little group would have ever come together if it hadn't been for Todd, he seems to be the link to everything. Jonathan is already talking about him coming to visit when we get home, maybe we can organize a summer week at the beach?"

"Maybe," Alana smiled but said nothing else on the subject, it was only early February and summer was months away. Alana couldn't, wouldn't, look that far ahead, it was today and as much as she wanted to she couldn't promise more.

Todd wasn't in the room and his radio sat on the vanity desk where he'd forgotten it again and it was way past his curfew. Alana had the funny feeling he might be purposefully late and chose to forget his radio intentionally so she would have to go look for him in the obvious place of the basketball court.

"Todd Gibbs," Alana said it as sternly as she could when she found him where she suspected.

"Oh, Mom! Am I late?"

"Tomorrow in St. Lucia I am buying you another watch and this time I'm using super glue to attach it to your wrist. And super glue your radio to your other wrist." She then looked at Matt's wrist. "And Matt has a watch, why didn't you ask him what time it was?"

"I did. He said it was eleven o'clock just a few minutes ago, I don't have to be in till eleven thirty."

Alana looked at her own watch that had the correct time of twelve thirty then saw the guilty look on Matt's face.

"Sorry, watch must be wrong," he shrugged and playfully looked the other way not to connect with her eyes. Alana stopped herself from laughing.

"Jonathan!"

Amy joined them at that point when she hadn't found Jonathan in the room either, and Matt raised his hand in confession.

"My fault Amy, my watch was wrong, guess it stopped. Sorry."

Amy stood beside Alana and whispered low, the others unable to hear her words. "Please explain to me why I never took up basketball. I thought he was the finest man I'd seen in a long time with clothes on, now I see he's even finer if that's possible."

Amy verified the dilemma Alana felt when she saw him play basketball shirtless. She previously thought she found him so attractive because she'd been celibate for so long.

"Todd, go on down to the cabin and take a quick shower and get ready for bed."

"It's the end of the night for you too, Jonathan, come on." Amy called, and then whispered to Alana before she left. "I'm going to go take a cold shower myself."

When they were alone, Alana walked slowly across the court with a playful menacing look in her eye as Matt dribbled the ball lightly.

"I didn't do it on purpose. By the way, what's punishment these days? Restriction? Early curfew? Just out of curiosity, not that I did anything, really, it must have stopped at..." He blabbered on as he looked at his watch again.

Alana grabbed his wrist and looked at it herself. "Twelve thirty five. Funny, looks like it started again and it even caught back up to the correct time, imagine that."

"Yeah, some watch, huh? It's late, I'd better..."

Matt backed away from her as if his intention was to get away but she held his wrist and pulled him back, pulled him closer to her this time, so much closer. Feeling flirty, she tipped her mouth up to his as if she were going to kiss him, then stopped just short. Her voice was low and seductive.

"I suggest you have your watch checked out, and since it's a first offense, you won't be punished. Goodnight, Matt." Then she pulled back and walked away.

"Whoa, what was that? Not punished? Not punished? That was punishment, Alana, excruciating punishment. You can't do that, it isn't playing fair." His voice portrayed the aggravation then he laughed in disbelief.

CHAPTER TEN

One of the Windward Islands of the Lesser Antilles, between Martinique and St. Vincent, you find the lush tropical gem of St. Lucia that beckons visitors to its rich beauty. Only 27 miles long and 14 miles wide one can bask in the great Atlantic Ocean on its eastern shore and kiss the west coast breezes of the calm Caribbean Sea. It was reminiscent of an island in the South Pacific with its commanding twin coastal peaks, the Pitons, that soared 2,000 feet up from the sea where it sheltered a rain forest abundant with wild orchids, giant ferns and birds of paradise.

Endangered species, the St. Lucia parrot, was indigenous to the region, and brilliantly plumed tropical birds abounded as travelers tried to catch a glimpse. Only when they could avert their eyes from glorious surroundings did they stand a chance. Green, rich, luxurious fields and orchards of banana, coconut, mango and papaya trees contributed greatly to a region with a rich past.

Small villages of warm and charming island people pulled one in and offered a peek of their many different traditions as one traveled a steep coastline around a mountainous interior. St. Lucia awaited them and Alana was anxious to explore.

****

The top deck was fairly empty, there were few early risers as Alana poured a cup of coffee and saw Matt against the banister alone.

"Good morning," She smiled as he looked up to her. "Looks like another beautiful day in paradise. I don't know what I'll do when I get home and have to brave the cold of Chicago."

"You're up early." Matt suspected she would brave the cold well, from what he knew about her so far, she had courage. The cold of Chicago was the least of her battles.

"Always, I sleep very little." She didn't tell him of the times she nervously waited through the dark to wonder if she'd have Todd for another day. When dawn broke, and he was still breathing, only then could she relax.

"I've always found it overrated, too much to do to waste time sleeping. And when I go on vacation, it's hard to get out of the habit."

As she stood next to him, there were many things she wanted to know about him, but didn't ask. What was the point? No sense getting to know someone she'd never see again after it was over.

"I know I said it in anger one night, but I want to say it again. I really do appreciate you being nice to Todd when I was the last person you wanted to see."

"It's hard not to be nice to Todd. Grandmother thinks he's going to be president one day."

Alana laughed. "I've had many tell me that. He's already campaigning and gaining loyal supporters along the way." Then she paused. "I don't care if he's president, or a trash man, as long as he's here to be something."

"He'll make a fine man one day. The only thing I can say is to have faith that he will be here, unfortunately, I can't make promises or I would."

"I don't want to go back to Chicago, I never want to return." She was open and honest with him, found it odd since she rarely opened to anyone, but he was accommodating as he listened with compassion in his eyes, eyes that promised her a warm and safe place. "This has been like living without the cancer, and the illness doesn't exist here. I always feel like I'm trapped and spinning wheels, but I don't feel that way here. It feels like a guilty pleasure though, like I shouldn't be having such a good time."

Matt saw the vulnerable pain flash across her eyes and then it was gone, the pain she tried to hide. "I've always been one to believe things happen for a reason. Maybe that's the reason this trip came about for you, to make you see what it was like living without it, maybe to strengthen your faith."

Alana had an odd feeling in that instant, she thought of her father and didn't know why but she turned and looked across the top deck as if she'd see him there, but of course she didn't. "Maybe," she said lightly and thought it could be a little slice of heaven her father gave her glimpse into. But then she'd have to believe he was with her, and for the first time since his death, she truly suspected he was.

"What about you, do you believe things happen for a reason?" Matt asked.

"Some things have no possible explanation." She couldn't believe the illness of cancer, the threat of death, would serve any logical purpose. "But I guess some things do happen for a reason."

"What about us?"

She looked at him. Again, logical purpose didn't come to mind, but he'd woken up in her things she'd never felt before. Was it all part of fate? Things that were meant to happen? Or just as it appeared on the surface, a casual fling that threw them together.

She felt foolish thinking of her father again, but Matt was everything her father would have loved, everything he would have wanted for her. And just being in his presence she didn't feel that relentless loneliness, that void in her life. It was strange but it was impossible for her mind to think there was reason to their chance meeting even if her heart was telling her otherwise.

"Is that what you think?" She avoided having to answer with a question.

He couldn't believe it wasn't true, couldn't believe the anguish and feelings he had for her after only a short time didn't mean something more important. Matt smiled with playful teasing in his voice as he rubbed his face. "The obvious reason was to show me I could be taken by a woman. I can still feel that slap."

Impulsively she placed her hand gently on his cheek and laughed, "I told you I was sorry."

When she went to pull it away Matt held it close with his own hand. "I obviously won't be so quick with my words again."

"I was to blame."

Matt continued to hold her tender palm against his cheek as he bent to kiss her, his lips soft against hers and the feeling that enveloped them both was shared equally.

"What was that, Matt? I get cows for apology and you get a kiss?" Alana kept her face close.

"I didn't write island law, it's just the way it is, a man apologies with cows and a woman has to apologize with a kiss."

"Oh, so that was a required kiss. You didn't do it for any other purpose?"

"Of course not, I'm only abiding the island laws."

"The honest law abiding citizen," Yes, Alana thought in that instant second, he was everything her father wanted for her. Again, she pushed the thought away but that was more difficult with his next words.

"You don't believe there could be a reason for us meeting? I know your life hasn't been easy, but something special happens every now and then, even to those that don't expect it."

She looked at him with a strange expression, actually felt a chill as her father's words rang in her ears. They'd penetrated over her lifetime from a young child to adult.

'It's going to take someone special," he'd said. "But it will happen, and it will be something special.'

Matt watched her strange reaction. "Obviously you don't feel the same."

"It's just... I..." She had no words. How could she confess her thoughts? Her father had said them so many years ago, so many lifetimes ago to a young girl. And he'd repeated it throughout her adulthood. Thinking of it now wasn't odd, was it? It was imbedded into her brain.

****

That day was almost a repeat of the first she'd discovered Matt was on the ship. The group of them went on an island tour, only now, she was much more comfortable and relaxed. And Richard and his group were added to the mix. They stopped at several places and each time when they got back in, seats were randomly taken, as to who got in first. The final leg of the short trip, before dropping some of the men off for golf and others to the beach, Alana found herself next to Matt in the very back.

Todd was the one who insisted Matt get in before him, which placed him directly next to Alana. Then he ran off for a minute with the pretense of getting Jonathan.

"He makes it a little obvious, doesn't he?" Alana knew Matt picked up on it also, it was a little difficult not to.

He laughed, "He tries not to."

"I wouldn't be surprised if he suggested you two switch rooms."

"Would that be a bad thing?"

His hand accidentally brushed across her leg and this time she couldn't wait for him to get out of the van not because of uncomfortable anger, but because of desire. After some of the men were dropped off for golf, the others were taken to a beach, including Diana who normally went back to the ship and rested midday.

"I don't know why someone would want to spend the rest of the day looking at nothing but a white ball." Diana said from beside her.

Alana made sure she was comfortable then sat down herself as the others took to the water. "My father played, and I couldn't understand then, even less now. It's the most boring thing to me to watch on television."

"This is my speed, I could sit on a beach like this all day and watch your son, he's so entertaining."

They looked out to see him having a grand time in the water. He had boundless energy which was wonderful, a good sign, but of course she worried. When he was sick, when he was well, she always worried.

The beach and snorkel day was relaxation and quiet, doing absolutely nothing but bask on a sand edge of yet another glorious setting. It had become a life she could get used to, maybe they could just sail the Caribbean forever, if they never went back to reality, could it find them?

Alana waved to Todd when he took a moment to look up at her. He smiled and waved back with the wide grin that was so ever present on his face now.

"This reminds me of when Matt was young and we'd come to the islands. He'd do the same as Todd, just as I sat here on the beach. That was before he grew up and found girls and golf."

"I think it's nice, you two taking a vacation every year." Alana leaned back in her chair and dug her feet in the warm sand.

"He's been my sanity, especially after I lost my husband. He's a rare breed with a good heart, even kept his heart after that nasty wife of his wanted to break it, but he was smarter than that. Matt's very special."

There was that word again. How ridiculous it was for her to think anything of it. It wasn't her father trying to reach her, it was a word. "Todd thinks so."

"Todd picks out the good people, almost as if he knows which one's to talk to."

It was a nice secluded beach where very few people were. Tranquil and serene with the mountains as a backdrop, Alana could lounge and Todd could snorkel. All the rainbow hued fish he encountered as he swam around an old sunken tugboat didn't disappoint him and Alana had no complaints from her perfect spot in the sun until it rained.

It was a short rain that gave them an opportunity to eat until it stopped then they were back out again. Alana had purchased a small roll up foam raft and decided to lounge in the water to read while Todd paddled around her with his fins. She was comfortable and content until the raft began to shake from underneath and she thought it was Todd.

"That isn't funny, Todd." She thought it was her son but it was Matt's face that emerged from the water beside her. "Why you..."

"Hey, hey, be careful. This is a family beach you know."

"I could have tipped over."

"It's only two feet deep, you would have landed on your knees." He didn't know the fear she would have suffered, so his look was coy. "Besides, I'd have saved you."

She didn't feel like he'd save her then, she felt herself falling deeper to somewhere unfamiliar. Her heart raced at seeing him, she hadn't planned on him being there, hadn't planned on possibly seeing him until later that evening. It was nice to see his face.

"What are you doing here? How many beaches are in St. Lucia? Couldn't you pick another to terrorize people?"

"The course was crowded, so we decided to quit early. Kevin wanted to be dropped off here, so..."

"So here you are," she smiled.

"Figured I'd snorkel a bit with Todd, that's the only reason I came."

"Is it now?" She teased with flirtation in her eyes.

"Why else?" He touched her arm lightly before swimming off.

Later, Alana sat on the shore with the others as Matt and Todd took every last second in the water. Only now, when it was moments before they had to leave to catch the ship in time, did they meander towards the shore. Even then, it was a slow pace, neither wanted to give up the day.

Matt never let on to Todd that he knew about his cancer, left it up to him to talk about it if he wanted but didn't think he would. Now as they walked along, Todd opened up to him with no reservations. His boyish laughter of a moment ago had faded and he took the quiet moment with just the two of them to talk. His voice was hushed and serious, thoughts of his fate heavy on his little shoulders.

"I just want to let you know that I have cancer. I've had treatments and was operated on a couple times and it might be gone, but it might be growing again, I don't know yet. They've done everything they can so far and now I just have to wait and make sure it isn't coming back. A little while after we get home I'll go back in, and if it's come back, it'll progress more quickly than before and I'll probably only have a short time."

He'd come right out and said it. There was no emotion in his words, no sadness, and no gloom evident, he was straightforward as he continued with detailed medical jargon and told him the same story he shared with Diana. Including all the details of how Alana revamped his hospital room and shaved her head and painted a face on the back of it. He recalled those parts with loving smiles.

He explained how she never left the hospital once any time he was in even when they'd moved to a closer apartment that was just down the street. Matt didn't speak, just listened. What stood out most was that this young man stricken with cancer was more worried about his mother than he was for himself.

"Matt, do you like my mom?"

"Of course I like your mother."

"I mean like man and woman like, boyfriend and girlfriend, husband and wife. So do you really, really, really like her?"

"Very much so," Matt was honest.

"Like I know that she can be a pain sometimes, like when she makes you eat at least one serving of vegetables or one of those good-for-you muffins every morning along with the junky cereal. But the fruit for snacks isn't bad. She likes you to eat lots of fruit, and that's probably just me, she probably wouldn't make you. Do you think you could like being with her? Maybe even live with her? I mean, do you like her in that way?"

"I'm sure I could, even if she did make me eat the muffin." He had to laugh, Todd made it impossible not to.

Todd looked out to vast sea, he felt as if his mother's fate lie in his hands and he had to be so careful and gentle with it, as if it were a tangible object. "See, I don't want my mom to be alone if something happens. She's never been alone before, she's always had me around. And I've been doing a lot of thinking about this."

"I'm listening," Matt encouraged him when he looked as if he had a little hesitation.

"My grandfather is gone, and there is Dr. Lee but he's a friend. He'd never like my mom in a special way like I think you can. And I know she likes you, like when she went to get me water and got you some too. Or like when she brushed lint off your jacket last night in the elevator, just like she does me sometimes. I know its little things but it's not something she'd do to a stranger, someone she didn't care for."

Matt had noticed the little things but didn't think anything of them. The little boy before him put it into such simple but profound perspective and he listened intently as Todd continued.

"She's very protective. If we were back home in Chicago she wouldn't let me play basketball with some strange man every night. She trusts me in your care. That's the way I feel about you too, I know I can trust her in your care."

"I feel honored you would think of me in that way." Matt spoke the truth in a soft tone.

Todd paused and bowed his head down a minute before he took a deep breath. He knew the enormity of what he would ask and did not take it lightly. "I just wanted to talk to you man to man. See, if something happens to me I don't want my mom to be alone. She'll really need someone, someone like you, you'll be good to her and I want her to have someone to look after her. So do you think you could maybe take care of her if I'm gone?"

Matt squatted down, his eye level closer to Todd's. He couldn't believe what had just been asked of him. The seriousness of Todd's words and the words themselves evidence he'd thought a lot about it and knew his decision was best.

Never in his life had anyone asked such an enormous request of him, trusted him so completely to be given such a responsible role in a person's life, and it touched him. And never in his life had he dreamed he'd be kneeling before a thirteen year old boy and feel the swell of his heart that filled with both sorrow and awe at the same time.

When Matt spoke, his tone held the same seriousness as Todd's. "I give you my word, man to man, that as long as I'm in this world and for as long as your mother wants me to, I'll make sure she's okay. Take care of her in any way I can, in whatever way she needs me. She'll be safe Todd, I promise you that."

Matt reached out his hand to shake on it just like a gentleman would, and Todd shook it strongly. Then the boy unexpectedly leaned into him, wrapped his arms around his neck and Matt enclosed him in an embrace, held onto the small body as securely as he could.

Alana waited comfortably in the chair for Todd and Matt while the others either went to the restaurant or had already caught a taxi back to port. Diana and Richard had taken a walk earlier and she watched as they made their way back along the shore. Richard loved to get her worked up about something, he liked the debate. Diana's hands flew and you could tell she talked animatedly about something.

Alana watched the activity of her surroundings. People watched, a favorite past time of many. A young couple, probably on their honeymoon she guessed. A mother and dad with two small twin boys had a hard time keeping pace as the kids ran in different directions. A large group of what appeared to be two families combined had set up camp around children who dug a hole in the sand.

Then she looked closely at her own little space. How did they get here? Alana thought. Not physically of course, but in the realm of reality. How had they gotten here? They looked like their own little family, like the others that surrounded her, when in reality were basically strangers who'd come together in some mysterious way, maybe even for some unknown mysterious reason. She felt as though she didn't know them and yet at the same time felt as if she'd always known them.

Who were these people and how, or why, had they arrived in her life? Could Jenna's psychotic tale of moon and stars and stars under moons ring true? Alana pushed the thought away, almost laughed aloud at entertaining the notion.

Could Matt be right that they'd met for a reason? But it was simple. They were brought together as anyone would be, pleasant conversation, likable people with similar interests and types of personalities. It was how friendships formed, a natural process that occurred between people.

Whether you met them in the grocery store at home or on far away islands surrounded by turquoise and emerald beauty and distant folklore of days gone by. Even amid made-up tales of island law people came together for odd and natural reasons. Alana did laugh out loud then at the thought of Matt bestowing her with cows.

Some would pass through your life and others linger for a while. Alana wondered what would happen to the four companions then automatically pushed the thought away. Don't think about it now, don't think about it tomorrow, or the next day. Today Alana, you had only today.

When the two reached her chair, Alana looked into Matt's eyes and noticed something different, just the slightest hint of deep sadness. Within their time together Todd touched him the way only Todd could and she saw now a sad pain that could truly be shared with her own. He didn't have to live with her son for thirteen years to be able to realize the agony one would feel were he to be gone. She would never know what happened, neither one ever told her and she never asked.

CHAPTER ELEVEN

As they rode back to the port, Alana noticed Todd was a little quiet when Jonathan kept talking about windsurfing over the summer with his brother. He kept encouraging Todd that he could come to, but her son said little. Alana questioned him when they were alone.

"Hey, what's the matter?" She asked when her maternal instincts gave her worry.

"Jonathan keeps talking about spending some time together this summer. Said he had a cool boogie board at the beach they always go to and his brother can teach us how to windsurf."

These people didn't know it was possible they may never see Todd again. She thought how lucky they were to be able to walk off the ship and forever imagine Todd alive. It would never cross their minds the possibility that he'd passed on.

Alana and Todd stood quietly along the sea, her arm protectively around him. He had been so jovial but sometimes it hit him at the oddest moments.

"I don't see why you couldn't learn how to windsurf."

"Summer seems so far away."

"So we'll do it now." She answered quickly.

It always seemed to be an exchange of roles between mother and son. Alana would have a weak moment and it was Todd who brought her back up. Or now when Todd had a rare weak moment, it would be Alana to support him. They worked as a true team of two.

"Could we? Think we could find a place to learn?"

"We're in the Caribbean surrounded by water everywhere, I'm sure we can find a place to windsurf. Now if you had asked to snow ski, that would have been a little more difficult right now, that we would have to plan for later, but windsurfing we can handle." She rubbed his back. "We're going windsurfing sometime before this week is over, and that's a promise. I don't care if I have to get behind you and blow, you'll have wind."

Todd smiled but still looked a little pensive. To accomplish things he wanted to do was not his major concern, it wasn't his first priority thought when he gave in to feelings about possibly not being there for very much longer. First and foremost he worried about his mother. Would she be okay if he were gone? How could she take care of herself alone? If he had his way, Matt would be there to take care of her and as much as he wished for that in his mind, he had to admit there would be all kinds of factors involved in that scenario.

Was his mother going to be able to take care of herself if his dream scenario didn't work out? His mother was the strongest person he knew, or ever would know, but he needed reassurance she would be okay. It was his biggest fear, it was the only thing he worried about when he thought about dying, was her survival without him.

Other than possibly losing him, he knew her biggest fear was having her face in the water. He didn't know why, it was just something she'd always been afraid of, maybe if she could overcome it, it would validate for him that she was as strong as he thought. And maybe she would really be okay if he eventually had to leave her. He'd seen people windsurf, seen them fall off and their faces go underwater several times and he looked at it as the perfect opportunity to assure himself.

"I know you're afraid of the water mom, actually your face getting in the water, and if you went windsurfing with me it could happen. In fact, it will happen. But I think you can do it, will you try with me?"

Alana chuckled lightly at first, thought he was only kidding. But when she looked at his face there was no humor there, it was a serious request. He normally said things like that in jest, knew she would refuse, but she looked into his eyes and this time was different. This time he was solemn and in her son's eyes was an unspoken urge for her to defy her fears. All he had come through, all he had braved, uncertainties conquered with heroic pride. Now all he asked of her was to face her own fears.

"I'm sure you can do it, Mom, I know you can."

"You really think?" The thought of it already frightened her.

"I know you can." The small voice was full of conviction.

"Of course I'll try, anything for you."

"Really?"

"Really."

"It'll be great mom, just wait and see, we'll have a blast." His face looked so promising it was hard not to smile.

When she called Jenna, Todd talked quickly to her then ran off with Matt once again. He and Robb were in deep conversation with a few local fisherman and Jonathan and Todd were enthralled with the catch of the day.

Alana called both Jenna and Dr. Lee from a payphone. Jenna's phone call was done quickly. Todd was fine and she hadn't had sex again with her 'Puerto Rican' as she continued to mistakenly refer to him as.

"He's from New York Jenna."

"Whatever, have you had sex again yet?"

"No. And quit asking."

"You were swept away in San Juan. You blamed it on the moon, the stars, the water and the wine. It's the same atmosphere where you are now. No different. What are you waiting on?"

Alana knew it would already be difficult to pull herself away from Matt and she didn't feel she needed any more of a connection, but she didn't tell Jenna her feelings.

She dialed the number to Dr. Lee's private phone she could envision ringing on his walnut desk. He picked it up on the third ring and Alana immediately began to talk.

"We're not coming home. You should see the wonders the Caribbean is doing for Todd, so if we just keep sailing around for the rest of our lives I think he'll be fine. Would you come visit us if we stayed?"

"Alana, I've been waiting to hear from you again."

She could hear the smile in his voice. "We're having the most glorious time, why didn't I listen to you a long time ago?"

"Because you haven't wanted to look past today to see tomorrow for so long, you'd forgotten how."

"That's right, I forgot. See? That's proof this atmosphere does wonders." Alana looked over and saw Matt and Todd, and they looked over at the same time and she waved. "He's looking wonderful but I do worry about him. He's not sick or anything, quite the opposite, I'm afraid he's going to wear himself out. He's up early and he doesn't go to bed until midnight, sometimes after. All the walking, snorkeling, basketball, is it good for him?"

Dr. Lee laughed, "Of course it's good for him. He's gaining energy and strength back, that's always a good thing. His body will slow down on its own if it needs to. Is he taking all his vitamins and meds?"

"Religiously, but..."

"Then they're working, let them work. Alana, listen to you, you are in the Caribbean with your son who is as active as every other boy his age, when four months ago he was so weak he wasn't able to pick up a soup can. He's doing things some adult's only dream about, having the time of his life and you still worry."

"I know how ridiculous it is but I can't stop until I know for sure it's gone. What if..."

"Stop. Stop right now and I hope I said that with as much authority as I meant to. You know I won't entertain any 'what if' thoughts."

"Did I mention windsurfing? He wants to go windsurfing and I promised I'd go with him."

"You? You're afraid to get your face wet in the shower." Dr. Lee knew her fears and knew where they came from.

"We all have to overcome our inner terrors sometime, Todd's taught me that."

"Todd's taught us all quite a bit. And if he can get you windsurfing with the risk of your face going under water..." He paused, didn't want to scare her anymore than he knew she already was. "Let me know how it turns out. So he's having a wonderful time, what about you?"

"It's great." Her voice came off confident with just a slight tinge of reserve that didn't go unnoticed.

"But?"

Alana looked over to Matt. "I just feel like I'm in limbo, I can't move forward until all this is put behind us and yet I don't want to come home, I don't want to find out the answer. I just want to keep sailing around the Caribbean then maybe I can avoid it. Just live in limbo for the rest of our lives."

"Enjoy it, Alana. Rejuvenate yourself, that's what it's for."

He almost added that she needed to be recharged for the next stretch ahead but stopped. Although he held high hopes, and all signs were good, the statistics on Todd's cancer being completely gone were not in his favor. He could be perfectly fine now, but if the slightest bit of his aggressive cancer showed up again it would move much more rapidly and he would be in the same ill position he'd been, start the process all over again. Only this time, they would know that treatments would not work. It would only be a matter of time, and very little time.

When she hung up and walked towards them on the pier, Todd pulled a fish from a bucket to show her but it slipped from his hands and almost landed on her feet. Alana jumped and was saved from falling off the pier and into the water by Matt's strong arms as he caught her.

Todd scooped the fish up quickly and put it back in the bucket and looked to her with fear in his eyes, and apology. "Sorry Mom."

"See? Like I told you earlier, I'd save you." Matt said quietly as he eased his hold.

"If I didn't know any better, I'd think the two of you conspired on that one." She smiled but slipped out of his arms quickly.

****

After they returned to the ship, showered and dressed for the evening, Alana and Todd found a party going on pool side. A Caribbean party had begun just as the ship was leaving port and the sun set in the distance.

"Look, Mom, it's Mrs. McCray."

Todd pointed to Diana on the stage doing an island dance the band instructed the participants in. Step by step directions called out and hips swung back and forth then side to side. She was doing great and kept up better than most of the young one's. Alana got the feeling she'd done it quite a few times.

Automatically she scanned the crowd for Matt then saw him smiling at her from the top deck as he leaned over the open rail to watch his grandmother. Every time they exchanged a smile lately, it was as if they shared a private confidence. A silent knowing that passed between them. The exchange of a secret inner happiness at seeing the other was the only way Alana could describe it to herself. A few moments later he was at their side.

"Hey buddy." Matt shook Todd's hand as he always did.

Todd loved it, always made him feel like one of the guys as Matt treated everyone that way, Todd no exception. He then looked at Alana and his sweet smile was something she'd been eager to see.

"How come you're not up there?" She asked and nodded towards the stage.

"I could ask you the same."

"I have an excuse, we just got here."

"They aren't done yet." He challenged and it was all she needed.

"Come on, Todd, let's show Matt how it's done."

The two joined Diana with Todd on one side and Alana on the other. They had to catch up but they quickly got into the rhythm with specific instruction. Laughed when they goofed up and Todd held onto Diana's hand a few moments to give him a better edge until he got it down on his own. They began to call a little faster and the music sped up, then a little faster as hips swung everywhere. Some had it, others were lost, but the three of them held their own. When they finally stopped everyone was laughing.

"That kind of felt like sex, hell, at my age, I think it was." Out of earshot, Diana said it to Alana and she cracked up as they exited the stage.

"Impressive, you even kept up with grandmother." Matt smiled. "Remind me never to throw out a challenge I won't get enjoyment out of."

"Hey, Matt, wanna play in the ping pong tournament? I can't find Jonathan and mom was gonna play but mom's... well..." Then he stopped and looked guilty but continued and tried to make up for it. "She's a better dancer. Didn't she dance good?"

They took off to play in the tournament and Alana joined Diana for the Martini tasting where they found Amy, Rita and Richard.

"Todd's been looking for Jonathan."

"Same with Jonathan, they must have been running circles around each other on opposite sides of the ship."

"Where have you been?" Richard shouted and kissed her in greeting. "I feel like I haven't seen you in days."

"We just saw each other a little while ago," Alana laughed. "I just went to take a shower."

They all sat together and as usual chatter and high spirits ensued as the bartender prepared martinis with skill and a comical flare. Plentiful and outstanding they continued to flow like water and as time passed no one was sure how long they'd been there, but no one made the attempt to leave and the drinks kept coming.

"Weren't we all going to meet for dinner? Can we eat here? Do we have to walk somewhere?" Richard prattled on as his words rolled together.

"I think we already ate," Diana raised her glass. "But we forgot to toast."

They all cheered and toasted, long ago lost count how many they had, both toasts and drinks.

"Hey, Richard, where's Kevin?" Amy asked.

"Spa, sauna, pool, facials, the works, hell, by the time he gets out of there he'll look like Joan Rivers." He squinted his eyes to look across the room at someone. "But that's okay, I'll take that instead. Oh, never mind, he's Alana's and I know as much as she like's me she won't share."

They all turned to look and saw Matt leaning against the wall with his arms crossed in front of him, ankles crossed, and he had a quirk of a smile as he shook his head at their antics.

Hadn't she just left him? Hadn't he only possibly thirty minutes ago gone to play ping-pong? Alana glanced outside and realized it was dark, dark as in night dark.

"Oh my Gosh, Todd, where's Todd?"

Matt walked up slowly and eased her fears. "Todd is getting ready for dinner, same with Jonathan."

He surveyed the drunken crowd that remained still and quiet as if they'd been caught doing something wrong by a parent. Each tried not to giggle and it was Diana who broke the silence with her statement.

"I had sex today, right up on stage."

It sent the entire group over the edge into hysterics.

****

Matt told Alana and Amy not to worry. The plan was for Robb to take the boys to a late dinner in the buffet area and they could join them when they were ready. Then he took his grandmother to her cabin and ordered room service when she said that was what she wanted, but she was asleep before it arrived. And when he joined the group of three at the buffet he assumed the same happened to the other women.

"Where's mom?" Todd asked eagerly.

"They were at the spa and said they'd meet us later for a show, but after those massages they looked so relaxed I suspect they went to shower and fell asleep. I wouldn't count on seeing them till later." A little fabrication of the truth wouldn't hurt anyone at the table. The part about them being asleep was probably true, but he didn't see any reason to tell the young boys they were drunk as sailors.

With the meal over, the boys wanted to go off to kid's karaoke and Matt gave them a time he would meet them at the basketball court. When Todd mentioned going to check on his mother first, Matt told him to go have fun and he would check on her and Todd was grateful and gave him his cabin key before he left. When they were gone he explained to Robb the full story and as Matt suspected he thought it quite amusing.

Matt didn't want to intrude but didn't want Todd to check on her either. Not that it was a bad thing, she'd had a few too many drinks, it happened, but he saw no need for Todd to know. When he opened the door to complete darkness, the only light coming from the moon through the window, he saw her still form lying on the bed with her back to the door. She was fully clothed just as she had been.

He chuckled to himself as he closed the door behind him but hadn't realized she wasn't fully asleep until she spoke. When she did he knew she was trying hard to sound as normal as possible, to sound sober. Her attempt made him laugh.

"Todd? Mommy's tired honey, and I have a headache. Please just turn the bathroom light on if you need it."

"Wow, that was good. If I were Todd I would have fallen for it."

She swung around on her back and spread her arms wide as they fell to either side of the bed. "Thank you, thank you, thank you." She thanked someone unknown and sighed in relief. "I thought you were Todd and I'm still sooooo not feeling myself."

"That's quite an understatement. I had to check on you, I wasn't even sure you and Amy would find your rooms."

"Who told you we got lost? These hallways all look the same, it wasn't our fault."

"Did you get something to eat? Coffee at least?"

"I tried the coffee, didn't work. And dinner was chocolate mousse' from room service."

When she opened her eyes fully she saw him standing across the room, he hadn't come any closer and she patted the bedside. "Come here, come sit a minute." He did and she took his hand. "Thank you for taking care of Todd. I wouldn't have sat up there and drank so much if you hadn't been with him. I'm not that kind of mother, I would have played ping-pong and... gone to trivia and... games and... stuff." Her mind was slow as she thought of the activities. "I wouldn't have been up there drinking, but I knew he was safe, I knew he was with you. And I just, I don't know, I haven't had that much to drink in... I can't remember. But he was with you and I didn't even worry about him, I knew he was with you." Then she paused. "It's actually your fault, that's why I'm going to blame my hangover on you in the morning."

"I'll confess to the crime if I have to. Get some sleep, Todd will be fine for the rest of the evening, I told him you had a massage that made you so relaxed and tired so he already knows you're asleep, and he's at karaoke now and we're playing basketball later. I'll walk him down and make sure he's in by his curfew. Eleven? Twelve?"

"I can't sleep. I have to plan for windsurfing tomorrow. I have to find out where to go." She worried about it now, didn't want to rush in the morning even though the thought terrified her.

"I'll take care of it."

"But we have to do it in the morning, he's going off with Jonathan in the afternoon. As soon as…"

"I'll take care of it," he stated with more intensity. "Don't worry about it Alana."

"Are you coming? I won't… I have to windsurf, Matt, I…" The fear was about to overcome her, she wasn't asleep but nightmares almost entered at the thought.

"It's okay. I'll plan it and I'll come. Why are you getting so worked up?"

She sighed heavily and closed her eyes. She'd get through it. She'd get through it. Was all she repeated in her mind, "Where did you come from?" Alana asked softly.

"We ate at the buffet, I just came from there."

"No. How did you get here?"

Matt had no inkling of what her words meant or how he was supposed to answer. "I took the elevator?"

"Matt," Alana hadn't sat up, still lay flat on her back and she pulled him down to her. "I know the questions don't sound right, but they're not drunk questions. I guess what I want to say is how did you get here into my life?"

"That, I don't have an answer to."

Alana's hand was firmly on the back of his head as she pulled his mouth to hers and kissed him passionately. Her inebriated state had not affected her ability to make him ache with every touch and it took him several minutes of enjoying her pleasure but he pulled away.

"Alana, you don't want to do this."

"I don't or you don't."

"Oh no, that certainly isn't an issue."

She pulled him in again and he kissed her but objected, tried to talk her out of it. "We're in your room, Todd could come in."

"He never comes in until the very last possible moment," she gingerly bit his bottom lip. "Besides, you have his room card."

This time he pressed against her more as she kissed the side of his neck, her warm breath against his skin. He emitted a throaty moan as he trailed down to press his lips and taste the sweetness of her. Finally, the smooth skin he yearned for. His hand began to unbutton her shirt and she arched her back in urgency but again he stopped, this time it was much more difficult to do so than the last.

"Alana, you don't want to do this," he said breathlessly and rose from the bed. "I look at you everyday and crave you so badly I feel like a man without water, and I can't believe I'm going to leave you there in that bed alone, but I am." Matt ran his hand through his hair and wanted to pull it out, every strand.

"Why?" She quickly propped herself up on her elbows and when she did felt the blood rush to her head, or was it liquor that rushed to her head, she would guess both. It still didn't stop her from wanting him terribly.

"You're not exactly sober and I'd feel like I was taking advantage."

"You're not, I swear, I promise, Matt you can't do this."

"Sleep, Alana. Todd will be fine, I'll walk him down and check on you again but don't worry about him."

"I didn't worry about him when he was with you, and look where it got me. It's all your fault, won't you at least give me a kiss goodnight?"

She said it so innocently that he almost did, but when he looked at her he knew he wouldn't pull away this time. "I can't," he groaned honestly and ignored her as he walked to the door.

"Don't be noble now, not now, be noble and good tomorrow." Then she almost screamed her next words. "You owe me four cows for this one. That apology of yours where you offered cows? I want four of them."

CHAPTER TWELVE

Warm steady winds seemed to blow them into the largest of the British Leeward Islands. Antigua offered a vista of complex coastline with safe harbors and a protective, nearly unbroken wall of coral reef. Those unique characteristics attracted the Royal Navy and Antigua became Great Britain's most important Caribbean base when Admiral Horatio Nelson sailed there in 1784.

Alana rolled over the next morning and looked at Todd's still sleeping form with his even breathing she'd trained herself to see under the covers, and as always she smiled. She'd been showered, dressed and looking a new woman by the time he'd arrived back to the cabin the evening before, and he never suspected otherwise.

The ship arrived in Antigua at seven that morning and Alana and Todd met Matt and Diana for breakfast. Later, they were joined by Amy, Robb and Jonathan. Matt smiled coyly at her and she playfully barely looked at him as if she were still mad.

The evening before, Matt had planned both the morning of windsurfing, and a surprise for Alana as he'd made a call to his friend Jack in Barbados and set in motion the perfect day.

"Hey Jack!" Matt greeted his friend when he answered the phone.

"Matt, don't tell me, you're on your way back to Barbados, decided to become a golf pro after all."

"I told you, I'd starve. I was calling because I'll be on the ship overnight and won't be able to plan anything, so I thought I could use your island expertise."

"Sure, what do you need?"

"We'll be in Antigua and I wanted to plan an afternoon for someone. Something relaxing and nice but I don't know what. You're the expert in the islands, and I needed some suggestions other than the touristy stuff."

"Ahhhh, the dancing queen from the bar by chance?"

Matt laughed at the name he'd used, "As a matter of fact yes. Her name is Alana Gibbs."

"So I take it things have improved. You don't need my suggestions you have enough experience of your own. You have a great looking lady, take her to the beach, some frozen cocktails to get drunk on and wham, you're in."

"It isn't like that Jack."

"Whoa, you're looking for something special? She really means something?"

Matt was quiet for a minute before he confirmed the words to Jack and to himself. "Yeah, she really means something."

Jack heard it in his tone and for a split second he was a little envious. "So a little more than the beach thing is required."

"She's been through a lot. Maybe there's an exclusive spa on a beach, a plane tour, I'm not sure but I thought you could give me a few numbers I could call, or make the arrangements for me."

"I have some favors to call in, don't worry about a thing. What time do you want?"

"Noon should be good."

"At noon tomorrow just look around the dock at the ship. There will be someone to meet you."

As they walked alone along the port that morning, he told Alana he'd made plans but wouldn't tell her exactly what. Only then did the thought cross his mind that he just assumed they would spend the afternoon together and he didn't know what he would do if she said no, it hadn't crossed his mind.

"How do I know I want to go if I don't know what it is?" She argued.

"You planned this whole trip as a surprise for your son, excursions as a surprise for your son and he's told me about surprises at home. Isn't it about time you had some surprises of your own?"

"Just give me a hint."

"No hints, you just have to trust me, Alana."

She looked at him for a long time then moved slowly close to him, her hands moved up his chest until they rested on his broad shoulders and she kissed him lightly.

"How do you expect me to trust you, when I can't even trust myself anymore?"

"You'd better be careful. I might not be as noble as I was last night."

Alana kissed him slowly again, this time she lingered. "Do I get a hint?"

When her kisses left his mouth and softly trailed to his neck he laughed and moaned at the same time. "That's wrong." He would have broken and given her a hint at that point, but he didn't know a thing.

She pulled away, didn't want Todd to see them and knew he would be there shortly. "Maybe I won't go."

"And maybe I'll just take you to shark infested waters for your windsurfing."

"Think I can tell Todd I don't feel well? I really don't. Windsurfing with a hangover can't be fun."

"I can't wait to see you in these stingray infested waters. You know, it's said that Antigua has the most shoreline stingrays per square inch than any other island. The beaches are swarmed with them, swimmers have to practically wade through them." He hadn't looked at her but when he did she had the most serious look on her face he laughed and had to confess he was teasing. Saw the look of relief wash over her.

"What beach did you find anyway? I did a little quick research this morning and I think Hawksbill might be good, it's actually a resort but I think we can get in for the day." She looked to Matt who had a quirky grin on his face. "What? It's not a good beach?"

He hesitated only slightly before he answered. Hawksbill had the only clothing optional beach in Antigua, for a moment he was going to tell the truth which would have changed her mind but decided against it. "It's fine, they have a nice beach. We can go there if you want."

"You going to windsurf, Mrs. McCray?" Todd only half teased when they were on their way, he wouldn't have put it past her.

"These old legs can barely hold me on solid ground, believe me child, they wouldn't hold me on moving water. I am going just to watch you."

The cab ride was a small tour of the island, only things pointed out along the way until they finally arrived and it couldn't have been soon enough. Todd was so excited Alana thought he'd jump out of the cab before it even stopped moving and she wanted to get it over with as quick as possible. Matt lagged behind them just a little and spoke privately to the cab driver to ask him to wait.

After she wandered a bit, she went through a gate to a beach that didn't seem to be as crowded as the others, Alana first wanted to get Diana settled in a nice comfortable place. She looked out over the water where several windsurfers glided.

"Don't they look cool? Look at that one, the blue and red, he's really going." Todd excitedly pointed to the windsurfers. "Look, there's three of them."

Bright colored sails spliced through the water and Alana watched and her fear already high she looked to study how easy they were to fall off of. It was obvious the one's there were experienced surfers, as they smoothly caught the small waves and one further out where it was rougher, was literally going airborne. The most important thing she saw was when someone did fall off, completely off, they went underwater. It didn't look easy to control and her stomach churned even more.

"Oh wow, she doesn't have any clothes on."

"What?" Alana looked and Todd was right. The woman surfed casually as her breasts bounced along.

Todd began to look at others along the beach and realized there were more. "Look at all those people that don't have any clothes on, hey most all of them are naked."

Alana looked on the beach and saw the rest of them. Men, women, some partially clothed, but most totally nude and her hand flew up to her mouth instead of her eyes and all she could do was stare and gasp. A somewhat pot bellied man walked down the beach and all she saw was a dangling penis. It was what her eyes were automatically drawn to, naked people were everywhere, it certainly wasn't the site she expected to see and she could hear Mrs. McCray giggle from behind her.

"Hey, look at that dude, whoa, he's got beads." Todd laughed and Alana hoped no one heard him as she quickly turned him around and they headed back to the cab. Matt chuckled to himself, had a smile that pointed him out as the culprit.

"You knew, how could you do that? And Todd saw!" Alana smacked him on the shoulder when she realized it.

"Todd saw what any normal teen boy would want to see, he'll be the hit of school when he goes back and tells all his friends."

"Why didn't you tell me? And where are we supposed to go now?"

"We're going someplace to windsurf."

"It isn't like that beach, is it?" She looked at him slyly, unsure now of any of the beaches.

"Four beaches at Hawksbill, and only one nude beach in Antigua, you just happened to pick it. I don't know how I knew, but I knew you were going to wander there." He laughed as they got back in the car.

Matt now asked the driver to take them to Dutchman's Bay where there was a windsurfing center that had available both rentals and classes with experienced instructors. A man made reef separated the sailing areas, inside the reef flat water was perfect for beginners, and outside the reef for the more experienced and advanced.

Once they'd rented the equipment and had someone to help them they entered the water and Alana began to sweat even though the early sun was not that hot and the water cool. Todd looked over to her and saw the fear that was apparent. Maybe he asked too much of her.

"You know, Mom, you really don't have to do this. Maybe you shouldn't."

Alana almost turned back, almost took the 'out' he offered but she took a deep breath instead. She'd promised, she could do this, he'd overcome so much it was the least of her fears to cover. Only water, Alana, it was only water.

"I can do this." Her statement was to reassure them both.

Todd was still worried, hadn't realized before how deep her fear actually was until now. He thought it was just a tiny frivolous thing but now saw the enormity of it as her eyes filled with a grave terror he'd never seen before.

"No really, Mom, maybe you shouldn't." When he took her hand she was shaking.

Alana squeezed tight, both to stop herself from shaking and to draw confidence from her son's strength then she took one more deep lungful of air. "I'm going, Todd, and if I learn well my face won't be in the water, will it? If I don't fall off, I won't have to worry about it."

Each of them had their own instructors because Alana knew she wouldn't take to it as easily as Todd, and she didn't want him to not be able to move forward when it would take her so long, so she'd gotten separate teachers. Matt opted out and watched the two from close to shore as Mrs. McCray sat in a chair under the umbrella.

It wasn't long before Todd could balance himself but Alana struggled. "I'm sorry," she kept apologizing.

"Don't be sorry, you've never done this before, it's understandable."

"It looks easier than it is, I think I'd be okay if the wind would just stay in one direction. Then again I'd probably just sail straight across the ocean and you'd never see me again."

The tan young man smiled. "I'd come after you."

Matt overheard his comment and chuckled to himself. Couldn't help but hear and see their interaction on occasion as it was a short distance and the beach was not crowded. Matt guessed he was college age, probably dropped out and escaped to the islands to bum around, live the carefree life of the perfect beach bum doing what he loved. The beautiful women he encountered were probably more than bonus enough to keep him there. Heck, Matt couldn't blame him, had he done the same he wouldn't have ended up in a ten-year miserable marriage.

Matt knew he was falling in love with Alana, if he hadn't completely fallen in love already. How she felt about him he didn't know. He knew she wanted him physically, just as desperately as he wanted her and there was undeniable intense passion, but there was so much more.

Alana was a content and complete woman until the discovery of Todd's illness. Matt came to know her as a woman who'd submersed herself in her son's life both before and after they found out about his cancer, content and happy with the small family of the three of them that included her father until he passed away. And she loved her schoolwork as a secretary and also volunteered, substituted and worked on her teaching degree when it didn't take time away from Todd. That's why it was taking her so long she explained. Her plan had been to become a full time teacher by the time he graduated high school and moved on to college.

"My life after motherhood when Todd doesn't need me so much anymore," Was what she'd said.

She felt lucky her father had left her financially comfortable enough so she didn't have to concentrate so much on paying her small bills and could devote all of her time to Todd. She didn't have to work at least two jobs as she'd seen other single mothers do in their day-to-day struggle.

From what Matt could tell she hadn't dated all that much as a single mother, she mentioned times she called her 'nightmare dates' when her friends secretly set her up. And even though they pushed her to date she refused. It was probably why she didn't even seem to take notice that the young man who helped her surf, flirted with her at the same time.

It was all one sided on the part of the admirer as Alana fully concentrated on her task of staying above water. Only Matt noticed that he held onto her hand maybe a few seconds longer than necessary or the way he caught her when she was going to fall, or the way he held his hand on her thigh to hold her in place. Alana took no notice of his interest. Her inattentiveness was not a coy hard-to-get game, or not wanting to reciprocate just because Matt was there, it was pure innocence, she didn't even know.

"Here, I'll hold onto each side of your legs and hold you up and you concentrate on keeping your balance."

"Don't let go!" She screamed.

"I have no problem standing here all day holding you up." His palms held onto either side of her hips.

"You just might have to, we might be here until tomorrow."

Alana was concerned with making sure her feet were placed correctly to balance her. Once she set her mind to the notion that if she were on the board, her face would be further from the water, she managed to stay up for longer periods of time. It was fairly shallow where they were so when she fell off she could easily stand and her face didn't go in. Her instructor was so very patient with her and when Todd took off on his own it was the push she needed.

It wasn't much longer when she was finally able to stay on long enough by herself to be carried by the wind. Although she screamed over the smallest ripple of a wave, she didn't fall off. It was when she turned that she fell. Water enveloped her face, suffocated her and it seemed like forever before she could get to the top for air, even with her buoyancy vest. She came up gasping and her lungs filled with sea water as Alana grasped the board and held on tight. Visions of murky water clouded her mind and the fright of a six-year-old child returned. The child who fought the nightmares for years, now it was as if she relived it, every gasp for air, and it took her a few moments to recover.

"You okay?" The instructor called to her several times but she never answered him.

He thought maybe she hurt herself and was just about to swim out to her when she finally waved to him that she was okay. It took her a few more seconds to get back up on the board and this time she was more determined to stay on top but would fall again. And this time she felt like it took longer to reach the top.

The briny sea threatened to take her, that was how her mind viewed it and panic set in. The fear threatened her, made her desperate now. She almost went back to shore but from somewhere within, she pulled herself back up on the board. Her inner fright both motivated her and made her want to quit at the same time. It became a battle to be overcome, just like the battle of the cancer that filled their lives except Todd had fought most of that battle, physically anyway. His strength was what pushed her on.

When it took Alana quite a while to recover from her fall and she now sat still on the board, the instructor was going to swim out to her but Matt stopped him and he swam out to her instead.

"You don't look like you're having too good a time." He was concerned about her, even more so now that he saw her face and could see she was petrified.

"It's lovely," she said it sarcastically with just a hint of nervous laughter and her hands were shaking so badly she could barely hold onto the board.

"You're torturing yourself, are you okay?"

"Not really."

"Maybe you ought to come in." Matt was troubled by the look on her face, there was something buried deep in her eyes he couldn't describe.

"I'm okay, Matt, really. I have to do this."

"Alana..."

"I have to do this," she insisted with a little more force. "You can't save me from this, I have to save myself."

He didn't understand and was afraid to leave her, but she was adamant and he reluctant swam back to shore. Each time Alana fell, each time she landed in the water the memory terrorized her over and over again but she'd come right back up to the top, come up to air, to life. Although the panic never went completely away, it subsided a little with each and every fall. Her thought not so much the long ago murky water and death, but getting to the top where there was life.

As long as she wasn't in the water and forced her mind from a memory, Alana found herself skimming along ever so smoothly and eventually managed to turn it and get herself in the right direction several times, or the wrong direction. Every time she headed out to open sea she quickly turned back, didn't want to go far from shore.

At one point her and Todd sailed close together and he took one hand off and waved, she of course not so brave.

"You go, Mom!" He shouted with pride.

Todd was just as thrilled with her success as she was, and when she had enough and they glided into shore together they laughed and he gave her a high five. He would never know the agony she'd just endured, but it was nothing compared to what he'd gone through. She didn't even place it in the same category.

"See, I said you could do it."

"Yeah, it really wasn't that bad," she lied.

Alana was still shaking a bit but it was unnoticeable. In her son's eyes, she was a success, which was all that mattered. For that, it had been worth every horror stricken memory she relived, a memory she had run from for many years and she was just glad the experience was over.

"I think you might be ready for competition." Her instructor smiled at her.

"I'm ready for a pina' colada, that's the only thing I'm ready for and a very strong one."

When they reached Diana she was standing and smiling, congratulated Alana as if she'd just won a race.

"Bravo! You looked great out there, I was waiting for you to start doing flips, catching air, and all those other things they do."

"I would have but the thought of a nice frozen drink called." She joked. "My mouth is so full of salt water, I could put a cucumber in and it would come out a pickle."

"I was just going to get a drink, do you want me to bring you back one or do you want to walk up with me?" Diana asked but Todd quickly dried off and was ready to go with her.

"I'll go with you, Mrs. McCray." His mouth too needed refreshing fluid.

"I'll be up in a minute, I need to dry off a bit."

When they were gone, her and Matt alone, Alana picked up a towel and held it to her face, pressed it deep into her eyes as if she could erase what she'd seen over and over again. The murky water she was trapped in, the struggle as she tried to free herself, her mothers face so clear before it faded away. She saw it all, the pain and fear in the face she'd lost to death. She almost jumped out of her skin when Matt squeezed her arms from behind.

"What happened to you out there?"

Alana turned to face him. With the others gone she didn't worry about being seen and raised her face to his, kissed him gently. "I needed that. I'm fine now."

"You worried me to death, I didn't know the water was that bad for you. Alana you were petrified, are you sure you're okay now?"

She leaned into him, took the comfort and warmth of his arms around her, her head resting on his shoulder. "I've had this fear since I was six, when my mother died. She drowned."

"I'm sorry. You never said she drowned, I didn't know."

Even though Matt didn't ask for specifics, she found herself telling him. "When people ever asked, all they needed to know was that she died. Like you, no one ever questions how, not even Todd. When he was old enough to know that his grandfather was supposed to come with a grandmother, he'd asked where she was and was simply told the truth that she died when I was six years old. I didn't leave details out on purpose, he just never asked how." Alana paused before she continued.

"My mother always dropped my father off at work, he was an intern at the hospital then, and on that particular night it was raining really hard. After she dropped him off, on the way home, a truck skidded across the center line and hit the car making it spin around and roll over an embankment and into the water. It sunk almost immediately."

Alana didn't add that she'd grown up with the guilt of her mother's death, always wondered if her father ever looked at her and wished her mother were alive instead. If he had a choice to make, would it have been her who died? He loved Alana, that had never been a question and it wasn't that he made her feel that way. She was the light of her father's eyes, she knew that, and they never talked about it, neither one spoke one word about that night. It was just something Alana harbored deep in her thoughts.

When she spoke again the words shocked Matt, he hadn't expected it. "I couldn't get out. I was drowning and there wasn't a thing I could do, I was strapped in."

"You were in the car?"

"I was in the back seat. She always said the back seat was safer, said her worst nightmare would be me flying through the windshield. So here I was in the back and she couldn't reach me. I remember my mothers face looking back to me, all she could do was stretch over the seat to try and reach me, but as much as she struggled, she couldn't."

No wonder she was terrified, and yet she'd gone into the water time after time. Matt spoke quietly, her revelation gave him the understanding he sought, the reason she'd put herself through it. "You went out there for Todd."

"I had to. I've spent the last year watching my son go from being a healthy energetic boy to a frail, weak child who couldn't hold a pencil. Every fear, every step along the way he braved with not one complaint. Matt, when he was huddled over a toilet throwing up his guts because of the treatments, he'd look at me with those big eyes and say, 'I'm okay, mama, it really isn't that bad.'" Alana paused and a few tears came at the memory, she couldn't speak for a moment and took a deep sigh as Matt wiped the tears away. "I had to go out there so I could look him in the eye and tell him I was okay. It's all he needs to know."

Without saying a word he put his arm around her and pulled her close. The pain in her eyes tortured his soul.

CHAPTER THIRTEEN

"Man that water taste good, I had to get that salt out of my mouth. Here, Mom, we brought you and Matt water. Want to go back out again?" Todd handed her the bottle.

"I'm going to hand my board over to Matt now if that's okay, but we don't have much time. You have to meet Jonathan, remember?"

"Cool, you going Matt?"

"Are you going to teach me? I'm not the one who had lessons remember?"

"Yeah, but I don't know if I was as good as mom, you might want her to teach you. She's great, isn't she?"

Todd beamed as a proud son would and Matt looked to Alana, his answer had nothing to do with her skills as a windsurfer as he spoke softly, "Yeah, she is."

Todd ran ahead and Alana walked down to the water with Matt.

"I'm not worried about you and horny Henry but you might want to keep grandmother away from him, it's her I'd worry about."

"What do you mean horny Henry?" Alana was momentarily confused and didn't know whom he talked about.

"That instructor of yours, he's been trying to pick you up all afternoon."

"No he hasn't, he's a sweet kid, why would he flirt with an old lady like me?"

"That sweet kid would want nothing more than to take you back to his tiki hut."

Alana smiled sweetly, enjoyed their secret flirting moments. "Hmmm, a little jealous?"

"Maybe if he wasn't just out of high school, but I have nothing to be jealous about. I can't offer you a tiki hut, but I know whose bed you want to be in, and it isn't his."

"You sound sure of that."

"Here you are, Alana." The instructor handed her the biggest Pina' Colada she'd ever seen. "You worked hard for this one, it's on me."

Matt laughed as if he proved his point and joined Todd in the water. It didn't take him quite as long to pick it up as it had Alana and he was on it and gliding in no time. She watched from the shore with the delicious drink in her hand. Her instructor, horny Henry as she'd come to think of him now, was called away elsewhere.

The thought of what kind of affect their relationship would cause on Todd, even though Alana hid any sort of romance between them, was something Alana had to think about. She knew how much her son cared for Matt and vice versa. Todd already asked if Matt could come visit them in Chicago after the cruise and Alana stressed the friendship, stressed it was important not to look beyond the end of their two weeks. If anything, of course they would probably keep in touch.

When Alana went to join Diana the woman sat under an umbrella with her eyes closed and she quietly took the seat next to her.

"Drink up girl, so that nice looking young man can come back with another."

It made Alana jump because she thought Mrs. McCray had slept. Then again she was still a little jumpy from nerves that had not calmed all the way. "I thought you were dozing."

"No, just closed my eyes a moment so I could remember what it was like when I was your age. I remember what I looked like, but I surely don't remember young men looking like that windsurfer guy of yours."

"Cute guy, Matt told me he was flirting with me but I think he was just being nice and polite, making an old woman like me feel good."

"Made this old woman feel good just looking at him, I don't care how nice and polite he is, he doesn't have to open his mouth to say a word, even better if he doesn't."

It made Alana laugh, she always joked about men, she was an eighty some year old woman who meant nothing more than shock effect. One never expected some of the things she said to come out of her mouth. It was one of the things Alana loved about her. "Do you need something else to drink? Something to eat?"

"Oh no, dear, I'm perfectly fine, just want to sit here and take in this beautiful day and this beautiful beach. This is one of my favorite spots in the world. Not this particular beach, this is the first time I've been here, but any beach. Give me sand, a chair and an umbrella and I'll just while the day away. I could have really enjoyed whiling the day away at the other beach though."

Alana giggled. "My God, I've never seen such a thing. I don't want to appear prudish, but that was the last thing I expected, a beach full of nude people. I keep trying to think of a way to get back at Matt but I can't come up with anything to top that one."

Diana thought about their relationship, whatever it was, but something was developing between them. And Diana knew, as a mother herself, she would never be able to focus on what would be an added encumbrance of falling in love, if that's what Alana was doing, or thought she was doing. Diana wanted her to know she had plenty of time to figure it out.

"You know something, Alana, I may be talking out of my mouth, and this has nothing to do with anything, it's what happens in old age, we don't make any sense. But there's a time for everything in life. My late husband and I were together early, but it wasn't our time. I went off, he went off, and six years later there we were again. After that we had forty-six beautiful years together. I don't know what you feel for Matt and it's none of my business, but you have enough to fret about, you don't have to fret about that. If it's to be, it will."

"There's so much going on in my mind." Then she couldn't help but laugh as she thought of something and decided to share it, knew even if she was his grandmother she would appreciate the humor. "And elsewhere, I can't deny he would make a very nice side dish."

They laughed together then Alana continued with a deep sigh. "I'm not sure how I feel Diana."

Diana took her hand and squeezed. "You'll know when it's time for you to know. Love isn't the way someone makes you feel when you're with them, it's how you feel when you're without."

****

As promised, Matt didn't have to worry about a thing that afternoon and didn't, knew Jack would take care of it all and his friend did so in splendid style as a limousine picked them up by the ship to transport them to a luxury yacht for their afternoon in Antigua. The Lady Dream was a true five-star vessel at 118 feet of rich and dramatic elegance of lavish proportions. Opulently appointed, its design conceived for both festive crowds and personal privacy for those who desired the ultimate extravagant vacation and wanted to pay the small ransom of sixty thousand dollars a week for the personal charter.

"Good afternoon, Ms. Gibbs. Welcome aboard our Lady Dream." The captain, dressed in full white uniform, greeted her by name and kissed the top of her hand. How did he know she was coming when she didn't even know? "I'm Captain Andrew, I'm sure you'll enjoy the voyage today and if there's anything you need or want the entire crew will be at your disposal. If you'll follow my first mate, he'll make you comfortable."

"Good afternoon," Matt shook his hand.

"Welcome aboard, Mr. McCray, as per instructions I think you'll find the rest of your day as requested. If there are any changes please let me know."

"I'm sure there won't be." Matt didn't know what the instructions had been, but he would trust whatever Jack had requested.

"Then we'll be on our way."

"Thank you." Matt smiled.

The main salon and dining salon greeted one with the warmth of high gloss Italian walnut complimented with furnishings of leather, posh carpet and marble. Five sumptuous staterooms with marble bathrooms offered deep comfort for a night of sleep as one anchored off tropical shores. They wouldn't be sleeping, but it was theirs for the day.

The state of the art entertainment system emitted soft music from hidden speakers as they walked through the plush ambiance of palatial proportions intended solely as a world that existed for only pleasure. There were no limits to the pampered perfection. He followed Alana towards the back of the boat where a table was set with white linen and fresh flowers, and another crew member stood in white uniform with a black vest and held an open bottle of champagne ready to pour. Yet another person appeared and placed napkins on their laps when they sat down. All accomplished with complete silence.

"Matt, this is beautiful." Alana wasn't quite sure what to say, she was overwhelmed with everything.

"I can't take full credit. I called a friend last night that lives in Barbados who has a little experience in, shall we say, impressing the ladies. Quite a reputation around the Virgin Islands I'm sure. Said I needed a special day planned and he told me he'd take care of it."

"Nice friend." Then Alana realized something. "So this morning when I was all over you, you couldn't have given me a hint even if you wanted."

"And it killed me. I would have blown it, believe me. Instead I suffered excruciating pain because of my lack of knowledge and I've decided that surprises are not for the weak."

Their champagne glasses were constantly filled as they were brought strawberries, bananas, pineapple and various melons and fruit on a tray. All followed by caviar, then a delicious crab dish, along with anything else they desired.

A backdrop of emerald mountainous terrain flowed to a sapphire sea and the clear sky promised smooth waters as the yacht motionlessly navigated off shore of the sandy coastline. There were no limits to the pleasures aboard. There was dive and snorkel equipment, water ski's, Jet Ski's, tubes, all available for one desiring more adventurous activities. For those seeking more relaxed pleasures a large sundeck provided cushioned lounges and various other places promised endless lounging in sun or shade, along with several Jacuzzi's open to warm breezes.

A complete tour gave them more insight to its magnificence and it ended in the Master Bedroom Penthouse on the top deck where more champagne awaited them. It would serve as their private quarters for the rest of the day. It was splendid grandeur awash with more Italian marble and accents of gold with a king-size bed and soft leather furniture, the connecting bath just as sumptuous. A state-of-the-art multimedia center with satellite television and surround sound. Two private terraces and a window encased Sky Lounge that put you above silky seas below. A sitting area and fully equipped bar made the generous space its own fully contained living quarters.

A crewmember poured them a glass of champagne. "There are necessities provided in the bathroom and you'll find the closets are provided with anything you may have forgotten or need. If there is nothing else I'll leave you to get settled."

Already feeling its effect from lunch, she knew she didn't need another but took the glass offered. It was all a dream. A lovely hazy dream as she felt like she'd crossed over and floated on top of a world reserved only for those whose pockets were lined with gold. She sipped the delicious liquid and the man simply stood there before her but didn't leave. She wasn't sure what was expected, foolishly thought maybe a tip until he spoke and she realized he simply waited on a reply.

"Will there be anything else?"

"It's all been too much already, thank you." If she asked for fried chicken it would have been brought. Things rolled around in her mind and had she been a different person would probably have tested them. A blue bathing suit, five kosher pickles, a pair of ruffled knickers with purple bows and oh, of course, exactly 239 olives to go with the pickles. She giggled in her mind as the champagne's bubbles floated through her senses.

"Mr. McCray, will you require anything further?"

"No thank you, however, I'll be using one of the other staterooms for the day." Matt began to move towards the door but Alana stopped him.

"You're going to be noble again? Ever the gentleman?"

"Always the gentleman."

"Matt, don't be ridiculous, we're only here for a little while and it's just for showers and such, I don't see why we can't use the same room."

When they were alone again, they stepped out onto the terrace and Alana watched as Antigua passed by and they glided through crystalline water towards the sea. "I've never seen anything like this, I've never been so pampered in my life."

"It's about time you were." Matt thought of her struggle. If he could have planned the day himself he couldn't have done better than Jack had, at least not with the limited time he'd given him. He made a mental note to begin thinking about repayment and couldn't begin to imagine what he'd come up with for all he'd arranged.

Alana closed her eyes and leaned her head back, let the warm sun heat her face. "If I didn't know any better, I'd think you were trying to seduce me."

"I can't be blamed for anything that happens to you today, I'm innocent, remember? I didn't have anything to do with it."

"Ah, that's right, the friend in Barbados. Was it the same one you were with in the bar that day you dragged me out like a cave man staking his claim?" She laughed at remembering. She could now that the pain of their argument that ensued was long ago over.

"As a matter of fact it is."

"How far we've come." As usual, Matt kept a physical distance between them, Alana knew he left it up to her to initiate any closeness and she now moved in front of him, squeezed herself between him and the railing and he put his arms on either side and held onto the bar behind her.

"I went to college with Jack, he gave up civilized cities for Barbados. Kind of like a late college graduation phase to go off to Europe and find one's self except he landed in the Caribbean."

"Lucky us, and if he impresses all his lady friends this way, I can't imagine he's alone much."

"Jack doesn't suffer for lack of female companionship. He's a good guy though, you would like him."

"I'm sure I would and you'll have to thank him for me, but it isn't Jack I'm thinking about right now."

"Oh no?" Matt kissed the side of her neck softly. Forget the eggshells that surrounded her, she'd already crushed half of them herself.

"I'm scared, Matt."

"There's nothing to be afraid of," he whispered softly against her ear.

Oh but there was. She leaned her head back and fully exposed her neck to his tender lips, knew she could lose her heart right here in Antigua, right here in this dream she found herself in, and never get it back. But she didn't have to wake, not just yet.

In sun washed solitude of the private terrace, they enjoyed a vigorous rub down from the onboard masseuse, then slipped into the large Jacuzzi. With uninhibited abandon beneath cerulean sky above, Alana let go of all her inner defenses and let them quietly slip away into the wind. Amid islands with castles made of sand along white beaches, she made love to Matt with a slow tenderness that was indescribable in his mind.

Afterwards, the boat perused by places that went unnoticed then headed out a ways to sea where Alana was enchanted by dolphins that jumped in the wake. They relaxed undisturbed on lounges in the sun, enjoyed more food the chef prepared, and of course the champagne that flowed abundantly like water in a fountain. And although they could have gone ashore in a tender or Jet Ski if they wished, instead they slipped into the blue water for a refreshing dip off the back of the boat.

"I can't stand up here, Matt, I don't go into water I can't stand up in." She protested and sat on the edge of the swim dock with her feet dangling.

"Come on, I'm right here and you have a life jacket on, if you need any more than that hang onto the boat."

She finally slipped in beside him but didn't move from hanging on and the water did feel good but she quickly scrambled back up on top when she felt something brush up against her leg. Probably a fish, a turtle or harmless small stingray but she protested it to be a shark and refused to come back in. After she removed the life jacket, she perched herself on the back again, this time cautiously dangled her legs, on a constant lookout for any fish life in the clear water below.

From her safety she watched Matt as he swam around and at times snorkeled below and bought up some of the treasures found beneath the surface. Then she lay back on the flat platform flush to the blue sea, let the ripple of cool water filter over her as the sun beat down and heated her body. The slight rocking of the boat almost lulled her to sleep until she heard Matt and smiled seductively, Alana never opened her eyes during the enticing conversation that followed.

"You can't lay up here like that, it's against all marine rules to tempt other passengers. Back in the old days, the pirates could have used you to lure ships closer before attacking."

"I didn't realize I was tempting anyone. And if I am, why aren't you up here, is there a marine rule that says you have to resist temptation?"

On the back of the boat, their bodies cooled by Caribbean Sea, warmed by intoxicating sun and fresh breezes, they made love again.

"I can't believe we did that, I've never done anything like that before in my life." Now dressed in her bathing suit again, Alana lay on his chest and covered her face playfully in embarrassment.

"It's a little late now."

"I don't know what's gotten into me, I blame it on the champagne."

"You don't have to blame it on anything, I'm certainly not complaining."

"I've never done things like this before, Matt."

"I hope you've never felt like this before either." Matt needed something, he needed to be sure it wasn't just him falling in love.

"I haven't, that's what terrifies me. Thank you for this day, I've never had a day like this since... actually never." Alana watched the island become larger and knew it was almost over. Hoped her legs would work and they wouldn't have to physically drag her out of the fairytale.

"You needed it, deserved it."

Their last moments on the yacht were spent dancing. Music flowed almost unnoticeable and Matt pulled her up to dance to a slow melodic tune that mesmerized her. One strong arm around her, his hand rested easily on the small of her back, he pulled hips close and held her against him. Even though the cloth of her sundress was separation she could feel his hand burn like fire against her skin. His right hand held onto hers and pulled in close to their chests.

Neither one spoke. Alana looked into his eyes as their bodies swayed together slowly as one and let him pull her inside his trusting soul. Every movement was felt. His leg against hers, the movement of his hips, the one hand that glided tenderly up her back to hold her even closer made it a physical presence in this dreamlike state. A dance of slow seduction she felt in every blood vessel, every nerve ending.

Alana had never been in love before. Todd's father was a long-term relationship that was over once the pregnancy hit and they went their separate ways and she'd never seen him again. So she had nothing to compare her feelings to, just knew it was the first time she'd ever felt consumed by someone. As if his eyes transferred his soul to fill her body completely with his presence. If he pulled away from her at any moment he would take it back and she would be cold and empty again.

Matt made her feel safe, protected, but at the same time vulnerable to his intense force. With his gaze and touch he silently willed her to let go of everything and she was defenseless, willingly complied to his silent plea. And then he kissed her so softly, so lightly their lips barely touched yet the sensation so powerful she could hear her intake of breath.

Alana didn't think of love as he held her tight in his arms, it never entered her mind. Passion, friendship, closeness, a need buried deep inside or the desirous want blatantly on the surface but it wasn't love she thought of. To Alana, love between a man and a woman was a romantic tale such as the ones in books, all make believe. Love was a foreign notion. It wouldn't be until months later in the coldness of her lonely bed she would look back and realize it was the moment she'd fallen in love with Matthew McCray. The moment she felt they were the only two people in the world.

CHAPTER FOURTEEN

With a little time left before the ship sailed, they waited for Todd then went to Nelson's Dockyard in the limo, the only remaining Georgian Dockyard in existence in the world. Developed as a base it catered to the British Navy in a great age of sail long ago. The English Harbour served as headquarters of the fleet of the Leeward Islands during turbulent years of the late 18th century, but was abandoned in the 19th century. It had been completely restored for the modern century with its historical buildings now occupied by a myriad of shops, boutiques and restaurants that lie next to the quay, where some of the world's most luxurious yachts moored.

They took an easy stroll through some shops and stopped at a fruit stand, enjoyed freshly cut black pineapple they shared with the driver. He'd joined them at their encouragement rather than sit and wait, and he made an impressive guide as he knew about most of the buildings. If he didn't know about a particular one, there were signs posted that explained their original use.

Todd enjoyed the history just as he had with other places in the Caribbean. Alana saw the entire trip as a wonderful teaching lesson and he learned more than he ever had in history class because it was all there for him to see, it was much better than listening to a teacher lecture about far away places and events or reading a chapter in a book. Being there made it all more real, it was all in front of him and he took in every bit of information.

As Todd soaked up the culture, it was hard for Alana to keep her mind off the afternoon she and Matt shared. A couple of times as they walked side by side, Alana found her and Matt holding hands and hadn't even realized when it happened, but she'd quickly pull away before Todd saw. She didn't know what would happen to them but she didn't want Todd to read more importance into their friendship. Matt understood and would smile at her, enjoy her subconscious moments when he could. She'd hold his hand, or put her arm through his, it came to a point she would purposefully walk further away from him to avoid doing it.

"You're family has enjoyed your vacation?" The cab driver looked towards Matt and Todd who wandered off elsewhere as he smiled to Alana.

He didn't know it wasn't her entire family, but she didn't correct him with explanations. "Yes, we've all had a wonderful time."

"Your son is quite the gentlemen and charmer."

She laughed. "A young man much wiser than his young years."

"I have a daughter, she just started school this year." He smiled proud. "She will keep me on my feet until my very old age."

"They grow up much too soon." She looked to Todd in the distance and remembered his first day of school so clearly. It seemed like yesterday and a lifetime ago at the same time.

With their day over, they headed back to the ship and Todd made sure they had definite dinner plans before he went to shower, Alana decided to spend a few moments on the top deck as the ship prepared to sail away, and Matt went to check on Diana. After he did, she was easy to find.

"How's Diana?" She asked when he joined her.

"She's already ready for dinner, going to play bingo with some friends and she'll meet us for dinner at eight." He laughed. "She almost objected, but I told her Todd picked the time and place."

"He's trying not to be so obvious."

"I'm just glad he likes me, if not, I wouldn't stand a chance."

She smiled coyly and teased him. "And who says you stand a chance?"

He shrugged his shoulders. "Just a guess, and the way you threw yourself at me this afternoon."

"Threw myself at you?" She laughed. "Okay, you have me on that one, but you don't make it easy to resist you. You swept me off my feet today."

"Did I?" He looked at her with a serious expression, he'd seen her hesitation at times, and it began to worry him as he questioned where they were headed.

"It was actually all the champagne and the sea air, how could I not have been swept off my feet."

"So I get no credit at all. And when you come into my room tonight you won't have the champagne and the sea air, what will be the draw then."

Alana almost blushed. "You seem to think there isn't a question I'll be in your room tonight, that's awfully presumptuous of you."

"It's confidence."

But there was no question on either part as late that evening a note was left for Todd just in case he woke in the middle of the night that explained she couldn't sleep. He was to call her on the radio, which she always carried with her, if he needed. Then she realized that being without Matt in public only served to intensify her feelings for a night together when she quietly slipped from her room and into his. The need for him she was beginning to feel scared her.

She'd fallen asleep in Matt's arms and woke just before the daybreak and stood wrapped in a robe on the balcony, enjoyed a few quiet moments before she'd have to leave. It wasn't long, almost as soon as she'd left his arms, when he woke and joined her.

"Good morning," he wrapped his arms around her as she stood against the banister, her back warm against his chest.

Alana snuggled to him, inside protective arms that surrounded her, then took a deep breath and leaned her head back into his shoulder. How perfect a morning it was, she thought, it felt so real, so normal, to wake up beside him as if they'd been doing it for years. It felt like the safe place she'd searched for.

And yet reality was much different, and that reality loomed up at her with every sunrise and it was time they at least discussed what was to come. She didn't want Matt to have any false notions of where they were headed and if Alana mentioned it now, perhaps it would give them both a chance to let it sink in.

"In a few days, we'll have to say goodbye, Matt."

"That's taking it to the extreme, goodbye sounds a little bleak. I think we both know this relationship is a little more than a shipboard romance, isn't it?" The certainty he heard in her voice scared him.

"There's nothing more I want than to be a normal person right now. A single mom who came on a cruise with her son and happened to meet a man she could possibly have a future with. To carry on from here would be a natural thing, if things were different, but things aren't different. It can't happen right now."

"I don't want anything from you other than to share your life. I don't expect you to toss aside everything else, this is monumental, Todd's cancer is first and foremost and I want to be there for you and for him. You've been through so much, but you don't have to do it alone anymore, Alana."

"It's best this way. I don't want to think about it but I have to. Death changes people, Matt, if something happens to Todd, I'll never be the same person again. I'll never be the Alana you're holding in your arms right now. I've seen what it's done to married people who had years together, a much stronger relationship than we have right now. And I pray every day death isn't something I would have to deal with, but I don't know, Matt, I just don't know."

"We can get through it together." He tried to persuade but she was silent and he knew she was about to shut him out of her life. All he kept thinking was that she couldn't do that, couldn't share so much of herself then pull it all away. "We can't just pretend we never met. So what happens? We leave and put each other on a Christmas card list?" His voice was sarcastic.

"I have to concentrate and deal with what's to come, that's all I can do right now."

"And what am I supposed to do?"

"Go back to the life you have. I don't want you to contact us after we leave. If Todd's going to be okay, I'll call you."

"And if he isn't? Will you call me then?"

"If I don't, won't you be the lucky one to never know for sure. You'll be able to spend the rest of your life at least thinking it's possible he might still be alive, and if you never see us again you can smile about a boy you once knew."

"I want to know, Alana."

"You say that now, but it might be easier if you don't. If you don't know, you can at least pretend he's in this world somewhere."

"You can't ask me to do that, this isn't right, we can deal with this together if you just…"

Alana turned to face him, saw the fear and pain in his eyes and she knew she was hurting him but it was the only fair way. "He is my world, my entire life, probably the only reason I was put on this earth was to give birth to him. He's my reason for living, Matt, there is nothing else and without him… I'll lose myself, I know I will."

"I don't have a right to demand to be in your life, and I know you think this is best for you, but I don't."

"It's a decision I've made and you don't have a choice."

Her mind was made up, her words final, and she didn't need him to second-guess any conclusion she'd come to. Maybe her words had been a little hard but it was important for him to understand, important for him to let her deal with what was to come in her own way.

When Matt quietly pulled away from her she could feel the instant cold. He stepped into the shower and she dressed and left for her own cabin.

CHAPTER FIFTEEN

Tortola came much too soon. Their last port materialized through the morning haze as Alana and Todd stood on the top deck and watched the sunrise.

"This is it, Mom, our last stop."

Todd didn't have to remind her, she'd thought of nothing else. "I wanted you to see the sunrise again, I hope you're not mad I woke you up so early."

"I like seeing the beginning of the day. I can always sleep later, tomorrow we'll be at sea all day and I can catch up."

"Sounds like you have it all worked out."

His back to her, she laid her arms in front of him across his chest and held him close, Alana could feel his heartbeat with her hands, each throb of life. Her son, her love, so many things he had seen and experienced for the first time in his life, and she couldn't help but wonder if it would be his last.

Every ecstatic smile that crossed his face was etched in her mind for eternity, she memorized it in picture perfect detail, even the sound of his voice she would be able to recall in years to come along with elated laughter at every new joy, every little surprise. If something happened, Alana never wanted anything to fade away, wanted to always remember, so she made it a point to deliberately commit everything to memory. A place in her mind reserved only for him.

Matt secretly watched the two from his spot across ship. His heart ached to be a part of them, to belong in their world, but he stood alone in his solitary isolation. He would have to find the courage to watch them walk out of his life just as they'd walked in. Could he? Could he actually let go of the first thing to come into his life he felt he couldn't live without? Matt spent years chasing the dream of recognition in his work and he'd achieved it, sought a comfortable financial position that would give him the freedom to easily enjoy the things life offered, he had that. Now was the first moment he realized none of it meant anything. And neither his hard work nor his money would buy him another day past the two they had left.

When Todd thought Jonathan would be up, he ran off to get him for breakfast and Alana remained behind, lost in thoughts. She was doing the right thing, they would say goodbye and move back into their old lives when the ship docked a few short days away. If Matt didn't want to talk to her from here on out, she would deal with that but she couldn't deal with dragging him into her life right now. She had no life to offer.

Alana felt him before she saw him. He'd placed a soft kiss upon her cheek where it lingered for a moment then moved down as he kissed her neck. It was soft and slow and Alana didn't move, just enjoyed the moment even though it was a risk. But Todd had left and it was quick and discreet. It was her first sign that he would at least talk to her for the next few days.

Matt turned her to face him. "This doesn't mean that I like or agree with your way of thinking when it comes to the future."

"I didn't expect you to agree with me."

He stared at her for a long time before he kissed her with longing. "Good morning. You wake up in my bed and I didn't even give you a proper kiss this morning."

"Don't let it happen twice. I'll have no choice but to demand more cows." Alana held his face close to hers.

"What am I up to now?"

"Six."

"I thought it was four."

"I'll let you slide on the good morning kiss, but you didn't even tell me goodbye this morning, you jumped in the shower, so it's six cows now. And the next time I wake up in your bed and don't get a kiss, I'm doubling the six and it will be twelve."

Matt had to wonder if she'd ever wake up in his bed again. "You're a lucky mother, Alana. Todd loves you very much." Matt felt it was important for her to know. "He talked about you before I knew you were his mother. I remember thinking what a special person you must be. There was something about the way he talked, you could hear it in his voice, see the pride in his eyes. I certainly can't remember talking about my mother when I was thirteen, I probably was, but it wasn't nice things. Normal stuff like she put me on restriction or wouldn't let me watch television on a Saturday morning because I forgot to take the trash out, but I never talked about her the way Todd talks about you."

"So Diana was right. She joked once that you were a demon child," she teased.

"When I was Todd's age I didn't love my mother the way he loves you, I didn't appreciate her until years later."

Todd told her he loved her and of course she believed him, Alana didn't have a doubt, but as a mother it was nice to hear it from someone else, it solidified what she knew all along. And in her position it meant a great deal to truly know it.

****

Matt rented an open jeep and the four of them would travel on their own to explore the wonders of the small island of Tortola, or as it was also referred to because of its shape and beauty, Turtle Dove. The tip of the central mountain spilled down the sides and into azure blue sea and contained within the waters boundaries was an incredible view from almost every spot on the island.

Driving in Tortola was to be an experience in itself. Hairpin turns required the placement of mirrors to be able to see around the bend. Climbs and downward slopes that felt almost vertical sent one breathless for a few moments and all that coupled with the task of driving on the left side of the road, and Alana was grateful to have Matt at the wheel.

They began their drive through Main Street where historic character was evident. Most of the structures older wood frame buildings and were marked by traditional red tin roofs and Victorian trim. Narrow streets crowded with cars and pedestrians but they meandered through easily towards Windy Hill where Cane Garden Bay Road and the North Coast Road joined at the western end of Ridge Road. The road squiggled around and they went one direction and switched backed another to traverse the mountain.

Todd sat in front with Matt so Alana and Diana were in back. From his driver's position Matt could watch her face in the rear view mirror and laugh as her face made as many twists and turns as their drive. A donkey marked the intersection where they would take the turnoff on the Channel side towards Mt. Sage and it wasn't the first time Alana spoke up.

"How do you know to turn here and not there? What if we get lost on this mountain?" Alana tried not to sound worried but felt she had to be the sensible one. Matt simply jumped in the open jeep and was ready to go.

"I looked at the map, we can turn off any of these roads and they'll all go to Road Town, back where we started. I know where I'm going, Alana, trust me. It's an island with few roads and we're not going far." Then he turned his attention to Todd. "Why didn't you tell me your mother was a backseat driver? Is she like this all the time?"

"What do you think? Is there any duct tape or anything in the back?" Todd teased, the two chatted as if she weren't there.

"We could find something, course we could drop her off on top and let her make her own way down since she doesn't trust my driving." Matt swerved closer to the edge on purpose and Alana screamed.

"Stop that!" Alana slapped his shoulder and playfully explained it was because of Diana. "You're going to give your grandmother a heart attack."

"Not me dear, I'm just hanging on," Diana laughed.

They hit a little traffic on the section of Ridge Road where traffic traveled from Road Town to Cane Garden Bay, but after that it seemed they were the only vehicle on the island. When they did pass anyone else the locals always smiled and waved, some honked their horn as if they were old friends and passed each other every day.

Alana finally calmed down enough to get used to Matt's driving. After that she could sit back for the most part and enjoy the views but didn't want to trade seats with Todd when he offered. It was bad enough having to look at the road with limited vision, she didn't want to see it from the front seat, would have been much too close to the curves.

They almost missed a turn because it looked like nothing more than a driveway off the main road, when actually it was the road they needed to continue up. The views were amazing when Alana could concentrate on them. The steep hillside was without guardrails and Matt continued to drive her crazy as he swerved for no reason or drove a little faster than she'd have liked.

No one else was bothered but her, and they all chuckled under their breaths when she screamed, even Diana who hung on tight and laughed around every hairpin turn. They gradually came to what was known as the highland Caribbean suburbs of Upper Hope. It was a fascinating drive as the view changed from sea and distant islands, to ridges and valleys as they followed the contour line and Matt skillfully navigated the next peak.

The top was the most level part and here they found a country life. Rural fields that rolled on for miles then appeared to drop off the side of the mountain at a certain point. They passed Island farmhouses with the traditional red tined roofs.

"Look at all those cows," Alana commented once and looked towards the mirror where she could see Matt smiling broadly as he tried not to laugh out loud at her private teasing of his debt.

They stopped along the side of the road on occasion to stretch and take in the stupendous views. Certain vantage points allowed one to see the splendor of the other islands beyond that rose out of blue surf and all of them were surrounded by their own white sand.

A piece of hand-lettered poster board announced that a shack they stopped at on the roadside was Rudy's Outside Bar. The bar stools poked out toward the road and a nice view of Brewers Bay could be found in a secret lower level in back.

"Ahhh, beautiful ladies to brighten my day." The man behind the bar greeted them kindly, came out and took Diana by the hand and helped her up onto a barstool with a broad welcome smile and continued as if he knew them. "Where have you been? I've been waiting for you."

Diana answered. "Well, you aren't the easiest place to find, and we almost fell off the mountain twice."

"But you are safe now, you are in my hands and I make your afternoon unforgettable. You wish for cold drinks, I have coldest on the island. You wish to not worry on your way back down the mountain? I have Rudy's rum punch."

Alana immediately ordered the punch and drank almost half of it in one swallow. She imagined the little road side bar would never suffer the stress like that of a Chicago yuppie bar after work hours. It was so remote, happy in its own little world atop the ridge. She imagined the biggest problem of the day would be a stray goat that chewed on a wall.

With their thirst quenched, Matt took the road to Cane Garden Bay, another beach in the Caribbean said to be one of the worlds most beautiful, and also one of many Jimmy Buffett sang about. Although most beaches in the islands offered seclusion in less developed areas, Cane Garden Bay was one of the islands most popular and offered more to enjoy than just beach.

Yachts anchored in translucent water that covered emerald reefs below as white sand moved with every small ripple along its shore. Overhung palms offered the sun lovers and sailors who'd come ashore, shade from the heat of day. Plenty of beachfront bars offered cool liquid and food to nourish. One's day could easily be fulfilled in this one place but they just stopped for a little while.

Alana and Diana decided to shop while Todd and Matt enjoyed some time in the water then they met up for a drink and snacks at a beachfront place. A decor of cement floors and pink painted cinder block walls, it sat right on the beach and they looked out over the sand and water and passing people as they paraded by.

Because it catered to boaters with a grocery and gift shop and a Laundromat among other things, it also offered showers for three dollars which Matt and Todd took advantage of. Alana also noted it seemed to be the place to catch a taxi and she teased Matt once more about his driving abilities when she threatened to take one back.

"I think I've been doing pretty good, I missed those chickens didn't I?"

"You missed the chickens. How, I don't know. But you forgot to go back for my stomach which came out of my mouth and is still in the road."

"I think the roads are cool, like a roller coaster ride. We don't have roads like this in Chicago. Hey, Matt, after we get back, when are you coming to Chicago?"

The question caught everyone off guard, only Mrs. McCray pretended not to be as she sipped her drink.

When no one answered Todd continued as he looked to both Diana and Matt. "You're going to come visit, aren't you?"

"I'm sure I'll get there sometime, but after two weeks of vacation my office might need me to take over again. I'm sure everyone else has been a little relaxed in my absence and it'll take me a while to straighten them all out." Matt answered with a casual smile without once looking at Alana who was the only one that noticed the hard edge to his eyes.

"That's okay, we can come visit you, can't we, Mom?"

"I'm sure we will someday Todd but we have quite a few things to do ourselves when we get home. Like work and school, remember those?"

"We've got spring break coming up and..."

Alana smiled and tried to stop him as inconspicuously as she could. "Todd, this vacation isn't even over yet, I can't think about the next right now."

Their road journey continued through the switchbacks across the mountain, and all its unseen bends and twists. Along the way they passed the occasional goat or chicken that crossed the road with lazy inattention to oncoming cars, and Alana was caught up in all of it. The glorious day, the magnificent views, every moment embedded in her mind.

The treacherous spine of the mountain behind them, Matt took the coastal road that ran the perimeter of Tortola, and would eventually lead them back to Road Town. But they continued their tour of the North Beach Coast with Apple Bay and the most famous North Coast beach, Long Bay. Then on toward the West end, that included Smuggler's Cove and Soper's Hole.

Apple Bay was a series of charming spots and seaside villages. If you asked locals they would answer it to be Cappoon's Bay where Bomba's Surfside Shack was located. Famous throughout the West Indies for its wild and notorious full moon parties that spilled out over the beach at night as locals, boaters and tourists gathered for party central. And if one wanted to push the party envelope, they could imbibe in Bomba's special mushroom tea. Although most well meaning locals would advise you to stick to the plentiful rum punch.

Under a tree across the road from the Shack, Bomba would stir and brew the pot of tonic himself over a fire. A late-night elixir prepared from indigenous mushrooms that grew over the island after a good rain, referred to as psychedelic fungi. Said to be hallucinogenic from those who drank it.

Generally packed on Wednesdays and Sundays, it featured live entertainment, but during the day a little less walking on the wild side. On that particular day there were more subdued patrons, only a handful of customers. It lived up to its name and was truly a ramshackle shack. A bar perched precariously on the beach with a floor of sand.

It was basically constructed from driftwood that often found its way there due to hurricanes that sliced through the Caribbean from time to time, and the more driftwood found, the more extensions that went on.

Inside and out walls were painted or decorated in some way as the intriguing spot had been visited by many that left a small token behind. Tokens in the form of business cards attached to the walls, flags, t-shirts, underwear and bikini tops. All plastered everywhere there was a spot. One had to wonder what people wore after they left their panties, bra's and swimsuits.

"Hey, Mom, can I write something and leave something?"

"Sure."

In true Kilroy form, he simply wrote 'Todd was here' and left his new baseball cap as tangible proof. A simple thing that would probably go unnoticed to its many visitors that would come over the years ahead, but Alana couldn't help but think that if something happened to Todd, she could always come back to this very spot, and remember. She stood there and looked at his young scribbled handwriting when Matt approached silently.

"Hey." He'd come up from behind her and reached his arms around her then kissed her neck, and she automatically looked around to see where Todd was. "Grandmother and Todd went out to the beach, he hollered to you when he left, but you were over here in a trance."

Then Matt noticed what she'd been absorbed in. The statement 'Todd was here' struck him as not a simple nondescript writing on a wall, but a statement of his existence he'd been in this world. One would think nothing of it unless they knew the threat that could possibly take his life.

Matt held her closer and whispered with his lips intentionally brushing against her ear. "Do you know how hard it is to spend the entire day pretending you're merely a good friend?"

"I know but..."

"But you don't want Todd to assume I'll be in your life after this and then disappointed when I'm not. I know. I also know your son is intelligent enough to figure out on his own that we're a little more than friends."

"Maybe he suspects something, but..."

"But it's better this way." Matt finished for her, heard it before. "Better for who? I don't see anyone that comes out ahead in all this. Is it so wrong for your son to see you in a relationship with a man who loves you?"

"You're in love with me?" She asked softly.

The notion hadn't crossed her mind. Alana didn't try to examine her feelings or think of what he could be feeling. She didn't want to look closely at something she considered and treated as simply two fantasy weeks that divided her life. But now, in this ramshackle pieced together hut by the sea with its bikini's, goat skulls and beer labels, he confessed his feelings.

"I love you, Alana. Somewhere along the way between our first hello on a plaza bench on a sunny day in Puerto Rico, an innocent drink in a bar, through all the craziness. Then you in my arms again and our days together as some sort of nice little family, when we're not. I don't know when it happened, but it did. It's insane, and everyday I wonder why and how you and Todd ended up in the middle my life. I fell in love with you somewhere in all that madness, and come the day when you plan to walk away from it, at least I'll no longer have to pretend I didn't."

Matt continued on with the day in the same jovial mood as before. He had learned to switch himself easily between the two separate worlds of private and public and his smiling face revealed nothing of what he pondered on the inside. Had he been right to tell her? Would it make a difference? Maybe it would help change her mind, maybe it wouldn't. Regardless, he wanted her to know how he felt even if she decided to stick to her plan and go on with her life alone. There was only one full day left of the cruise, and he felt urgency as it approached.

The coastal road took them past Sugar Mill Restaurant, considered the best in the Caribbean, but they didn't stop there. They stopped at Nan's Gallery where Alana wanted to purchase the souvenir of a Moko Jumbee mask. It was made from Calabash, a tree gourd, and hand painted in different motifs.

Then they moved on to Long Bay where from a strategic spot on the mountain one could see its famous vista. You could look straight down the line of white sand that was the division of green lush hills and crystalline water. Often a photo on postcards, it depicted the true to life tropical Caribbean scene people envisioned it to be.

On to Smuggler's Cove they found a beach honor bar where you put your money in a cigar box on the counter and got what you needed. The film 'The Old Man and the Sea' with Spencer Tracy was filmed there and the bar still had props from the movie. Diana enjoyed a lively conversation with an English gentleman before they headed back to port where each had just a tiny bit of energy left to expend.

Diana and Alana took to a few shops while Matt and Todd took to a restaurant, Pusser's Landing. They met up later, and even Diana enjoyed their famous Painkiller drink. A mix of pineapple juice, orange juice, cream of coconut and of course rum, all with a dash of nutmeg on top. She didn't finish the entire thing but Alana had no qualms on helping her with the leftovers, even ordered another after Diana and Todd decided to return to the ship.

"Don't make me leave here." Alana laughed as she looked to her watch and realized they only had a little time before the ship would pull away. "We drove the entire island all day and I still feel like I didn't see half of it. All kinds of little nooks and cranny's and beaches we missed."

"We can always come back, Tortola isn't going anywhere." Matt noticed her look of uncertainty. "There is a future out there, Alana. Regardless of what comes, the years will go on." As much as he tried, he couldn't keep the edge out of his voice.

"If Todd isn't here I can't imagine that, but unfortunately, you're right."

Matt stared at her. Like her, of course he didn't want to concentrate on the possibility of what could happen. But if death did occur, she would have to move on somehow. And it might just be that she'd move on alone. "And you still think it's best to drop everything when this ship docks? Forget we ever met?"

"I didn't say I could ever forget."

"It's what you're asking me to do."

"Right now I'm asking you to understand."

"I can't." He finished his drink.

"Maybe one day you will."

Matt ordered another drink. He knew that day would never come for him to understand he couldn't be in their lives. She needed him, Todd needed him, and it wrenched his insides into a knot of turmoil to think he couldn't be there for them both whatever may come.

Alana changed the subject, didn't want to spend the last moments on a beautiful island arguing. "By the way, in case you've forgotten, this is our last island and you won't have another chance after this, did you make arrangements to purchase the cows you owe me?"

"I can't do that. It's a package deal, Alana. The cows and me come together, I can't just send you the cows alone." He smiled easily, not wanting to feel angry anymore, didn't want to talk or think of a few days away anymore than she did. "It's island law."

"Tortola law? You offered the cows in St. Vincent, maybe their law is different."

"No, all islands are the same. It stands in the whole Caribbean. Clearly states if one offers peace in the form of livestock, specifically cows, that such offered party must agree to accept the combined two, both livestock and the offering party. If further offenses require the addition of more livestock, the law stands to the original island where the agreement was initiated. And the partnership between the two, the offering party and the livestock still applies as to the original agreed terms. Now..."

She laughed at his amusing tale. "That didn't make any sense to me at all, is it the drinks? Or are you trying to confuse me on purpose?"

Matt stuck his finger up as if to really get his point across. "Now this is the interesting part of the agreement, you have to pay attention to this. If you don't want me and still want the livestock, it's the only way I don't come with the cows."

"I'm listening." She never said she didn't want him, she wanted him desperately.

"In lieu of a package containing the cow livestock, the offering party, that's me, at their discretion has an option of substitution. And the offered party, that's you, can agree to accept various other livestock chosen by the offering party, but it has to be a mixture."

"A mixture?" She smiled into his eyes, liked the way he held tight to her hand.

"The endowment of livestock has to be an assortment, such as a few pigs, chickens, lizards, snakes, birds, whatever the offering party so chooses. But it must be a combination of animals. So the conclusion is, it's a literal farm of outcast animals, or the cows and me." He stopped and took a drink then added to his story. "Oh, and I guess the answer is no. I didn't make arrangements for your cows because you have to decide on which it will be."

"I think you've had too many Painkillers."

Matt stopped her chuckling by leaning across the table and kissing her full on the mouth, lingered there with a sweet tenderness and compassion. He thought to himself the Painkiller drinks weren't working, he hadn't had nearly enough as they were killing no pain.

When he looked into her eyes he knew that unless things worked out, he'd never be able to visit Tortola again. Never be able to visit the other islands they'd seen together. He wouldn't be able to look at the Caribbean as carefree paradise, not when there was so much he'd have to give up and leave behind.

Before boarding the ship again, Matt pulled her to the waters edge that looked over the harbor and took her in his arms. When he kissed her she felt just as she had when they danced on the boat. As if he transferred his soul into her body, all senses consumed by him, and when he pulled away she felt empty and cold. Again, he'd taken another part of her with him.

"Whatever comes, Alana, remember this day, remember I love you."

CHAPTER SIXTEEN

Their day at sea before a return to Miami and the end of their trip was quiet and subdued for Alana and Matt. The others in the group of them carried on as carefree as they normally did. Only the two of them more reserved but they participated in the ships many activities. Todd had all of them running around doing all kinds of things, wanted to take advantage and not miss a moment.

"Mom, Mrs. McCray is going to do the belly flop contest." He'd found her sitting in the sunshine with Richard on the top deck.

"You can't be serious." She looked worried for a moment, wouldn't put it past her, then he laughed. "You scared me for a minute."

"I think she really thought about it."

"I'm sure she did. That little old lady's a pistol." Richard looked down below, almost expected to see her positioned alongside the pool.

"She's only going to be one of the judges."

"I know she's disappointed in that." Alana too looked below, and just as Richard did she almost expected to see her ready to throw herself full throttle into the water.

"Jonathan and I are going to the kid's pool." He kissed her quickly and gave Richard a high five before running off.

"That's one little dynamo too." Richard commented. "I've never met a little person I like more."

She smiled proudly and looked to him as he caught up with his friend and they disappeared together. "Neither have I."

"Out of the hundreds of people on this ship, I don't think there's anyone who's enjoyed this cruise more than Todd. He knows how to live, doesn't he?"

"Yeah," The word almost stuck in her throat at the words Richard spoke totally unaware of their meaning to her.

"You've been quiet today, what's up? You and that gorgeous hunk of yours have a fight? I haven't seen much of him today."

"He isn't my gorgeous hunk."

"Oh please," Richard waved his hand through the air. "You can try to hide it, and maybe others don't suspect anything, but this is me, Alana. This is Richard, and I know better."

"Not really a fight. There's a misunderstanding between us. Not really a misunderstanding…" She didn't know how to explain it and didn't try. "Let's just say we aren't in agreement over something."

Richard looked her in the eye as much as he could before she averted them, but before doing so, he saw the sadness. "So I guess we're not in the sharing mood and that's all I'm going to get."

"Yeah, Richard, that's all you're going to get."

"I hope I'm at least invited to the wedding."

She smiled, but the sadness was still there. "Don't expect an invitation anytime soon. It doesn't fit into my life right now."

"Love always fits."

She looked at the puzzle of her life at that moment and couldn't see a place for it, refused to see a place for it when there were too many extra pieces of her life that had to fit first.

"Where is Rita today?"

"Spa. Between her and Kevin, they're going to be the most relaxed, best looking people to leave this ship. You'd think they'd never have access to one again. There's one right around the corner from where we live and neither has ever gone. Something about the Caribbean that makes everything different."

There was truth in his words that could explain many things. Everything was different. She'd forced herself to see it as something that wasn't real, it was better for her that way. There were many things she would think about when they returned home, many things she would try not to think about. That day she tried desperately to get away from the battle that went on in her mind but of course her head was attached to her body, so where her legs took her, her battle went along.

Did she walk away from him? Invite him into her life to share every pain there? Would that be good for Todd? What if it was only a beautiful shipboard romance that would fade with reality anyway? As Richard had said, something about the Caribbean made everything different. That certainly wouldn't be good for Todd. And if that were the case, she would be crushed.

If not for the cancer, maybe she would take the chance. But she certainly couldn't compromise where her attention belonged and have to deal with a broken heart on top of all else if it didn't work out. Matt told her he loved her and she had no reason to believe it wasn't true. Did she love him? What if she didn't? And if she did, how could she develop that love with the threat of impending tragedy that was ahead of her? God forbid, she would fight as long and hard as she had to, but if something were to happen to Todd, she had told Matt the truth. She would never be the same person again.

Through all her thoughts, Alana came to the same conclusion as before and didn't change her mind, felt she had to say goodbye no matter what. She had to walk away with no plans or intentions of being with Matt, no thoughts of any future together and insist he do the same. She couldn't think about love now, and didn't know if there would be a 'when', but she had to do it this way. The two glorious weeks in the Caribbean had been magical as they shared their nights and days in beauty and splendor. But it served as another dividing line for her life.

She categorized it as before Matt and after Matt, everything in between served as a diversion, a wonderful reprieve.

She would return to Chicago and the hard reality of her world where she couldn't find a place for him just yet, she had drawn an invisible dividing line and he wouldn't be allowed over. What they had in the Caribbean she would leave there, it was where it belonged right now.

That night Alana stood alone on the deck at the aft of the ship, watched the wake of the boat and looked to where they'd come from, tried to catch a literal glimpse of what she was leaving behind. She said a silent prayer to any Caribbean Gods or Lords, or even any long gone Pirates with hearts of gold who could help her, who might listen. She asked them to take good care of the love she had to leave behind, maybe one day she could come back for it.

****

That night in his arms, he took her a zillion miles away. Took her to a different place where there was no pain, no impending doom, it was only two souls lost in a world they'd created just for them. He made her a different woman, one who could take the love he gave her, and he gave so freely, even knowing there were no promises she would ever be able to return it.

When dawn approached she moved to leave and he held tight, his words revealed his pain. "I'm afraid I'll never see you again."

"I know."

It was a repeat of what they'd said in San Juan when both of them thought they'd quietly leave the others life. So much had happened since then, yet they were back at the beginning as if none of it happened at all. In the quiet of their own minds each wondered what the next phase of their lives would bring. If they'd ever have the chance to know how it would feel to not let it go.

****

They had breakfast with everyone on the outdoor deck as they all waited together as one by one their disembarkation color was called. One by one the group whittled down as goodbyes were made, promises to call and keep in touch.

Matt and Diana had an early flight and had to catch a cab immediately to the airport when they disembarked. When the time came and they stood along the sidewalk of the port, Alana held strong even though she felt she could break at any moment. She'd already talked to Todd and told him not to expect, nor ask for, any visits or such from Matt and Mrs. McCray. They were friends but they all had things in life to get through and if it happened one day it would be great, but he was not to push it to try to make definite plans. It didn't stop him completely from bringing it up.

Todd said his farewells to Diana with promises that once they knew he was really better he thought his mother would plan a visit then. Either to see her or maybe she could visit them. He was excited as he spoke of the plans for their future.

"Mom said we're going to get a new house, we only moved into the apartment because it was close to the hospital. But once they tell me it's definitely all gone and hasn't come back, we're going to move somewhere where there's a yard and stuff. We'll have a guest bedroom and all, hey, I'll get you some of those little shampoos just like on the ship. We're going to get a dog too maybe. And I've already decided, I'm going to name him Bomba."

"I want to be the first in your guest bedroom, save me a reservation." Diana hugged him tight and didn't want to let go but had to, afterwards he walked off with Matt.

Alana too hugged Diana close. "I'm going to miss you, I really am. And reservations won't be required because if we get to that point of buying a new house I want you to be our first guest."

"He's going to be okay, Alana, I feel it in my heart. Besides, he has to be, who else would take care of a dog named Bomba?"

"I think I'll get him two, he can name them both Bomba. Actually he can have a dozen, as many as he wants once this is over."

Diana took her hands. "Thank you for sharing part of your son's life with me, I feel like he was a gift sent by my late husband. A reminder of how life should be lived. Our deceased loved ones send us gifts every now and then, you know. We may not recognize them, but the signs are there."

A chill ran up Alana's back as she thought of her father and mother somewhere above. She thought of the several coincidental signs, but that's all they were, just signs, she told herself. She couldn't read more into them, couldn't believe if her father were looking out for her he'd have put her and Todd in the position they now faced.

Diana squeezed her hands tight as she continued. "I'm a miserable old lady sometimes because I'm old, Todd showed me an appreciation for every day and I'll no longer sit around and feel sorry for this old bag of bones. I'll take each day I have and appreciate it." Diana had tears in her eyes. "Whatever is to come, I know you'll see yourself through it and maybe you'll find your way back to Matt."

Further away, Matt sat on a wall ledge and Todd stood in front of him. They were eye to eye as Matt's face was serious and he tried hard not to let so much of his pain through to the outside. "I needed to talk man to man again, Todd."

"Yeah, guess this will be our last time for a bit. Mom doesn't want me to talk about visiting and stuff, so…" Todd shuffled his feet and shrugged his shoulders. It was difficult for him.

"I want you to know that I love your mother, I know we've just gone along like friends, but I'm in love with her and I thought you needed to know that." Matt didn't want to add in case he never saw him again.

"Oh I knew that." Todd said it as a matter of fact with no hesitation. "I knew she just tried to hide it from me, you two are way more than friends. But mom... she's just scared right now. After everything's fine things will be different."

"I'd come to Chicago right now, and if your mother says the word a week from now I'd be there to go through the rest of this with you, but Alana wants to do this her way. Of course I have to respect that."

"I understand."

Matt looked into young eyes that did understand, young eyes that had to understand so much more than he should have, "I don't know when we'll see each other again, but I'll never break my promise to you. No matter what happens, if she wants me to be there for her she'll always be loved and cared for. In the meantime, it's up to you." As if it would help Todd to will the cancer away, Matt gave him the most important job he'd ever have in his life. "You have to take care of her for me, you can do that, can't you?"

"I try, but I..."

"She won't let anyone else. It has to be up to you."

He was quiet for a time but when he spoke there was a conviction in his voice, as if it were the first time he realized that he could take care of his mother on his own. He'd always thought it had to be up to someone else, but Matt trusted him to do it and he would. "I'll take care of her." Then he repeated his words with even more strength, "I'll take care of her, Matt."

"I know you will." Matt's voice was soft. "I do love your mother, Todd, and I love you as well, always know that."

"I love you too." The young boy hesitated a moment before he continued. "Ya know, if I could pick a dad, I would have picked you."

Alana watched the two hug from across the way and the sting of tears was immediate, she had to take a deep breath and turn away but her emotions were under control again when Matt approached. The two of them would now share their own private moment, but it wouldn't be what she pictured their goodbye to be. She thought maybe it would be tender and bittersweet, she didn't know he would have only the bitter part right, she would find that out when one of the dockworkers approached them.

"You need a cab?"

"Yes please," he answered quickly.

"Four people and luggage?"

"No, two separate cabs, we're not together." Matt's aggravation was evident in his words. He didn't think this was how it should be, and maybe he was wrong, but he wanted her to know it. Especially since he'd just had to walk away from Todd not knowing if he'd ever see him again or ever know what was to become of them.

"I thought many things, but I didn't think you'd be this angry for our last time together."

He looked at her with hard eyes, "Our last time? You already have it set in your mind, don't you?"

"It'll help me get through it." She said with honesty.

"Then I guess no sense prolonging it, what are you waiting for?"

"I'm sorry, Matt."

"There it is, Alana, your life is right there sitting with your luggage so just pick it up and walk back into it without me. Pretend none of this ever happened."

"I never said I could do it easily, I said it was the way it had to be done."

"To just end it right here on the sidewalk? Me not knowing if I'll ever see you or Todd again? My God, Alana, have you thought about what you're asking me to do? You're asking me to just walk away and basically forget you two ever existed."

"If we get back and the news is bad, the cancer is back, the doctor's say there's nothing else we can do but I'm not ready to give up, Matt. How can I? I don't know how long I'll try to fight it but I will. And that's not your life, you have a nice life in New York, it's not fair for me to pull you into one so painful."

"At least let me decide for myself what I want my life to be. You're not even giving me the choice."

"No, I'm not. I've been through it and I've watched my son suffer. You love Todd, I know that, but you know him like this. Happy, healthy looking, you don't know what it's like."

"I pray to God I would never have to experience it, but if I had to go through it, I would. I could help you, Alana, I could help him." It was his final plea.

"It's easiest to end it here. Anything that happens between us after this is a second chance, a bonus in our lives. Maybe another time, but not now, Matt, not now." Her voice was a whisper but the tone of finality came through loud and clear.

Matt looked at her for a long time. Neither made an attempt to move towards the other and she pleaded for forgiveness in her eyes, forgiveness he couldn't give at that moment. His hand came up and he wanted to touch her face, take her hand, something to feel close to her when he felt so far. Then it fell to his side again and he walked away.

Alana stood on the sidewalk and watched as he got into the cab and it began to pull off. She couldn't believe this was going to be it, she would have to end a two week romance with resentment and hostility from a man she shared so much with, and had only just discovered she possessed the capability of loving in that way. Todd got into their cab and she was about to step inside when she saw the other cars brake lights. It backed up and stopped and then Matt got out and approached her.

Without a word he placed his strong hand behind her neck and pulled her mouth to his. For several moments she was lost in a world that belonged only to them, no one else broke through even though the sidewalk was packed, the surroundings busy. Only the two existed. When he pulled away he took with him yet another piece that would never be returned. It belonged to him now, and always would.

Nothing else was said as he got back in his cab and left for good this time. Matt held onto his anger and couldn't let it go, maybe because it helped him not to feel his heart.

****

Had she made a mistake? What she had been so sure of, she now questioned over and over again. She'd previously arranged to stay in Miami a few days to extend their vacation. After they checked into the hotel she even looked at her watch once to see if it was too late to stop him. She had his cell phone number, all she had to do was call and he would be standing in front of her, but she didn't.

Alana saw Matt everywhere, was surrounded by him. Everywhere she looked he was there and she knew she hid it well from Todd but felt he too suffered from missing both Matt and Mrs. McCray. They were to stay for three days after the cruise, but by the second day they were both ready to go.

When Todd suggested they just go home, she didn't try to talk him out of it and made arrangements for an earlier flight then called Jenna who was to pick them up from the airport.

"Where have you been? Well, I know where you've been but I've been dying here, I was about to fly down and make sure you got off the ship. Why haven't you called?" Jenna began a friend's tirade because she hadn't heard from her.

"I've been busy," Was all Alana answered with.

"You've been having sex, you've been having sex with the hot guy all week." Her joking words were met with Alana's cold iciness.

"Yeah, Jenna, and now I'm coming home."

****

Chicago was much colder when they returned. The wind whipped through to the core of the bones and Alana had to let the warmth of the Caribbean, and the warmth of Matt, slip away to the recesses of her mind. It was difficult to get back into city life with the constant noise of traffic, bright lights outside the windows, and the gloom of a winter snowstorm within the next week. Her mind certainly had some adjusting to do.

When the snow came, her and Todd huddled inside with comfort food and watched the travel channel. What was it about snow that made one feel domestic? Alana baked fresh bread and plenty of brownies and they watched the television as island after island appeared and talked of where they would go next and reminisced about where they'd just returned from. Once, each of them closed their eyes and told their favorite memory.

Todd recalled his snorkeling trips. How it was like another world to him, like a different planet with all its coral and formations and multi colored fish. All his time in the water changed his view of what was under the sea, whereas before he simply thought it a hole filled with water, now he'd experienced the other side of it and looked at it differently.

Alana's favorite memory was standing on the top deck and holding her son on his birthday as they watched the sun rise. She described the warm breeze that morning, just the slightest whisper of wind. The striking pink as it first crested over the water and sent shots like parallel lightening bolts straight across the blue-black sky. The way the air smelled and the sound of a distant boat motor setting out for early fishing.

"If the airport wasn't closed, I think I'd book us a flight right now. Why did we come back early? Where were our minds?" Alana sighed.

"Our minds were with Matt and Mrs. McCray. It was different when they were gone." Todd stated it simply and Alana didn't deny it wasn't the truth.

"Yeah," she said quietly in agreement.

Todd hadn't mentioned them since they'd been home. She thought at first that he would bring their names up every day, want to call them or write, but he hadn't. It was as if he understood in his own way.

"I know Matt loves you." Todd blurted it out and didn't care. "And I don't know if you love him or not, but I know he makes you happy. Don't you want to be happy, Mom?"

"Oh, Todd, life is so much more complicated than you think."

"Why? He likes you and you like him."

Alana couldn't help but think of Jenna's same argument as she said the same thing to her over and over. "It isn't that simple. I'm not ready to have anyone else in our lives right now, I'm selfish, I don't want to share you."

"I told Matt that if I could pick a dad, I'd have picked him."

In that moment, Matt's words lashed out at her again, she could hear them so clearly... "My God, Alana, have you thought about what you're asking me to do?"

She hadn't really let the full meaning of the words sink in until now. He not only had to give her up, but also a child who wanted to belong to him. Her heart went out to some unknown place in New York where she pictured Matt alone in an empty apartment, and she ensconced in her life with this wonderful child. Alana knew how he must be hurting and he didn't have a choice to change it no matter how badly he might want to. She'd made a decision for all three of their lives. A decision she couldn't look back on, they could only move forward now.

CHAPTER SEVENTEEN

Work had piled up in her absence. It seemed there was no one who correctly tended to the simple tasks of her everyday habits of filing, scheduling substitutes, and other simple activities. She thought at least one person would have been skilled enough but her desk was piled high, and although she hadn't been there, she received the messages that came with the substitute no shows and complaints. They hadn't even bothered to clear her voice mail so Alana took a deep breath and set about to get things back on track.

"Welcome back, Alana." One of her co-workers smiled. "Wow, you look... different... great. What did you do, go off and get some kind of makeover on a reality show or something?"

"A vacation, but looking at this mess, I'm calling for another one. Who was trying to take care of this? Whoever it was, was lousy."

"We couldn't get a temp so we all kind of pitched in."

Along with her work back up there were college classes to be caught up on and she had to get back into volunteer duties and help with the organization of the fundraisers scheduled. She also spent time dodging Jenna and all her questions about Matt which she didn't want to share just yet. Told her bits and pieces, but most she wanted to keep all to herself. Felt as if she told her intimate details they'd no longer belong to her and it was the only thing she had to hold onto.

Thoughts of Matt were with her every day. Whether she filed papers at the office, stood in front of a classroom of children, shared a quiet dinner with Todd. It didn't matter what she did, he was always there. Most times she successfully pushed him to the back of her mind, but in the silence of night, alone in her bed, thoughts of him overwhelmed her.

Alana's busy schedule at least made the time go quickly. At times she wasn't sure she wanted it to, and at times she couldn't wait for their appointment with Dr. Lee. A month after they returned from the cruise, she thought she was ready to walk into his office. They were scheduled for extensive x-rays and other tests and afterward would meet and finally see if the cancer was really gone.

The night before the appointment, Mona had insisted they come for dinner. Alana knew that specific night was planned because both Mona and Dr. Lee knew it would be torture for her to get through, and she enjoyed the distraction, needed it.

"Ms. Mona, why don't you have any pets? I think you and Dr. Lee need a dog."

She laughed as she placed the last of the dishes in the dishwasher. "I don't know why we don't have any pets, Todd. I've never really thought of having one."

"Maybe you need some fish."

Alana had helped her with the dishes until coffee was ready and she took a cup into Dr. Lee's home office. "Mona said you'd need this." She placed it on his desk, noticed the enormous amount of papers scattered everywhere.

"I've been helping out a friend in research, all this paperwork is why I'm a practicing physician. I have enough of my own, I could never have this much on a regular basis."

Alana was about to leave him to his work when a picture caught her eye. It hung on the wall just by the door, one of her father and Dr. Lee when they graduated from medical school, full of smiles and anticipation towards their future and what it would hold. It brought her sadness to look at it now.

"I still miss him so much." Alana hadn't meant to speak out loud.

"I have to believe your father is up there watching over you, right alongside your mother." Dr. Lee said.

Her fathers smile was broad, he was proud and in love, she remembered Mona telling her years previous that her mother had taken the picture. Alana had previously thought that after her father's death, maybe the guilt would fade, but it hadn't. Again, she didn't mean to speak words out loud, but her thoughts were voiced.

"I suppose the guilt will never go away."

"Guilt about what?" He questioned.

She turned around to him unaware he'd heard her thoughts, and then she turned back to the picture. Alana decided to reveal the truth she'd never revealed. "Guilt that my mother died. He loved her so much, I often wondered if he ever wished they saved her instead of me."

"Alana, your father would never have wished that, you were everything to him." He rose from his chair and stood by her side. "And who is 'they' you refer to?"

"The person who got me out of the car, whoever it was. I've just always wondered if he'd have had a choice who it would have been to survive."

Dr. Lee was quiet, stunned she had never known. "Alana, your father had a choice. Your father is the one who rescued you."

The words sent her mind into a complete blank. There was nothing that surfaced but astonished silence as she tried to grasp what he'd said and still couldn't, it didn't make any sense. "How could... how could that have happened, he wasn't there."

"He saw the whole thing."

Her mind began to return as she recalled the events that filtered vaguely in again after all the years. "I thought we'd dropped him off. Yes, we dropped him off at the hospital and were on the way home, it wasn't on the way, was it?"

"No, you dropped him off, but your father was in a hurry that night. He was running late and when your mother pulled up to the front he jumped out of the car so quick he forgot something. When he turned back around your mother had already pulled away so he jumped in a cab and tried to catch her. He was right behind the car when it was hit. Saw the whole thing."

"Oh my, God, I never knew. I... how could I have not known that?"

"You were six. Your father never talked about it because you never did. And you grew up well adjusted, other than your fear of your face in the water, which was understandable. By the time you were older and could understand more, you never mentioned it so he didn't either."

"You said he saved me, it was him?"

"The car sunk fast. He jumped in, and once you were safe he kept diving in after your mother. Almost drowned himself trying, but... he couldn't save her. During the crash it pushed the dashboard in and her legs were trapped. Your father never once regretted getting you out first, Alana, don't ever think that. Sure he wished he could have saved your mother also, but that was the only thing he ever regretted, never that he saved you first."

Alana was in shock. The events of that night now came into full view, not the hazy dream of a scared child. They had never talked about it, what would there have been to say? It happened, her mother died, and as Dr. Lee said, she was well adjusted. She had always loved her father and the only obvious problem was her fear of the water, and she could understand why they'd never talked about it.

She stared at the picture of her fathers face as she asked the question. "What did he forget? What was so important?"

"He forgot to give your mother a kiss."

"One last time," she whispered, her voice a scant noise in the quiet room. Words from a lifetime filtered through her brain and ran over and over in her mind.

She could see his face and hear his voice clearly as she remembered, pictured the look as she was about to run out and play and he'd call her back. Whenever she went off to school or he dropped her off at Mrs. Carmen who watched her. Whenever she left his side he'd say 'One last time' and give her a kiss. It was something he always did and there wasn't a time she couldn't remember him not saying it, she just never knew why, never knew what it meant until now. In case something ever happened, he didn't want to forget again.

That night alone in her bed, all the guilt she'd ever felt began to ebb away and slowly she let it go to feel release as she was liberated from years of remorse and speculation. The news freed her. It didn't change how she felt about her father, she always loved him with the whole of her heart and still did, that would never change. But it made her feel better to know. It made that little six year old insecure girl know that her father never wanted anything, but for her to live.

"Oh, Daddy," she whispered to the dark. "I can't live without Todd. Help me live now, please help me live now."

****

Dr. Lee called at six a.m. that morning. "I called to see how my favorite patient's mother is. I know Todd is fine, probably still sleeping sound, but I know you didn't sleep all night."

"I closed my eyes once. I think."

"I wanted to call just to see how you were. I'll be out of the office all morning but I'll be back just about the time we're scheduled, so if I'm not there at exactly two, don't worry, I will be."

"So you won't be seeing the x-rays before we do?"

"I'll be pulling them out of the envelope and we'll be looking at them together."

"It's going to be okay, isn't it?" It was part question, part statement and part prayer to God. One of many she couldn't stop saying.

"Alana, if you prepare yourself for the worst, which is the cancer has returned, you'll be better off. This is a tough battle, the odds aren't in his favor and I just want you to be ready if the news is bad."

"I've been doing some research online and..."

"Alana," Dr. Lee stopped her. "If the news is bad, there's nothing else to be done. We've talked about this at great length."

Dr. Lee wanted to tell her to do all the research, to find the miracle drug, the homeopathic remedy that would cure her son, but he couldn't encourage her when there would be no hope if his cancer were back.

Todd and Alana had a little time to enjoy that morning and Todd took the opportunity to search the newspaper real estate ads, began his search for a home and a dog, something she'd promised after the day they got good news. She could see the promise bright in his eyes, the promise that they could move from the tiny apartment. It made the hospital visits convenient, but that was its only purpose. It was tiny and cramped, and both of them would be anxious to get out and leave it all behind.

"This is a pretty one, and it's on the beach." Todd handed over the paper and showed her the picture.

"Todd, this is at Lake Michigan."

"So? Why can't we live on a beach? Call and make an appointment, let's go see it today after we see Dr. Lee."

"I can call tomorrow."

"Call now, Mom. We'll be out of Dr. Lee's by two thirty, make the appointment for after that."

Alana stared at him as if he'd said something so odd. She was still feeling as if their life was on hold and he planned their future, that day just another one to get through. He looked so insistent and she called the number, set their appointment with the agent for four thirty and it would take them at least an hour to get there.

"Cool, now we can get a dog."

"We haven't got a house yet, Todd, all we have is an appointment."

"And remember, the dogs name has to be Bomba."

Alana pulled him close and hugged him, silently prayed to her father, wanted desperately to believe he was with her, felt she could possibly channel him through Todd. Her need for him the greatest it had ever been, but she couldn't cry out, he wasn't there. She was helpless and had to leave it in God's hands.

Later, as they walked up to the front doors of the building, Todd took her hand in his. "Hey, Mom, remember it's the best day ever. Whatever happens, it's the best day ever. We had today."

"Yes, Todd, we had today." She held his small hand tightly in hers, felt every ridge of his fingers, the smoothness of his palm, and wanted to speak out loud but only whispered in her mind. Don't let go, Todd, don't ever let go.

Tests were done and everything was expedited and rushed off to where it had to go so that it was in Dr. Lee's office at the appointed time of two where Alana and Todd waited. Dr. Lee called and said he would be there in ten minutes and although it wasn't a long time, Alana stopped herself from pacing the floor. Her entire life had been put on hold for this moment.

She'd long since pushed the Caribbean memories away, had concentrated on nothing but this and here she was. Life or death would stare her in the face less than ten minutes from now and she wasn't ready, would never be ready. Maybe they could just walk out and not know. Would it be easier just to go along as if they had every day? What would she do different if she knew the cancer was there again? She'd only be left with nothing to do but count the days until death, how would she live that way? Thoughts of just walking out and not knowing grew in her mind.

Todd sat casually in a chair and flipped through a car magazine. "Hey look, I've got a model like this one."

He held the page up and she looked at it but didn't see it, answered as if she had. "Yes, you do." Did he? She didn't know, and at that moment she didn't care. When the door finally opened Alana was quickly on her feet.

"I'm sorry, the most important day of our lives and I was late, it couldn't be avoided." Dr. Lee truly felt bad. He kissed Alana on the cheek and shook Todd's hand and spoke again. "Mona wants you two for dinner this evening again. Actually, she's made it a command performance and won't take no for an answer, no matter what."

His wife catered to every whim of Todd's and always made meals a special occasion. But she couldn't think about dinner, or food, or anything else but the moment. Alana's palms broke out in a sweat and her hands began to shake, then her legs felt weak and almost buckled as she walked over to the light box to view the x-rays.

He pulled the film out of the large envelope and placed it in position. Alana and Dr. Lee hovered over it while Todd still flipped through his magazine. She'd seen so many x-rays, studied every one of Todd's, and could literally say she knew his body inside and out, and she could read the film as well as any physician.

Dr. Lee pulled another one out, then another as she stared. Different angles, different areas the film concentrated on, he continued slowly one by one and through it all neither said a word. She wasn't breathing, not one breath escaped until he pulled the very last one. It was then Alana began to cry.

CHAPTER EIGHTEEN

Three months later, Alana stepped out of her car with a handful of wild flowers and walked towards the marble headstone in Fairview Cemetery. Spring was warm in the air, it was welcome after the cold chilly winter of Chicago. The trees were green again and flowers burst forth with new life. It gave one a sense of new beginnings.

Alana rubbed her hand along the cool headstone, stretched her palm out fully and felt the smoothness. So many words formed in her head and her heart, but there was nothing to say now. The only sound was the birds in distant trees and the rustle of the wind that filtered through branches just now getting their buds. She stayed for a long time, her mind on the past, her mind on the future, and then she lay the flowers down softly and left.

Her trip out of Chicago would be hampered by traffic, everyone in the city tried to get home and all she wanted to do was get out. She reached over for her coffee cup, all she had survived on lately, but found the travel mug empty and stopped for a refill. It was the sustenance she'd survived on, black liquid that carried her through the days.

Crammed boxes overstuffed her car. She left her new home in Lake Michigan reluctantly to go back and forth to the city all week to tie up her loose ends and she wasn't going back after this last moving trip. She made sure of that when she left two boxes of things behind for a neighbor, they were added to the others she'd left previously.

It was dark when she pulled into her new driveway but remembered the garage door opener on her visor and pushed it. She'd never had a garage before, then again, she'd never had a house like this before either. One she needed, for Alana had to leave the city behind her.

She had splurged on the 3-bedroom home that even had guest quarters that included a kitchen and living area along with a bedroom and bath over the garage. Jenna already claimed it as her own and picked out colors, said her things would remain in the closet so she wouldn't have to bring a bag every weekend for visits.

The house was quite large and Alana didn't know what she would use all its space for but had fallen in love with the location and the beautiful house came with it. It was open and airy with vaulted ceilings and a stone fireplace in the great room along with a spacious all glass sun room that overlooked one of the most beautiful parts of Lake Michigan. The expansive decking gave a generous view across the water and a few steps took one to the sandy beach below.

The weather had already warmed up to look to be a promising summer and in the week she'd owned the house she'd already gotten used to a morning walk along the shore. It was a secluded hideaway, felt like her little piece of the world, a pristine, sandy and private beach with gentle dunes, the northern sky, and Lake Michigan splendor.

When nightfall came, the sky was filled with thousands of stars. Another thing Alana had already become accustomed to was to sit on the deck at night and blanket herself in the silence. The only noise the rhythmic sound of water that lapped along the beach. Then she'd leave the door open to the deck of the master bedroom when she went to bed and let the soothing waves lull her to sleep.

Furniture delivery was scheduled for nine the next morning and she'd just made it back from her walk when they arrived. Since every room had new furniture, it was late afternoon when they finished the job.

The rest of the day was spent distributing boxes to the rooms they belonged. She hung a few curtains and began to unpack boxes marked miscellaneous to determine where they went but one of the first boxes she opened contained cruise vacation pictures. She'd had them developed and never looked at them, now held them in her hand and wondered if she wanted to look at them, knew she wouldn't get another thing done if she opened the envelope.

With pictures in hand she retrieved the one chilled bottle of wine she had in the fridge, a single glass, and then went out to the deck but before she could open the envelope the phone rang.

"Hey, Mom!" Todd's voice sang out to her and her heart instantly lifted.

"Hey, how was your day?"

"They gave me a going away party at school today, and Mrs. Baker cried because I was leaving."

"I'm sure she did," Alana smiled into the phone.

"Tommy doesn't want me to leave tomorrow, and I feel really bad but I can't wait to get to the new house. We were thinking maybe he could come stay with me next weekend." Todd asked with a hopeful voice, didn't know plans had already been made with his best friend Tommy.

The family had been long time friends since the boys started school together in the first grade. And when they offered for Todd to stay with them that last week of school, it saved her the hour drive commute back and forth, and they were only too happy with his company.

"I've already talked to his mom about it and she's going to bring him out. They'll come and stay for dinner Friday night, then pick him up on Sunday."

"Hey Tommy," Todd hollered gleefully to his friend in the other room. "It's already set, you're coming next weekend! Cool, Mom, thanks. Okay, I gotta go, we're going swimming, the Carson's just opened their pool."

"Be ready for Jenna tomorrow, she'll pick you up in the morning. I love you."

"Love you too, see you tomorrow."

Alana hung the phone up and looked forward to tomorrow, couldn't wait to see him. It had been the longest he'd been away from her since her father used to take him on their fishing trips. She didn't tell him on the phone, but she figured they would be settled in enough to go to the shelter and he can pick out his dog. One he still wanted to name Bomba.

She also looked forward to Jenna's long weekend visit. She'd taken off work a few days and wouldn't have to leave until Tuesday. So after they worked on unpacking boxes there would still be time for relaxation. After a week of moving and traveling back and forth to the city, she was anxious to finally be able to settle down.

Alana poured a glass of wine and began her journey through Caribbean memories. Todd must have taken most of the pictures as her and Matt appeared in many along the shore, in the rented open-air jeep, a few places on the ship, or standing in a beautiful tropical backdrop of azure water and palm trees. His face smiled out to her.

As she held the picture, her thumb moved along his arm as if she could feel him. Handsome and masculine dressed in a black suit and tie standing next to Alana in a black dress with a sheer top. They made a good-looking couple, a perfect fit together.

She looked out to calm water that was swathed in moonlight now. A breeze crossed the deck, brushed ever so lightly across her face as if it were his touch. How she missed him, thought about him every day and as she looked at his face again she knew it was time. The pain and sadness of her life before was over, she had a new life to offer now, one that didn't bind her to the pain and suffering of cancer. Both her mind and heart now free to concentrate on other things, free to rediscover the love again.

Upon the return from the Caribbean, as each day passed she felt closer and closer to him even tough they were miles apart. Alana had come to realize she'd fallen in love with Matt and guessed the exact moment she thought it happened. The memory that stood out in her mind was their dance on the boat as it floated in azure sea. The romance, the champagne and soft music, she felt they were the only two people in the world and he had quietly stolen her heart. And she hadn't even noticed at the time.

Now she was finally unburdened from what had consumed their lives and could take the next step but felt a little apprehensive and excited at the same time. She breathed deep, took a couple of good breaths and noticed there was a slight fear. But she had nothing to be afraid of now, did she? She dialed his home number and when there was no answer tried his cell phone. After three rings a woman answered.

"Hello?"

"Is... is this Matt McCray's number?" Alana stammered for a moment as the voice had taken her off guard, one she hadn't expected to hear.

"Who is this?"

"This is Alana. I'm sorry, I must have the wrong number."

"No, you don't have the wrong number, this is Matthew's cell phone."

"Is he available?" Alana was getting a sick feeling in the pit of her stomach. The slight fear she'd felt a few moments earlier was now beginning to magnify in its intensity and she almost felt physically ill. The woman sighed deeply as if she were quite disturbed.

"Of course he isn't available, this is his wife Katherine. He may have told you that he was divorced but we're back together and he's off the market now. So mark him as unavailable from here on out," then she hung up the phone.

Katherine quickly deleted the number from his recent calls list then set the phone back down on the table in its exact place before Matt could see it in her hand. She had just enough time to pick up her drink to look nonchalant before he returned from the restroom.

Matt sat down and noticed she ordered a scotch for him, a martini for her. "What did you order drinks for? We're not going to be here long, certainly not long enough to have a drink."

"We were married for ten years, the least you can do is have a civilized drink with me." Katherine pushed the drink further towards him and huffed when he didn't touch it.

"The least you could do is not pretend this should be a pleasant experience for me, we're not the type of ex's who can get together for a friendly drink. What do you want?"

"You seem a little angry. Where's the pleasant Matthew I used to know?"

"You mean the one who ignored the fact his wife was a lying adulterous bitch? That was just the me that wanted to flow on with my everyday life as if it were wonderful. I had work, and you had men."

"So you still have work, shouldn't that make you pleasant? Or is there a woman somewhere in the mix who's making you crazy. Someone you're interested in?"

Katherine had the feeling she'd just talked to her on his cell phone. Of course she would never tell him, the less money spent on other women, the more for her. Plus she'd always envisioned Matt pinning away for her, certainly never thought he'd fall for anyone else. Maybe he'd consider reconciliation. She was between boyfriends, a little time and he'd be back in love with her.

"What do you want, Katherine? I might consider it worth my time if you told me your mother was sick or needs something. I like her, but unless it's that we have nothing to talk about."

Katherine wondered which she should pursue first, the money issue or a possible reconciliation? Smartly decided if the reconciliation worked, more money would come later. If she asked for more money right away he'd be angry and the reconciliation point would be mute.

"Is it so wrong to want to see you just to sit and chat? We spent ten years in bed together, surely we can have a nice friendship."

"You spent ten years in bed and not with me, with other men."

"I was stupid and..."

"No, this is stupid, Katherine, what do you want? The only reason I met you here was because I didn't want you to come to my office. I don't want to look at you. I don't want to talk to you. I don't want to deal with you. So if you have nothing to say I'm leaving." Matt stood up but she grabbed his arm to stop him.

"Okay, just sit down for one minute and drink your scotch, I won't waste any more time."

Matt sat down but didn't touch the glass, just stared at her and waited for her to explain the reason she was desperate to see him. He hadn't heard from her since their divorce. He sent alimony on a regular basis to keep her out of his life and it had worked till now. As he looked at her he still wondered what he ever saw in her, felt it a wasted ten years of his life and the only good thing that had ever come out of it was that he built his company without distraction of her or any other female. That is, up until now when he felt he couldn't function on a day-to-day basis as he waited for a phone call from Alana.

Katherine decided she could forget all else and go in for the money. "I saw your firm in that big architectural magazine, that commercial piece they did, you've been getting bigger and bigger. Some pretty good things are happening for the company and I just feel I'm not getting my fair share."

Matt stared at her as if she'd lost her mind, seriously considered she had. How could he ever have found her attractive? Her perfect exterior presence of poise and beauty only served to hide the ugly greedy inside. "I agreed to pay you alimony even though we both know the courts wouldn't have ordered it, and a very generous amount it was. Did you get that word, Katherine? Was? Don't expect a check in the mail next month, or the month after that, I'm done. Our agreement for me to pay you through the end of this year is over as of right now."

"You can't do that!"

"I can do anything I damn well please and I just did. You have a problem with it, I'll see you in court." Then he stormed out.

****

From the moment Jenna and Todd walked through the door the next day, Alana didn't give them a second of rest. Todd was busy getting his room unpacked and put together and Alana had Jenna get the kitchen in order while she finished the bathrooms. All four of the bathrooms now equipped with towels and necessities.

She hung the rest of the curtains in the many windows and anything else that needed to be done. From one project to the next she flew through the house and busied herself between enormous tasks of rearranging furniture and the smallest thing like hanging a roll of toilet paper. All of it to try and take her mind off the phone call the previous evening.

After Dr. Lee examined all the rest of the test results and concluded Todd was in remission, the cancer gone, Alana set into motion the steps necessary to wrap up one part of her life before moving on to the next. They spent every free minute at Lake Michigan to look for the perfect house. She trained a new person for her job and had her exams for college courses, and Todd closed out the school year.

Her first thought after the phone call had been that she'd waited too long to contact Matt and he'd given up on her and moved on. But as she tossed and turned all night long, even the sound of the waves unable to soothe her, anger took hold. It had only been four months, not four years. If he had loved her as much as she thought he had, why couldn't he have waited?

It became obvious to her and she had to finally admit to herself that it was all a make believe dream. She'd been swept away in the Caribbean islands by a handsome stranger who'd taken advantage of her innocent vulnerability. She'd exposed her heart and was defenseless to his charm and personality and she'd been taken. He obviously had never really been over his wife.

As angry as she felt, it still didn't stop her heart from aching. It all seemed so real, his love, his passion, the intensity of it. Clearly in her mind she could envision the two of them standing in warm breeze over the water in Tortola, could feel his touch and hear the words so clearly, as if he were standing right in front of her... 'Remember this day, Alana, remember I love you.'... And she did remember that day, that moment. During cold lonely nights she pictured that exact time and it had gotten her through many.

My God, was she really that naive? Somewhere between dark and dawn, Alana's heart formed a shell of protection. Never again, never would she expose herself to the pain that now ripped through her.

By the end of the day, Alana could look around and actually see the house shape into a home. All their hard work paid off when she looked around and it felt homey, felt like them. Upon the mantle, in a prominent location with all her other important pictures, was a picture of her and her father. She was almost seven years old and it was their first Christmas without her mother and he held her in his arms with a smile. A proud smile, she was in her new Christmas dress he'd chosen himself.

It was blue lush velvet the color of midnight and she could almost still feel the softness of it now. It had a high cream lace collar and lace cuffs on the long sleeves. They looked so happy, and they were. They missed her mother terribly that year, but her father didn't crawl into a shell because he lost the only woman he'd ever loved, or ever would love. He did what was best for Alana, picked her up and they carried on.

"Daddy," she whispered to the empty room.

He had such strength. Bravery and courage she never suspected the intensity of when he was alive. Only the recent conversation with Dr. Lee revealed the extent of it.

He was with her somehow, he had to be. She now believed it was his strength he'd given her to get through the illness, now she needed more. He had to give her some of that strength to hide her pain, hide her broken heart so she and Todd could get on with their lives. Just as he did with that small little vulnerable girl he held in his arms.

"Mom?" Todd called from the top of the stairs, his voice a little hesitant. "Can I go to bed now?"

She gently placed the picture back on the mantle and walked to the bottom of the stairs to look up and see her exhausted son who stood on the landing, then looked at her watch and realized it was almost midnight. "Of course you can, I didn't realize it was so late." When she reached the top he literally fell into her arms.

"I was afraid to ask, you've been running around giving orders all day and I want to help, but I'm really tired now."

"Oh, baby, I'm sorry. I guess I got carried away with all that had to be done."

Alana hugged him to her and walked with him to the bed after he hollered a 'good night' to Jenna who was somewhere else in the house. They heard her faint reply.

A quick overall vision of the day and she realized what a tyrant she'd been. "Tomorrow we do nothing."

"Except go get Bomba, right?"

"Right. Our new house is now settled enough for a dog, and we'll go find him, or her, tomorrow at the shelter." Alana sat on the edge of Todd's bed and pulled the covers up around his shoulders.

"I hope whichever one we pick likes the water, we've got a lot of it in the back yard." Todd laughed, was still getting used to the fact that a beach was just outside his door and he loved it.

"You'll like sleeping with the window open, it will probably be the best night's sleep you've had in a long time, I can almost guarantee it," Alana pulled the covers up more to make sure he was comfortable. "I'm sorry, you're probably getting too old for me to tuck you in, huh?"

"Well, I am a teenager now, but it's okay."

"I can't help it, when you were sick there was no way I was going to miss a night. And I'll confess something now, there was many a night I tucked you in and came back when you were asleep. I'd sit on the floor and sleep with my head on the bed."

"I know," Todd said with a childlike tenderness. He remembered when he was really sick and he'd woken up a couple of times and saw her there. It was what helped him make it through the night, she became the reason he woke up in the morning.

Alana touched his face tenderly, they were so much like she and her father were. She had to think they too, would make it. When Alana spoke, she didn't make the statement lightly, wouldn't take for granted that everyone went through the natural process of getting old. She knew how fragile life was.

"I guess you're growing up, aren't you?"

"Yeah, maybe since we're in a new house and all, and since I'm okay now, maybe I should start taking more responsibility and just coming to bed myself." He paused before he continued, added the last statement for her benefit. "Well, I'm just thinking too because the house is big. It's not like that little apartment where your bedroom was right next door, your bedroom is downstairs now. No sense you running up and down the stairs when you don't have to."

Alana laughed. "Okay, just this last night. Your first night in your new bedroom, in our new house, and this will be it."

"I love it here, Mom. Having the beach right outside the door, hardly any neighbors, we can't see them anyway. It'll be so great living here."

"Our new life," Alana bent down and kissed him on his forehead.

"Yeah, our new life."

"I love you, Todd." She gave him another kiss before she left.

"I love you too, Mom."

Alana turned the light off and left the room with a heavy heart. Todd didn't need her, Matt didn't need her, was she useful to anyone anymore? When she walked through the kitchen Jenna asked her from the deck to bring a bottle of wine and two glasses. Alana let out a sound that was something between a chuckle and a huff and spoke out loud to the empty room.

"Jenna needs me."

CHAPTER NINETEEN

She opened the wine and carried it with the glasses outside. After she poured and sat down in the chair next to Jenna she leaned back, closed her eyes, and let out a deep sigh.

"You missed your calling, you should have been a dictator in some foreign country. It was like having Hitler in this house today. All week long you couldn't keep the excitement out of your voice, I think it was just to lure me here with visions of a wonderful weekend and then you turn on me. You were a totally different person. I've never worked so hard in my life."

"I know, I'm sorry, Todd just pointed that out to me. I'll be better tomorrow morning after my beach walk. Are you going to be up at six?"

"Oh, hell no, the beach will still be there at noon."

Alana took a deep breath of the fresh air and let it fill her lungs completely. Let it fill her mind with new beginnings that were just around the corner. No, Alana, she reminded herself, they weren't just around the corner, they were right now, and you were right in the middle of it.

They chatted quietly about Jenna's job, stores Alana discovered in the area, and what they needed to do tomorrow. And Jenna never mentioned her mood again until she went into the kitchen and returned with pictures in her hand and another bottle of wine.

"Okay, so you didn't tell me immediately but I know you would have explained eventually, so I won't be mad."

"Mad at what?" Alana asked and looked up to see the pictures with Matt in them she'd thrown in the trash.

"While I was inside I decided to empty the trash and there was a hole in the bottom of the bag and I saw these. I'm not going to ask, I'm just going to sit here and wait until you tell me what's going on." Jenna flipped through them again. "Very nice pictures. You said he was good looking but dang, Alana, you must have had to wear a blindfold to walk away from that man."

"I hate the cliché' but I have to say it because I can now say I've experienced it firsthand. Looks aren't everything."

Jenna looked at her long and hard, wouldn't stop staring until Alana explained.

"I called him last night," she finally confessed in a soft voice.

Alana finished her glass of wine and remembered every detail of the conversation, especially the strange woman's voice and her exasperated tone as it instantly gave Alana the feeling she'd interfered in their lives.

Jenna remained quiet, simply poured more wine for the both of them as she told her of it.

"Turns out, I was some sort of rebound thing, or fill in, or fling, something. Katherine, his ex wife answered the phone, said he was no longer available because they were back together."

"No!" Jenna gasped and put her hand over her mouth but it couldn't stop her from screaming out loud. The shock almost made her drop her glass and knock over the wine bottle at the same time. She grabbed it before it toppled but the pictures fell everywhere.

Alana looked down to the floor and Matt smiled up at her as if life were wonderful. Knowing what she knew now, it felt more like his face was laughing at her. Did she have to talk about it anymore? Relive it over and over? Why couldn't it just quietly fade away? Take with it her humiliation.

"I feel so stupid."

"I can't believe it. Not after everything you've told me, Alana, he sounded like a dream." Jenna's voice was still filled with the shock of her revelation.

"Because he was. Guess I made the right decision after all, didn't I?"

"No, if you'd made plans with him before you left him maybe he wouldn't have gone back to his wife."

"Jenna, obviously he wasn't over her to begin with. Four months ago, standing in some beat up shack beneath a goat skull he professed his love. And me, caught up in all of it. You'd have thought I had some of Bomba's mushroom tea, I believed every word."

"Goat skulls? Mushroom tea?"

"No wonder I never dated." She didn't explain, only sipped more wine but it didn't dull the pain. She imagined maybe a few more months and his memory wouldn't be as vivid, she hoped so anyway. He was a louse, an asshole, a bastard, maybe if she kept calling him names they would sink in, but she should be calling herself names, and she thought of many, Alana couldn't believe what a fool she'd been. "I do love this house. My son and this house, that's all I need. Actually, all I really need is my son, the house is a bonus."

"Hey, you had great sex, didn't you?" Jenna couldn't understand it, and knew it was more than that, but her comment was used to lighten the air just a little.

Yes, she'd had great sex, but it had cost her dearly and it wasn't worth the pain. Alana wanted to slap herself again, just like she'd done all night and all day. How could she have been so weak? Swept away in the Caribbean by a man who held her in his arms and made everything right, a stranger who knew just how to work his charm on her stupid innocence. Everything had been make-believe, nothing had been real and it hurt like hell even though she pretended it didn't.

"You don't have to worry about me ever making that mistake again. Don't you ever bring up dating. Not with your friend, your friend's friend, your mother or fathers friend. The guy you ran into at the bank. No one, do you hear me?"

"But, Alana, you can't just hide away now in this gorgeous house and become an old maid."

"Yes I can."

Left with no choice, she had to. Alana wrestled with her emotions and knew she would eventually gain her pride back and even though it would take her heart longer to heal, like Matt, she too would move on. Jenna didn't speak of it again and they were quiet for a while, enjoyed the soft night sounds of the water before Alana spoke again.

"Funny how things change isn't it? In one second, your whole life can be changed forever. I stopped by my father's grave before I left the city."

"I still miss him also. And yeah, in one second your whole life changed, his death was so sudden."

"I don't mean his sudden death. I've never told you, but I'd always felt guilty over my mother's death, Jenna. My father loved me so much, I know that, and never once did he ever make me feel he didn't. It was just something I felt inside. I always wondered if he had a choice, if it would have been me he'd have picked to survive, or my mother. I know now, but I've lived all these years with that guilt, now I know it was just a little girl's paranoia."

"What happened? I mean, what was it that made you feel better about it?"

"I had a talk with Dr. Lee." Alana recalled her conversation with her father's best friend, told her the things she'd just discovered.

Jenna screamed when Alana finished her story. "Oh my God, Alana, that's it, that's a message from your father straight from the grave, straight from heaven. It's the sun over the moon and the stars in alliance, kismet, fate, destiny whatever, and all that other garbage I've rambled about with you and Matt."

"What are you talking about?"

"That's proof of love. Your father forgot to kiss your mother, went to the extreme of following her in a cab even though he was late. Don't you get it? Matt came back for a kiss even though he was angry, it didn't matter, that's love, nothing else mattered but that. Don't you get it?"

A chill ran through her. How could it not be a sign? How could it all be so coincidental? Okay, she was level headed enough to think it didn't have anything to do with stars and moons, that was all too weird, but surely it meant something. Did it? Or was she just forcing her mind to believe that it was possible because she needed Matt so much.

"Alana, you have to call him again."

"Jenna, his wife answered the phone. His wife."

"There's something wrong, I'm telling you. There's something going on there and you have to call him again. If you don't, I will. I'll find his number, I'll find him. Maybe I don't know what I'm talking about, and maybe he really is an asshole but it will make me feel better if I make sure." Jenna was handing her the phone.

Alana couldn't take it from her hands, heard clearly Katherine's voice in her head and couldn't go through the humiliation again. She just couldn't do it. "I can't, I have to move forward without him."

"Is that what you want?"

"No."

"Do you love him?"

"With everything I have but..."

"Do you think he loves you?"

"Obviously not enough as I once thought. Let it be, Jenna, it's done."

"But I think it was meant to be, there was a reason you two came together."

She pushed the thought away. "What if it ended the way it was supposed to? If it were meant to be, we wouldn't have left each other. He would have refused to listen to me. Maybe it wasn't meant to be from the start and was only meant to be what it was, a two week fling in the Caribbean, nothing but a distraction." Alana's mind was set and she wouldn't put herself through more torture.

****

The next day after they found the animal shelter, Todd and Alana went home with not one, but three dogs. A mixed black lab type, another was a medium sized mix of unknown origin. And the smallest, a miniature French bulldog that had a strange flat face and big ears that stuck out on top his head like radar antennas, he was also the youngest of the motley crew that now gathered in her back seat.

"I think we went a little extreme Todd, three dogs?"

Alana still couldn't believe she'd agreed to his reasoning. If they were going to have one they might as well have another. Then when he couldn't decide he'd somehow talked her into three. She would really have to work on her vulnerability issues.

She looked in the rearview mirror and had to laugh. The three sat in the back seat, all different sizes, shapes and colors and they stared either ahead or out of the window with tongues hanging and tails wagging. Then they'd switch positions as if on cue, traded the window seat for the middle and one jumped over the other or the smallest, the bulldog, walked underneath.

Jenna, who'd been napping on the couch, was their first target when Alana opened the door and the dogs bounded inside. All three barreled through the foyer into the large family room as if they'd lived there forever. Then they jumped on the couch with Jenna, as if she'd be just as happy to see them as they were to see her.

She awoke with a start and screamed as she tried to get away from all the licks and kisses they felt the need to bestow on her. Then all three in sync moved on to explore new surroundings.

"Yes, I know. Nuts. Crazy." Alana talked as she walked to the kitchen to put all the new dog stuff away.

"More like insane," she was laughing now at the shock of it.

"That too. I didn't have the heart to say no, I never have the heart to say no to Todd. I still want to give him everything in the world he wants, I'm creating a monster but I don't know how to stop myself."

Jenna brushed herself off, ran her hand through her jumbled hair and wiped the dog slobber off her face with her sleeve as she walked over to get a rag. "Todd will never be a monster, but I'm glad he didn't ask for snakes."

It brought back the memory of the snake that crossed her path in a far away place. The day Matt swept her off her feet and carried her onto the ship.

"What did I say?" Jenna looked worried. "He didn't bring back snakes, did he?"

"No," she laughed, knowing there was so much she would have to erase. "And let's not bring the subject up. I probably wouldn't even be able to deny him that."

There wasn't much to do that day in the way of getting settled. She'd pushed them so hard the previous day, everything was done. Most of the day was spent getting used to the dogs, at the same time, the dogs were getting used to them and their new home.

Along the beach, one ran straight into the water then out again, one tiptoed along the edge, and the other, the miniature French bulldog, wouldn't go anywhere near it. They listened to direction well and seemed to be fairly well trained as Todd called them, or told them to sit. He was prepared with a box of bones to entice them into more.

Alana watched them run along the shore and her heart lifted at the pure joy on Todd's face. This was to be her life. This gorgeous home, her son, and three orphaned dogs that would now be included in their little corner of the world. Todd laughed and fell to the sand when all three jumped for the bones and Alana smiled in the distance. It was a good life, it would be a good life, once she had all of her heart back, once she put the pieces of it back together, it would be wonderful.

Jenna wanted to cook dinner that evening in what she now considered 'her' kitchen and Alana was only too happy to hand over the duties. The only thing she did was set the table and make salad. She wasn't the best of cooks but she watched as Jenna marinated fresh mushrooms, prepared a vegetable casserole, and actually peeled potatoes for homemade mashed potatoes.

"You're so much better in the kitchen than I am, how did that happen?" Alana asked from her comfortable seat on the stool.

"I've always had men to cook for." Jenna answered with a smile. "I filled their bellies and they, well, it was an even exchange, trust me."

"Well, men suck. I'll stick to my son who much prefers hotdogs and macaroni and cheese."

"Say what you will, but..." Jenna couldn't finish her sentence as Todd burst through the door.

"Hey, Mom, there's someone here to see you."

"Who is it?" Alana immediately suspected something. His face was flushed and bright, his broad grin revealed a knowing only to him.

"You have to come see."

Then she heard the dogs barking in the front yard, followed by strange noises, and when Jenna walked over to look out of the window she burst into hysterics.

"Oh, your new neighbors are going to love this one. And you weren't lying about the chest, my God, he's even more handsome than his pictures."

"What?"

Alana rushed to the window and saw Matt standing there with a pair of khaki's on and shoes but nothing else, and he was surrounded by animals that ran all over her yard and cows that grazed with disinterest. There were several other people meandering about trying to control the livestock, as the three new dogs tried to play with what they presumed to be new friends.

She didn't know where he'd gotten the animals and didn't care, but at least he had the sense to bring people with him to control the chaos he'd brought to her home.

"What is he... How...." Alana couldn't find words but she couldn't cope with this. He was back with his ex wife and now stood on her lawn. What did he want from her? Couldn't he leave her alone with her humiliation and heartache?

"There's a peacock, a sheep and a pig, a goat and look, a llama! You have a farm on your front lawn. Complete with an entire herd of cows. There must be at least ten cows, no, I just counted and there's a dozen. Of course that one is wandering down the street now, does he count?" Jenna just kept laughing at the chaotic scene.

"Go ahead out Mom."

She'd been hurt but she didn't want Todd to know or be hurt. And he didn't understand this couldn't work anymore because things had changed. How could Matt do this? She guessed his wife mentioned it and now he thought he could dump her again and come back to Alana?

What was the game he was trying to play? Whatever it was, she wanted out.

"Todd, things have changed, and..."

"Wait," he stopped her. "Don't say anything, just go out and see him. Remember in Antigua when you didn't want to windsurf but you did? You didn't want to get your face wet, you always had a fear of that, but you did and it turned out okay, remember? Don't be afraid now, Mom, just go out, it'll be okay."

Jenna remained at the window and Alana stepped outside and walked closer to him but didn't get a chance to say a word before he started talking.

"My wife tried to ruin my life for the ten years we were married and is still trying. I met her for ten minutes the other day and in my five minute absence she almost managed to succeed when she told you a lie, Alana, pure and simple."

"How did you know I called?" She was suspicious, refused to let herself be caught up in any charming trap he planned to set. Alana wanted to believe it had all been a misunderstanding, but could she? Was she going to fall into her vulnerable pit again?

"Todd called me. Apparently he heard you talking on the deck last night." Matt stepped closer to her with every word he spoke. Behind him he pulled two cows with the leather straps in his hands. "Alana, look at me. I'm standing on your lawn half naked. Three dogs are chasing the chickens all over your neighborhood and I'm trying to dodge cow shit from a dozen cows. You have to know I love you."

Her father's words ran through her brain... 'It will be special' and the other words he was sure of, 'You'll know what love is, Alana, you'll know' and she wanted to scream, 'But how?' Give me something here father, give me something, and help me out. I know you're there and I need you. It was a silent plea in her mind but she wanted to shout it straight up to heaven.

Then all of a sudden something came to her. She didn't know from where, maybe direct from her father straight into her soul. But she knew how to tell, knew exactly what to ask and something pushed her on, put the words in her mouth.

"Matt, when you left in the cab at the port then came back, why did you do that? Why did you come back?"

"Honestly? I didn't know at first. I was so mad I couldn't think, I couldn't see straight, then all of a sudden I knew I had to go back. I knew I had to kiss you one last time."

Alana's intake of breath was noticeable as her heart stopped beating. Everything was crystal clear now, my God, her father was there, right there with her and she felt him smile on her as if it were warm sunshine. Felt him embrace her in spirit as if he were right next to her and she were in his arms. He hadn't left her, he'd never leave her alone.

She looked into Matt's eyes and it was all there. Everything she remembered, and just by looking at her he quickly engulfed her again, emotionally swept her away where it was safe and warm. It had all been real, in her heart and soul she knew it and it scared her to think she'd almost thrown away the rest of her life. He dragged his cows closer still.

"I think the last count was six cows but I remember you said it was going to start doubling so I brought twelve to be on the safe side. By Island law, I've abided by custom and you have your choice, either an assortment of various animals, or the cows and me."

Alana's smile came slowly. "I understand the livestock, but why are you shirtless?"

"I was willing to do what I had to in case the cows didn't work. Did you think I didn't know why you watched us play basketball so often?"

An ostrich ran by, chased by something that resembled a goat, but she wasn't sure. And one of the cows was so close he nudged her arm with his nose and it startled her. She jumped and moved closer towards him with a little squeal and now physically touched the closeness of his bare chest as a small pig nibbled on her shoe strings.

Matt bent his head slightly and touched her lips with his in the soft way that sent her system into a tailspin. It was the lightest touch, barely a whisper of the passion that lay between them, but when he pulled away this time she held his love inside her. Didn't feel empty and cold any longer when he drew back. She could keep it now, it was hers.

CHAPTER TWENTY

TWO MONTHS LATER

"This is so cool, I can't wait to see Mrs. McCray." Todd was ready to board, almost didn't give his mother time to kiss him.

"Don't forget to give her my love and tell her I can't wait till the two of you get back. Tell her I've already got her a beach chair and umbrella that has her name on it."

"Take care of Bomba and Buster and Frita."

With a wave, Todd was on his way to New York where Mrs. McCray would be waiting for him at the other end. Alana watched him and just as he was about to round the corner she panicked, was actually about to stop him when Matt laughed and held her arms down so she couldn't motion for him to come back.

"Matt, he can't go."

"Let him go, Alana, he'll be fine. Who are you worried about? Him or you?"

"Me," she was honest. "He's never been off alone like this." She couldn't stop her eyes from watering and she was about to cry at the thought of her young son going off in the world alone, as if he were going off to college.

Matt hugged her securely. "They'll have a good time. Grandmother and my parents are so anxious they're probably sitting there right now waiting for him. He'll be so spoiled by the time he gets back you'll probably want him to go away again."

"He'll be meeting your parents before I do. That may not be such a good thing. After meeting Todd, they'll be disappointed in me."

"Never, they already love you, Grandmother told them all about you and when I told them we were getting married, they asked what took me so long. I thought my mother would have at least tried to talk me out of it, but she said even though she hadn't met you, she hadn't found a reason to dislike you."

"Did you want her to?" Alana teased him.

"I won't even dignify that with an answer. Speaking of our wedding, we have to go get the best man."

They had a few more minutes and Alana watched from the window as Todd's plane lifted off. She would miss him, but it would only be a week then he would return with Mrs. McCray and Matt's parents for the wedding, where he would walk her down the aisle. How her life had changed from just a short few months ago.

Todd had already been fitted for his tux and looked like a dashing young man, and he'd had the final say in her gown, which was a simple white sleeveless with subtle designs in seed beads. He'd helped her take care of their side of the guest list which included practically all of Chicago. Todd had made many friends and he wanted them all there to celebrate the day. Of course it included the friends they'd just met on the cruise, all of them more than ecstatic when they heard the news.

Other than doing the guest list and picking the place for the wedding and reception, she and Matt made their wishes known to a wedding coordinator. Everything was left in her hands as time was too precious to fret and worry about decisions.

Alana thought it the best choice to make. She had been so worried and stressed with much more important things in her life, and she didn't want her wedding day, the only day she would ever get married in her life, to feel like she was strained and frazzled when she walked down the aisle to the man she loved. It had formed into a huge celebration that was now only a week away. Close to four hundred guests were scheduled to attend and Matt said most of his family, friends and business associates were coming to actually see it happen. Couldn't believe he would ever marry again, especially after only knowing her for so little time. Most told him they had to see it to believe it.

One friend told him his ex wife was frantically trying to find someone to marry her just so she could get married before him. So she could tell their friends Matt only settled down again because he knew she wasn't going back to him. It didn't bother Matt, or Alana when she heard. Neither would ever let Katherine have any effect on their lives again.

They met Jack at his gate, had timed Todd's flight to coincide with Jack coming in and his plane was right on time. The two men greeted each other warmly, they shook hands then hugged. And when Matt introduced them, she loved the way he looked so proudly at her, as if he were showing off the most important thing in his life to someone so dear to him. She didn't need the reassurance anymore, but it felt good.

"Jack, this is Alana, my bride to be."

"I hope you don't mind, Matt, but I've waited too long to meet this one, I'm taking more than a handshake." He didn't wait for an answer and pulled her into his arms in a warm embrace as Matt laughed.

"I don't have to worry about a hug, I'll have to worry if you hand her the key to your house."

Alana of course looked confused and Matt just shook his head. "I'll explain later. By the way, you haven't given that key away yet, have you? I haven't talked to you in quite a while."

"No, I still have my key and keep it very close at all times. You will be the first to know, hell, I'll probably have to have a ceremony over it."

In the car on the way home the two explained what the key represented. If he was ready to give a key to his house to someone it was his sign of real commitment, a sign that he was ready to give up his wild ways and be faithful to only one. Both of the men suspected that it would probably rust before it was ever used.

Alana liked Jack immediately. Matt had told her so much about him, and she suspected she would. She knew he was a notorious fickle ladies man, but she also saw now that he was easygoing and outspoken. She suspected the two had their wild times in college, and probably after. Was sure she would hear more about them during the coming week, he would be staying with them so there would be plenty of time to get to know him better. She also wondered in the back of her mind how Jenna would like him. It would be interesting since she would be there all week also.

"I have to tell you upfront, Alana, I walked down the aisle at his first wedding grudgingly, tried to talk him out of it since the day he told me he was getting married to her. But I promise you, this time I'm doing it with all the love in the world for you two."

Alana smiled and spoke honestly. "I appreciate that Jack, especially coming from someone so opposed to settling down."

"I'm not so totally opposed to it, don't get me wrong, I just haven't been hit by a sledgehammer yet."

"A sledgehammer?"

The two men laughed, it was what Matt said it had felt like. And it had at the time it was said in Barbados, but he would explain the meaning later.

When they reached the house, Jenna was still sleeping and Alana suspected the amount of wine she drank the previous evening when Dr. Lee and Mona came for dinner would have her in bed till noon. The upcoming wedding made it like a party atmosphere all the time. Especially since all her friends were anxious to meet Matt and couldn't wait until the ceremony, so it had been a round of dinners and parties since he'd moved in two weeks previous.

Much to Alana's protesting, he moved into another bedroom, decided they shouldn't have any intimate encounters until their wedding night, which drove her crazy. Wasn't she the one who should have decided that? She wasn't even worried about Todd. They were getting married, Todd would have understood if he moved into her bedroom, but Matt insisted they do it his way, and left with no choice she reluctantly agreed.

It didn't stop her from teasing him and playfully complaining when they were alone. As she did when they took the dogs for a walk on the beach after they made Jack comfortable in the house.

****

Jenna rolled over and groaned, her head hurt, then again it seemed everything hurt. She almost couldn't wait for the wedding to be over so life could get back to normal. There had been a party or someone over since Matt had arrived and she was almost beginning to think she wouldn't make it till the big day. And what a day it was shaping up to be. Jenna smiled.

She'd never seen two happier people and with all the bad luck Alana had, it was about time God smiled on her. And smile he had. How romantic to have a man show up on your front yard with a literal petting zoo. Odd to think of it as romantic, but when she heard the story behind it, it was the sweetest thing she'd ever seen.

When Todd called him he immediately took the first flight he could and spent all day gathering a mosaic of beasts, whatever he could round up from various sources. Matt borrowed the cows from a farmer, actually three farmers since he couldn't get all twelve from one. A man didn't go to those extremes just to get a woman in his bed.

He not only won Alana's heart, but Jenna's as well. For her it was proof she needed that what he felt for her best friend was real. Jenna would go to whatever extreme she needed to insure her friends golden heart not be broken and she was confident Matt would treasure it for the rest of their lives.

Not that she knew much about the kind of love they shared. The biggest thing any man had ever done for her was show up at her office with Chinese food, and that was after hours when he thought it would be fun to have sex on her desk. It had been fun.

When she looked in the mirror she almost screamed but that would have taken effort and she couldn't exert herself. Her red hair frizzed out in all different directions. And she hadn't washed her face before she went to bed and now looked like a raccoon as her mascara smeared underneath her eyes and her large t-shirt she slept in was inside out. Jenna would have scared the most unshakable, pictured her face on the cover of the next horror novel or movie. But she didn't do a thing to fix it, again, it would have taken effort and she wasn't in the mood to exert herself. So she left herself as she was and walked downstairs.

She scuffed slowly across the floor towards the kitchen, the whole time she wondered why Alana had to buy such a big house because it took her so long to get to the coffee pot. She'd noticed the form of a body and as she got closer to the coffee pot she realized the man sitting at the island counter was not Matt as she first suspected. Jenna poured the last dregs of what was left of the coffee first, fixed it with cream and sugar, and then turned to face him.

"Who the hell are you?"

Jack had to chuckle. This woman certainly had no pretenses and couldn't have been more direct. "I'm the best man. I assume you're the maid of honor? Jenna?"

"I forgot, they picked you up this morning when they dropped Todd off, didn't they. I'm a little fuzzy right now, but its Jack, isn't it?"

"Jack Kendall."

"Well Jack Kendall, how long have you been here?"

He looked at his watch, "Almost an hour."

"And you don't know how to make coffee? This stuff taste like shit."

"Honestly? I don't know how." He didn't want to add that there was always a woman who was more than happy to make it for him in the morning.

"Do you drink it?"

"Sure, I drink coffee." He mistakenly thought she was asking to see if he wanted some in order to guess how much to make, Jack would find he was so wrong.

"Then you're going to learn how to make it. I might be the maid of honor but it's just a title, a figure of speech that means... well, something. But don't take the maid part literally. I'm not saying you have to make it every day, but we all pitch in around here and I'm going to show you how so you'll know when it comes to your turn."

Jenna proceeded to give him step-by-step instructions as she showed him where everything was and how to make a fresh pot. Jack watched her intently, afraid that if he didn't he'd catch her wrath and she was a woman with a hangover, he wisely thought it best not to get on her bad side.

Flaming red hair was everywhere with no rhyme or reason, her face was smeared with leftover makeup and the only thing that would seem appealing would be her long legs that ran out from her tattered shirt. At the bottom of the legs, a scruffy pair of dog chewed slippers. Odd, he thought, even in her disheveled sloppiness he found the whole package attractive somehow.

He was used to seeing ladies in the morning, many different one's over a period of time. But they made it a point to get up before him and primp so that when he woke they looked just as good as they had when they'd climbed into his bed the night before. But this woman had no airs. Right on the surface for all to see was who she was. He hadn't known either long, didn't know them at all, but from what he'd seen on the surface he thought her a huge contrast to her best friend Alana.

"You're not easy on a man, are you?"

"Men have it easy enough. You think making coffee is difficult? You ought to try having a damn period every month, we don't call it 'the curse' because it's a cute name, and how convenient and easy for a man that they can stand up and pee. Or try giving childbirth. Not that I've done that yet, but I went through every pain when Todd was born." She began to search through cabinets one after the other. "Or try unpacking a hundred boxes and making sure a kitchen becomes a kitchen. Where in the hell did I put the cutting board?"

Jenna searched through the cabinets, forgotten where she put it and wanted to cut a cantaloupe. She needed something in her stomach, something with liquid to help her dehydration.

"That's right, she has a son. I'd forgotten." Jack leaned against the counter and watched her.

"The best little guy in the world."

He hadn't really talked in detail to Matt, only bits and pieces when he called with the exciting news of the wedding. There was time for details later, but at that moment Jack's concentration was on the long legs. He almost laughed out loud at the freshly tattered and chewed slippers, one had a long string of binding she hadn't bothered to cut off, and the other so torn apart there was barely enough material to keep it on her foot.

"Anything in particular you're smiling about?"

Jenna's voice was a quick harsh tone that caught him off guard and he looked up to see her standing there with her hands on her hips and a defiant stance. He hadn't realized she'd seen him. "Nothing in particular," he answered.

"Then might I suggest you put yourself to good use and help me find the cutting board? I'm going around in circles here and all you can do is stand there with a stupid grin on your face."

****

The day was planned as a relaxed one, and that's what it was. The first one they were able to enjoy for quite some time as nothing was planned. No lunches or dinners, no company to visit and nowhere to go. The four best friends put together a leisurely lunch and then talked and laughed all afternoon. Before they knew it, they were having drinks and cooking steaks for dinner.

"Look Jack, Matt can cook. Since you mastered your coffee lesson this morning, maybe you can take on a steak or two eventually." Jenna commented with a smile before she returned to the kitchen to help Alana and left the two men to cook on the grill outside.

They'd had a friendly banter going all afternoon. Their wisecracks and teasing towards each other came easily, as if they'd done it every day.

"Are the steaks almost through?" Alana asked when Jenna entered. The potatoes were almost done and the salad already prepared.

"Almost. It's a good thing Matt doesn't need his help, Jack seems to be totally lost when it comes to preparing food. How on earth has he survived?" It was a rhetorical question, Jenna suspected he wasn't lacking for any number of females willing to prepare his meals or be his companion to eat out.

"He's a nice guy, I like Jack." Alana commented.

"Yeah, I guess. But since when have you known me to worry about nice. It's the sexual attraction I'm interested in."

"I'm sure there's plenty of that for you also."

"Not that I've tried it out yet, but I'm sure I won't be disappointed tonight."

"Tonight?"

"Hell, Alana, we only have a week, I'm not going to waste a minute of a good thing."

Alana shook her head and laughed. Wished Jenna would find something like she had. Security, comfort, and the love of someone like Matt, someone she could begin the next part of her life with. But Jenna's concentration on men didn't last long or go into too much depth.

Outside, the two men talked of the same thing.

"Man, Jack, she's been giving you a hard time today, isn't cutting you any slack." Matt turned the steaks and closed the cover.

"I didn't have a fresh pot of coffee made for her this morning," Jack laughed at remembering. "There certainly won't be any surprises the first morning she wakes up in my bed. My God, she scared the shit out of me this morning she looked so bad, that red hair frizzing everywhere, and a torn inside out big shirt. She just looked at me and said 'Who the hell are you?'"

"She holds no punches, but I like Jenna." Matt did like her. Could instantly see the love she had for Alana when he first met her, as he'd seen with all her friends.

But Jenna was closer, more like a sister because the two had shared the majority of their lives together. He sensed only a little hesitation on her part in the beginning, a little suspicion because she wanted to protect his future wife, but now she couldn't be happier. He'd convinced her that he truly loved Alana, and would for the rest of his life. He didn't really do anything, all she had to do was look at all three of them interact. He, Alana and Todd would now become the family each had longed for.

"Yeah, I like her to." Then Jack said more quietly, almost a serious tone that made Matt smile inwardly. "There's something about her."

"She isn't your type at all, you like the perfect blondes, the ones with enough silicone to build their own valley. Colored contact blue eyes, size zero, the typical model perfect."

"That's the strangest part, she's opposite of what I'm used to in both looks and personality. Most of the women I date are eager to please and vain as hell. Jenna doesn't give a crap about either." Jack looked inside to see her through the window and liked her smile. "I have no doubt we'll sleep together tonight, but I have a feeling in the morning instead of professing her love for me, she'll be shoving me out of bed because I stole the covers."

Matt laughed, knowing it was probably true. "Could it be that after all these years, Jack Kendall has met his match?"

"A corny pun but with that flaming red hair, I'm thinking a match with a hell of a fiery tip."

"You don't have much experience in getting burned, you'd better be careful."

"That isn't something I'd ever have to worry about, I'm the master, Jack." His voice sounded confident but in the back of his mind he had an odd suspicion that his skills to remain distant would be challenged eventually, his luck couldn't last forever.

They enjoyed a simple dinner on the deck as the sun set on another day and afterwards Jenna was firm in shooing Alana and Matt off to take their nightly walk on the beach.

"Jack's going to help me with the dishes, you two love birds run off and have some quiet time."

"I am?" Jack questioned with raised eyebrows.

"You don't think you're going to watch me, do you? Grab those plates and I'll get the cups."

He did as she asked, rather demanded, and picked up the plates and followed her inside. He was pleased when she was finally satisfied and they were through with cleaning up and could settle down on the deck again after he made coffee. Jack stood in the kitchen and smiled to himself that he was actually doing it, chuckled and shook his head as he prepared their cups and carried them outside.

"There's hope for you, this coffee is actually good, thank you." Jenna didn't have much to drink that day, the alcohol in her system was still there from last night and she was just beginning to feel normal again.

"Have you ever been to Barbados?"

"No, Alana and Todd told me all about it, it sounds lovely. The whole Caribbean sounds like heaven. I sat at home in the cold of Chicago and could only dream about them in sunshine."

"Come on down sometime and visit."

She looked at him with a half smile, there was a knowing in her eyes. "I have a feeling I wouldn't be the first woman you ever whisked away to your island love nest, Jack. I know your kind."

"My kind? What is my kind?" He asked with pretend innocence.

Jenna laughed, "Just like me. Get what you want, when you can, then get out fast."

"Okay, I won't deny that. So we're both on the same page, neither one of us want anything but to get what we want, when we can, and get out fast. Now that you know that upfront, does that mean you'll come to Barbados to visit?"

"If I don't have a good time, I want to be reimbursed."

"I'll even pay for it."

"Hell no," Jenna stated strongly, "You want me to feel obligated to you, don't you? The only way I'd be obligated to you is if you donated a kidney to my mother."

His offer obviously hadn't impressed her, and it wasn't his first taste of her independence, he'd gathered that information easily from being around her. Jack smiled and shrugged his shoulders. "So pay your way and don't feel obligated to me. When are you coming?" Jack of course meant to his home in Barbados but Jenna took it in another direction.

"I don't know, when do you plan to start foreplay? Or is this it?"

Jack's laughter boomed into the dark of night. Maybe all he'd needed after all these years was someone to put him in his place. Somehow he knew she could pose a threat to him losing his key, his symbol of commitment. The key that signified he was ready to settle down and be faithful. Matt had been right, Jack finally met his match.

From further down the beach, both could hear Jack's laughter as they walked quietly hand in hand. Alana chuckled and teased in her frustration. Matt thought it best they wait until the wedding night to make love and it drove her crazy.

"Even Jack and Jenna will probably get lucky tonight. I was celibate for years and you woke up my sexual prowess, now you take it away."

Matt stopped and pulled her into his arms. "They probably will, but you'll still have to wait."

"Why? It isn't that much longer."

"I don't know. It's different here, in your house. Just out of respect I guess, especially when Todd was here."

"He's not here now, he won't be back until the day before we marry."

"It isn't just him. We both know there won't be any surprises when it comes to the bedroom, all our body parts fit very well together. But I want to make sure you know it's not because of sex."

"I don't think that, Matt."

"You may not, but I want to prove that I love you for everything, Alana. I fell in love with you because of the way you brushed a piece of lint off my jacket. And the way you looked for me on the deck one day when you saw Grandmother on the stage and knew I must be around. But I especially love the person you are, the one who shaved her head for her son, and relived a nightmare of drowning when you went windsurfing. I fell in love with you for so many things."

"And I never knew I had so much to offer," She easily leaned into the safe and calm place he offered in his arms.

"Even when you risked losing the man you loved because your heart was full. As much as I hated it, I came to understand it and love you even more for it."

She kissed him lightly. "How can I complain about not having sex, when you put it so eloquently? I'm falling more and more in love with you every day. We've only just scratched the surface and it almost scares me of what's to come."

"There's nothing to be scared of anymore. I told you I'd save you." He kissed her lightly several times. "On Saturday, you will become my wife and yes, every day we will fall more and more in love. Like you, I didn't think it was possible either but I'm learning otherwise. And I'm glad Grandmother talked us into this big celebration, I think if we decided against it her and Todd would have planned it anyway."

"Down to the last white rose," she knew they would have. "I would have done the quiet affair, I know you've been through the big one once before and…"

Matt stopped her by interrupting. "That one didn't even count. I might have had the big wedding but it feels entirely different when it's for real. And I'm having a good time meeting all your friends and really getting to know some of them. They all love you almost as much as I do. I even think Dr. Lee threatened me last night, I'm not sure though, he said it so politely."

"What did he say?"

"Reading between the nice lines he spoke, basically, he said if I ever broke your heart I should pray to never get sick and in need of a physician anywhere in the world." Matt laughed at remembering, had seen the love in his eyes for someone who'd been like a daughter to him. "I think he was assured that would never happen."

"He likes you, both of them do. I thought Mona was going to cry when she left, she told me how happy she was for me and how my father would have loved you too." Alana got another chill when she thought of what else she said, just as she'd gotten the same chill then when she went on to share the conversation with Matt. "She said she didn't know how it happened, but she was sure my father hand picked you, that he had something to do with it because you are the perfect choice of what he would have wanted."

"And what do you think?"

"I think she's right."

He raised his eyebrows. "You think? That doesn't sound very convincing."

"Tell me again why you turned around that day at the port, why you came back."

Matt stared at the woman who had become a part of his soul, to that day still didn't fully understand exactly why but told her what he was sure of. "I had to kiss you one last time."

"Yeah," Alana's voice was as soft as the gentle breeze, "She's right." It was almost as if her father had spoken the words himself, as if the gift of Matt represented his last kiss before he actually joined her mother in heaven. He'd been with her all along, she knew that now, but she would let him go if she had to. His spirit in her heart would never disappear.

Alana leaned into the safe haven of Matt's arms again as she looked towards the sky and the stars that were just beginning to shine. "Thank you, Daddy," she whispered in the dark.